A Jersey Kind of Love

John Weiman

outskirts
press

INTRODUCTION

This is the story of three kids you can't help but like, their relationships, and their views on their parents marriages.

At the time I started writing this, I was drinking too much because I was alone. One night, this couple came in the bar and I just knew they had "it." I wondered about their story and I decided I would just write it. It was the first time in ten years that I didn't stay until closing. I went home and wrote for seven and a half hours. Half of the book was written drunk and half was written sober. I challenge the reader to find the difference. Please understand the book is not written grammatically correct because the kids don't speak proper English. Enjoy!

CHAPTER ONE

Who hasn't beach walked, in the dark of night, when the waves are crashing, and the moon is following the two of you? It's comforting and romantic to have the Moon follow. As the walk went on, the waves didn't crash, they gently rocked. It was as if they had a strong passion too, till it was time to fall softly asleep. We did.

The darkness of her eyes collided with the reflection of her deep dark hair. They brightened and blinded me. When she smiled, I wasn't old enough to be aware of how a smile can melt you. It's an innocent moment that lasts through a lifetime of memories.

I met Stephanie in 8th grade. We went to school together since first. It took me seven years to get the nerve to talk to her. Yeah, through the years we did the stupid school talk. At thirteen years old, I knew I was the luckiest boy on the planet... I was the first to see her innocent beauty. One day, we walked home together. Steph had a pimple or two. She didn't want me to see them. It was as if her face was emotionally naked. I didn't care, she looked beautiful to me. But girls are no different than women. They only believe they look good when they feel good.... About themselves.

We made small talk the whole way home. Both of us talking just made us feel something. Kids like us were happy talking to the other sex. I talked her to her door, and as she looked down, she had a girl's smile that reeked of happiness, inadequacy, and anticipation of something she, we, wanted to do, but weren't old enough to know how.

I dropped her off and felt the warmth within me. I knew why, and what made it happen, but I didn't understand it. Who cares?

My mind raced about kissing Stephanie. Days, weeks, and months would go by, and the thoughts of kissing dominated me. What happens when you kiss? Making out, something is goin on in there but no one is gonna tell me. And I'm not gonna ask.

It was a Friday night, May 25th. Steph's Dad dropped us off at the movie theatre. Showtime was 7:45. It was some stupid movie. We giggled about how bad it was and decided to live on the edge and walk the streets. We used our popcorn money to share a slice of pizza and a cherry Italian ice. Stephanie and I knew it was first kiss night and we were both alone in our anxiety and anticipation. It made us savor the ice even more.

My job wasn't easy. Your first kiss has to be in the perfect place for her, and for me. Across the street was an elementary school, I dared her to come with me and try to break in. We banged on doors and tried to open windows till we got tired and laughed. The little laugh brought our eyes together. It seemed so natural. Our lips met once, softly, twice, nicer. We stopped for a second. Our eyes met and overflowed with passion and confidence. As we kissed this time, our tongues met and got along a whole lot better than we did. We liked making out, I think we liked each other a lot more after we did.

When you're makin out for the first time, you remember it forever. I looked at my watch, time was up. Stephanie and I ran back to meet her dad as the movie let out. Piling into the car, her dad tried to make small talk and asked us how we liked the movie, we acted like small kids makin small talk even smaller. "It was ok"

Monday came, all weekend long, I thought about us kissing. When school started, I ran into Stephanie. She acted like nothing happened; even worse, she treated me in a way that was as if she didn't even know me. What did I do? . I musta kissed her wrong. I knew I should've asked someone what to do. She hurt me, hurt me so bad, at a time I needed acceptance and I know she did too. She rejected me.

Distracted, I had to keep going to school. My friends Tony and Jimmy thought I was acting weird. Family dinner sucked. Mom never put up with making spaghetti with meatballs and her son not cleaning his plate. Dad seemed to know that his kid would be ok, but he just got fucked over by a broad. He loved slurping pasta. He was right, but in such a crude way. Dad could do anything he wanted, so how could mom be that bad?

Tony, Jimmy, and I made the walk to school in the morning. Jimmy, in his make-believe bad ass way, grabs me and says..." you alright?'" I had no choice, I had to be. That's what friends do. Grab you and take you away from the darkness.

Tony chimed in and bragged about his newfound friend, himself. By accident, Tony learned how to jerk off and at 13 years old, he was in heaven He didn't care about the girls at school. Tony learned how to make himself happy. He loved the way he could love him-self. Sure enough, during those ten minutes between classes, Tony would be in the bathroom tugging the tiger. None of us could go in there while he was busy. But, when he came out, Tony's giggling smile shouted, "It's grrreattt!!!"

Tony was himself at school. And the walk there too. Only Jimmy and I knew how his father beat the shit out of him. Tony would show us his burns and bruises but swear to us he was okay. Tony didn't realize it, but he woulda taken any man down. Jimmy and me saw the anger in his eyes and would always fight for him. So he didn't have to. Tony could be a killer; he just didn't know it yet.

Locker doors slamming and kids struttin to class, made school a little better. As I was fumbling through my locker, Stephanie walked by me. I ducked but she smiled. Teenage girls didn't want guys to "talk" about them. I never said a word about our kiss. And I guess it took her a few days to realize it.

It was just a kiss; it wasn't a conquest moment. What made her freak out? It made me like her less. And it sucked, cause her relent-less smile made me feel more. She just said "Hi" as her eyes darted around everything that was good. I slammed the locker door in a way she knew I was pissed. Don't do that to me. Don't steal it... the kiss was good. I know you know that.

Class came and I didn't care. Neither did the teacher. Why

would anyone wanna learn from someone who had no passion about what they were teaching? I didn't listen to the teacher. I got lost looking at the girls I grew up with that now had tits. They didn't feel comfortable with them. Every boy was staring, especially Tony.

Girls with tits were scared of Tony, but also mesmerized. They had these newfound trophies hanging out for every kid. Yet, Tony was the only one who could say, "Nice rack". It was a defining moment of adolescence. The girls who looked at him with inadequacy and disgust knew they weren't ready for the changes their body was forcing them to accept.

But, the other girls, with their fresh fun bags, seemed ready for Tony to have a test drive. And he couldn't stop himself from doing the rock around the block. Girls didn't wanna be with Tony forever, a night was just enough. And he didn't care, the morning school bell would ring and there'd be another one waiting for him at the school door.

Jimmy and I were a little jealous, but we knew his life sucked at home. So, School was his happy life. He had a gift, at first, the worse he would treat them, the more girls would line up to get a chance. Tony would never let some girl get close to him. Me and Jimmy were the friends that he trusted. We were enough.

Jimmy came from a family that showed no affection. And he knew it. His mom and dad did nothing but provide for him. Clothes, dinners, and the country club pool were supposed to be enough. He couldn't be close to his parents when his parents weren't close to themselves. He learned more from Tony and me about love and loyalty than his parents could ever show him. Jimmy didn't know how to hate his parents. Since they didn't have any passionate hate or love, neither did he. Jimmy was scared of girls in a way his two best friends couldn't understand. He didn't want the emptiness of being with someone who's boring.

Thursday school came; it was almost a week since I had my first kiss. It seemed like a year ago. I was late for History class. Rummaging through my locker, looking for some stupid book about Alexander Hamilton, Stephanie shows up, stops and gets closer She tells me, "my dad isn't gonna be home tomorrow night. Want to come over and watch a movie?"

Fuck her, I thought, Ok maybe I could tomorrow night. But I had to make her sweat. I told her I'd have to ask my mom or dad and let her know tomorrow. Why should I go? It would be easier to diss her like she dissed me. I hate my hormones. I don't even know what they are, but they seem to rule me. Morning came, and I couldn't wait, to make her wait till the end of the day... "Yeah. I'll come over" She asked me, so she had to say ok. She told me to stop by about eight. Two hours later, it'd be ten and things were supposed to happen.

Walking home, I realized I needed an alibi. I told Jimmy he needed to cover for me, cause I was gonna go find love, on the wrong side of town. Southside was big in Jersey. Jimmy didn't understand, but he understood. He didn't ask anything. Tony did, "Kenny, you gonna go try and get some tonight?" How can you answer that question without lying and losing respect of your friends or telling the truth and losing the trust of the girl? It was easy; I looked at Tony, started laughing as I told him to shut the fuck up. He knew, and Jimmy wondered, but it was all cool cause we were friends.

Jeans and a t-shirt, I even put on deodorant. I hated seeing myself in the mirror and knowing how awkward I looked. Every pose I struck made me look worse. I ran down the stairs and said, "I'm sleeping at Jimmy's" Mom said be careful and Dad took another sip of his cheap beer.

Knockin on Stephanie's door, I didn't know what to think. I'm not good at thinking, being stupid seems a lot easier. The door opened, and her long legs trapped by tight jeans led to a pure white sweater that held and comforted her newfound bumps in the road. Her smile and confidence welcomed me in. I loved her hair, dark, silky, soft, and carefree.

Stephanie gave me on a tour of the house. Living room, family room, and kitchen. We made our way upstairs. Her Dad's bedroom was the first door on the left. Forbidden Fruit. Walking in made me take her, and we kissed with more passion. We made out at the foot of the bed for a half hour. I wouldn't let her go. She liked being taken. The kiss ended, she smiled, sighed and shyly looked me straight in my eyes and said "hi" I told her I missed her...Sometimes a week can last a lifetime when you're a teenager.

She liked the way I kissed, and my confidence grew. We giggled and I dropped her on the bed as we began to wrestle. She felt comfortable and we made out more. While my hands loved her hair, they loved the curves of her body more. As we kissed, I kept brushing by her tits. I didn't have the guts to feel her up yet. But the brushes by got me pretty excited. I knew there was something in her pants that she didn't want me to see, but there was something in mine that wanted to see her. I kept pushing it against her and she would carefully distance herself. Steph never lost the rhythm of our kiss.

I knew I wasn't ready to do what my body told me. but hers did. She stopped the kiss, pushed me aside and said she was gonna make dinner. Steph seemed confident as she reached in the fridge. Pulling out all sorts of foods, we made small talk about the dorky boys and girls at school. I never watched mom make dinner. It was just something you went to. Stephanie started boiling water. We were havin spaghetti and meatballs. They couldn't be better than mom's, but mom never wore a sweater like that, cooking dinner.

Two thirteen-year-olds, pretending they were grown up, sat down at the table to share dinner. She was beautiful as she lit the two candles before she sat down. She draped the pasta on my plate and asked me if I wanted any parm. I liked her a lot. "Yeah, put some on there" She sat down and looked to me for acceptance. While it wasn't as good as mom's, I would never let her know, at least till we got older. Dad taught me to slurp pasta, so I inhaled a bunch till my mouth was full "It's really good". She couldn't understand me but loved the look on my face. Making dinner was the first time she felt like she could be a woman.

We finished the pasta, cleared the table and washed the dishes together. I never saw my dad help, but it seemed like the natural thing to do. We talked and smiled at each other. Stephanie asked me if I wanted some ice cream. She made me the best sundae I ever had, lots of hot fudge, brownie bits, a cherry and extra whipped cream. At such a young age, she seemed to like pretending she was all grown up and married. But I realized she had to be, since her mom left, and her dad wasn't exactly the best at taking care of himself.

As kids, Friday night was movie night, so we sat on the couch and watched The Breakfast Club. Those kids were just a year or two older than us, but they all got high, so they seemed older. The one guy reminded me of Tony, but I couldn't let Steph know. We talked about the characters and who was like kids we knew in school. Steph thought that guy was like Tony, but I laughed it off and told her, "Believe me, nobody is like Tony"

We held hands the whole time and made out during the boring parts. There weren't enough boring parts for me. But kissing Stephanie, no movie would. I can't put into words how it felt. All I know is, it felt really good. And that thing in my pants started acting up again. Stephanie accidentally brushed by it and I got really nervous cause I thought I died and gone to heaven. I thought her accidental touch was born more out of curiosity than anything. I didn't care. And we never talked about it. She couldn't deny it happened. Silence really can be golden.

The movie was over, and it was bedtime. I let her lead me. I knew my wiener wasn't ready to do anything that it didn't know how. So, I followed her. Grown up again, she takes me into her dad's bedroom. She gave me the clicker as she hid behind the bathroom door, open enough for me to see. When she removed her sweater, I could see is the beauty of her back. With a flirting look, she turned around and teased me. The door shut as she was removing her bra. I was thinkin that's whole alotta girl!! She opened the door, with a long white t-shirt that showed the perfect shape of her shape.

"Anything good on" she asked as she pulled the bedspread down. I felt like an idiot when she asked if I was gonna sleep in all those clothes. With a false sense of confidence, I told her, "I usually sleep in my boxers". So, I undressed militarily, and got under the covers with her.

While the thought scared the shit out of me about what she wanted, she maintained her innocence as she put her head on my shoulder. She began to caress my stomach, in a way that relaxed her and me. She asked about my parents. I pretended not to know what she was sayin, "'Do you think they love each other?" It was a release, as I said "no". She wanted to know more, "why not?" At thirteen years old, how do you put a lifetime of snapshots and try to express something you don't understand.?

Comfortable in her arms, I felt safe answering. "My dad is miserable, and my mom seems cold around him. I hate it, being there. When I get older, I don't wanna be my dad, and I don't wanna act like my mom." Strumming through the channels, we both saw more love in a commercial than my parents ever showed.

Stephanie Demarino was nobody's fool. She asked the question for a reason.

"Dad's found a girlfriend and I feel left behind. I'm happy for him, but other than you, I feel so alone" I felt her pain and held her close and tight. "Steph, I know we're young but you're the most important person in the world to me". We shared one of those make out sessions. I didn't think we get could close as our tongues, but we were trying.

In mid kiss, I stopped. "So, what's gonna happen Monday?" "Where?", she asked. I remembered my anger and said... "Um at school, Cause if you do that again, I'm out. I would never do that to you" Stephanie said she was sorry and just didn't know how to act or what I was thinking. I asked, "So, do you know what I'm thinking now?" "Yeah, I do, you want me to brush by that thing in your pants again" We broke out into a laughter that couldn't stop. In the middle of a worry, she comes through. "Yes Kenny, I won't hide we're together anymore. I'll even tell my friends I like you. But, if I do this, my friends will.... go after you. It's just how girls are," I told her I can't wait to make out with her friend Fanny. I don't know if it was her real name or nickname, but both worked.

Everything was gonna be okay... we laughed, kissed and finally cuddled ourselves to sleep. Nothing happened but it was the happiest night of my life. The sky was slowly brightening as we fell asleep. I stayed up and watched her sleep. Her hair surrounded the pillow and her chest slowly moved up and down. I watched her just breathe for an hour. It wasn't long enough, but the sun was getting stronger than I was, so I had to drop my head on the pillow.

I woke up to the sweet smell of cinnamon and maple syrup. My girl, she had to be mine now, we spent the night together. I walked into the kitchen and my eyes found a plate full of my favorite, French toast. Did she make it cause of all the French kissing? I never understood why it was called French kissing... making out seems a lot truer. Stephanie turned to face me as she was pouring a tall glass of fresh orange juice. With a smile softer than the sunrise, she said "good morning" And it was. I took my place at the table and began to eat the stack. She sat across from me with a measly half of grapefruit. It didn't seem fair, but Steph knew she had to eat healthy to perfectly fill out those jeans and white sweater

"Do you like it?" As I was gobbling it down, I found the time to say. "Oh yeah" It was really good. I still couldn't believe how grown up she could cook. She picked at her fruit and seemed to enjoy a little bit of nothing. When I finally ate the last bite of the sweet toast, she looked me straight in the eyes, "So was it good?" I thought about it, long enough to make her squirm a little, as I answered the question with a question. "What? When you accidentally touched my wiener?" She busted out laughing and threw her empty grapefruit shell at me as she screamed, "I hate you" We were kids but, God, did we have chemistry. I looked at the clock and it was ten after nine. I had to get home before mom called Jimmy's house.

Stephanie completely understood and walked me to the door. I couldn't say thank you enough. In one night, She gave me a lifetime of good times. Maybe I don't expect much, but for this one night, she gave me everything. The date ended just like it started, I took her and kissed in a way that felt like the world was ending tomorrow. The more we kissed, the better it felt. I shyly said " Thank you" She appreciated my kiss and words as she sweetly told me "awwww you're welcome" We stared at each other as we held hands.

The hands grabbed each other in a way they never wanted to let go. But I had to … You know, how moms worry…I ran all the way home.

I got home and ran right upstairs. Mom was the first to meet me. "Did you have fun sleeping at Jimmy's house?" It was an innocent question, but my answer wasn't. Mom wanted to know about a home that was warmer than hers. She thought she could learn something. Mom didn't need to learn anything about warmth with me. She was my mom. I didn't want to talk with mom, cause it would be a lie. "Mom, I'm really tired and grumpy" Moms hate sleepovers cause kids stay up all night, so I knew she would leave me alone to catch up on my sleep.

I crashed on my bed and held my pillow as close as I held Stephanie. I couldn't stop thinking 'bout our night together. The kissing was captivating, but the laughs we shared, stayed with me. How many times can you laugh with a girl about brushing against your crotch rocket? We did twice, and it was only our second date. The pillow was too much for me and I fell asleep, till three in the afternoon.

CHAPTER TWO

Mom woke me up; telling me Tony was on the phone about our campout tonight. I completely forgot as she said, "Didn't you and Jimmy talk about this last night?"

"A little but we mostly told ghost stories, so I forgot" I hated lying to mom, but I loved being with Stephanie more. Mom loves me; I wished I coulda told her. She would've worried, but she'd be happy her kid found a feeling she and my dad couldn't see anymore. I fucked up, I shoulda trusted mom.

I got to the phone and Tony laughed, "So you ready to go campin by the "watah" and party?" With the accent that could only compete with Tony's, I answered, "Fuckin A right. How about Jimmy? Is he in?" Tony told me Jimmy's Dad is driving us there, so we got no choice.

Jimmy's dad honked the horn at 8:30. I ran to the car with a sleeping bag and marshmallows. Jimmy had a stuffed pillowcase. We found Tony on the corner. He had a pillow under his arm and a knapsack Tony got in and, immediately said Hi to Mr. Fortunato. Jimmy's dad couldn't hate Tony because he gave him the respect he deserved.

He dropped us off in the middle of a field of tall evergreens. We left the car as his dad said,"have fun". The look on his face seemed jealous. He wanted to be a kid again and have close friends that he never had when he was our age. But he pulled away, happy that his son had friends.

I hated walking through the woods after sundown. It's scary in the dark. Tony didn't care, and Jimmy walked toe to toe with him. I followed. He had to bring it up; we weren't even at camp yet.

"Kenny, you get some last night?" Ya better stand up to him or he would lose respect for you. I told him to bend over, and I'll show ya what I got. Jimmy busted out and Tony couldn't answer the bell. All he could say was "Fuckin Kenny!!!"

After Tony was done bustin my petunias, we all made stupid small talk on the two-mile trek to the shore of the lake. I couldn't believe that our parents trusted us enough to let us be out here all-alone. Maybe they just didn't care. Misery can give a kid alotta free-dom by accident... I heard the water and the singing of the bugs. We were close to our campground.

The water found us, and we settled in. Tonight, the three of us felt settled, but we really weren't. Tony pulls out this bag, and says, "Wanna get high?" I wasn't ready to do this, I looked at Jimmy and he had the same look on his face. We couldn't say no to Tony. "I never have but, yeah, I will" "Me too", Jimmy said. Tony had some-thing called a joint. It looked like a cigarette, `but it didn't have a fil-ter. It was a big fat wrinkly paper with something called pot inside.

Tony led the way as he fired it up. He inhaled deep and let the smoke out as if he was free. He coughed a little, as he looked me in the eyes and passed it my way. I did the same, inhaled, and coughed stupid. I didn't even look at Jimmy as I handed it his way. I felt peaceful in my first high. I got lost in myself when Tony hit me and passed the joint again. This thing took three trips around be-fore it was finally finished.

None of us said a word for at least a half hour. Jimmy was the first to talk. "What's it like where you live, in your house?" Tony looked straight down, I began, "My mom and dad don't even fake that they love each other anymore. I think they even fake loving me. Dad doesn't want me to love mom, and mom doesn't want me to be like dad. It's fucked up. What the hell am I supposed to feel?"

Tony started shaking, still staring down on the ground. He ran his hand through his hair like his hair pissed him off. Jimmy didn't catch it. He was too caught up in his own answer. "Kenny, fuck you", the pot was settin in. Jimmy was himself. "You talk about a house not being a home? That's bullshit. I live in an empty box. Tony and you can find a girl, but I can't. How could I? I'm so fucked up. Kenny, at least your mom and dad hate each other. I don't even know how to feel, and that really sucks. I live in a house, not a home."

Tony was completely silent. He wasn't ready to talk about the hell of his life. He needed to though. Me and Jimmy were scared to listen. Our sob stories were just what they were. Tony's was hell. He started talking about when his dad would come home. He'd be watching TV and his dad didn't like the channel, so he'd take his cigarette and burn him behind his neck. His hair covered it so no-body could see. Tony's dad burned him all over his body. "I learned to deal with that, but one time he came home drunk, and pissed on me cause I fell asleep in front of the TV" That's the closest I ever saw to Tony crying. I had to get up, put my arm around him to let him know, "We're friends forever, RIGHT?" He understood as he said, "fuck yeah".

Jimmy was kinda stunned by Tony's hard life. He knew his friend's life was hard but had no idea it was that bad. I could see in his eyes he felt ashamed. He complained about his life when one of his two closest friends had it much worse. Tony saw it in Jimmy's eyes, "Toughen up and get some heart my friend, cause ya gonna need it later". Jimmy acted like he didn't hear him. Tony got pissed and jacked Jimmy up. He smacked him around, not too hard though, but hard enough for Jimmy to take a pathetic swing at Tony. A careful smile wrapped around Tony's face as he grabbed his friend, held him, shook him, looked him straight in his eyes as he said, "Fight back, don't ever let anything ever beat you"

Pressure broke and adolescent energy seemed to fade as we got tired and had to hug a pillow. I know we all thought about what was just shared. Friends are something that most people don't ap-preciate enough. But we did. As my eyes closed, I thought about last night with Stephanie. It seemed like a lifetime ago. I missed her already but couldn't share the meaning and importance of my two friends. She'd never understand.

Morning broke and the sound of birds chirping woke us up. Birds only sing when they wanna wake you up. No one hears them throughout the rest of the day. Maybe we're too busy. We packed up our stuff and made the two-mile walk back. Each of us was scared about what we told the other two. We worked it out on the walk. It was pretty easy. We were friends, so nobody had to worry about a word being said.

Tony reaches in that bag, "C'mon let's get high again" Jimmy showed some heart, "hell yeah" It wasn't like him. He didn't have passion, but he was learning. Me and Tony looked at each other and knew the trip was worth it just to make Jimmy feel more alive. Tony took a nice relaxed hit off the joint. Jimmy, oooh he was different. He sucked the life outa that pot. He couldn't stop coughing and Tony and me couldn't stop laughing. Jimmy finally handed it to me, and I made sure I would breathe in and then breathe out without doing a "jimmy cough"

Friendship is a great thing. T and J were the best friends I ever had. I'll never understand why kids have best friends and adults don't. It must really suck to be an adult. Kids are much more loyal. Secrets shared, like the three of us talked about, we'd never tell anybody. But adults do. They lose their honor and loyalty. Piss a casual friend off and they'll bury you. Is it innocence or fear that keeps a kid's loyalty? I think both.

Tony's dad picked us up. With his bloodshot eyes, and alcohol stench, he told us, You're late!!! Get in the car" Tony sat in front and me and Jimmy were in the back. "Can't you do anything right? I told you; I'd pick you up at ten, but you have to fuck up everything." Tony meekly said, "I'm sorry Dad "Before he could finish his words his dad told him to shut up. Jimmy now saw the picture, crystal clear. He didn't even have the balls to look at me. He never seemed so scared. Tony just stared out the passenger window looking for a better world. Jimmy got dropped off first. He made sure he said thank you very much to Tony's dad. He got outa the car and ran as fast as he could to his front door.

Thank God I only lived a block and a half away. The first person I ever hated was Tony's father. I know my mom and dad have alotta hate. But that's different. It took years of being together to build their wall. I hated Mr. Matelli ten seconds after I met him. Maybe it had to do with what Tony said last night. I wanted to hit him. He pulled up to my house; I ran out of car and said thanks in a heartless way. "Tony, you're the best!!!" I turned and shouted, loud enough to make his father think about his son in a good way.

Tony got it. He knew what I was doing. I was fighting for my best friend.

Mom, Dad and my kid sister, Terry, waited for me to get home so we could go to the last mass. Going to church and "acting" like a family was a sin in my eyes. I looked around, and saw alotta families committing the same sin. Church was a place you go to convince yourself you're good. I can't believe they allowed my Dad in the building. Looking in the mirror as a teenager, you can't convince yourself you're good and you can't as a grown up either. Churches should have more mirrors.

The best thing about church was going to IHOP after. Terry got the blueberry, and I got the chocolate chip pancakes. Dad got eggs and Mom got coffee. Terry and me always tried to steal a bite from each other's plate. Stealing was easier than asking. It was just a game though. Having a kid sister is a kid's first responsibility. If you don't look out for her, then you'll never be a man.

IHOP was special. Mom was a good mom, but the only syrup I knew was "Log Cabin" This place with the sky-blue roof had five different flavors at every table!!!!! Sunday breakfast felt more like family time than church. Besides, the waitress would never threaten me with heaven, kicking me out and sending me to the hot place. But, The Priest did. I liked the waitress a lot more. She was nicer.

Once we got home, we spread out like the family, we weren't.

My kid sister comes into my room and asks me if I'm okay. I said, "Yeah, I'm just tired" "Tired of what?" I didn't want my little sister to worry, but her question was a good one. I farted out an air biscuit so she'd go away, and I wouldn't have to answer. Friday and Saturday nights never seemed as long as they were this weekend. Both nights were great, but they drained me. Fun and Friendship can do that to you sometimes, so I couldn't complain. Besides I got high twice. And last Thursday, the only high I knew was jumping.

Sunday TV was boring. I went to my room and did homework. Homework is a chore that a kid must endure. It's a rite of passage. Most of school is not about what you learn, it's more about how you deal with frustration. I can't believe people graduate from college learnin nothing about nothing. Maybe it's the trek that teaches them.

Me, Jimmy, and Tony walked to school in the morning. You can't be late getting there, but you can always take your time getting home. I saw Stephanie in between classes. As I was at my locker, she breezed by me, smiled and kissed me. I don't know what love is, but I felt something. She kissed me, in public. Whether she was my girl, or I was her boy, I didn't care.

School let out and the walks home are memories and treasures in your heart. Some are good, and some are painful. Tony wanted to talk. "My dad beat the shit outa me after he dropped you two off" Jimmy learned from Tony, so he thought he was saying the right thing, "Toughen up!!!" I grabbed Jimmy and said, "No!" this is different. Tony started crying.

"How long am I supposed to be strong?????" I got pissed and it was my turn to jack someone up. "For the rest of your life" He looked down and kept crying. " Did you hear me? Till the day you fuckin die" Then I held him in a way that he knew I'd never let him go. He hugged back and said "fuck you asshole, I aint goin nowhere. We both started laughing and then threatened to give Jimmy a wedgie.

Walking home, it's something you do as a kid, but stays with you as you become a man. I felt helpless cause there was nothing I could do but be Tony's friend. Terry crashed into my room saying she needed help with her homework. Two people I could never say no to, Terry and Tony. I loved being her big brother. So, helping my sister with homework was my release from thinking about my friend's hell.

Terry wasn't good at mathematics, and as the big brother, it wasn't easy to help her. Two trains in opposite directions, going at different speeds. Figuring out when they would pass each other?

Who cares? They're going in the opposite directions. But I helped Terry get the answer, even if I didn't care. Homework should be a lot smarter than trying to figure out when two trains will pass each other.

My kid sister liked the civil war more than math. It's a part of our history. Terry asked me why it was called the Civil War. There was nothing civil about it. I couldn't tell her it was the north against the south. I had to tell her something. "All wars begin cause one side thinks they're being Civil" My kid sister asked, "What about the other side?"

"They think they're being Civil too"

Civil wars happen in your own country. Terry learned it was no different than the way mom and dad fought in our house. They weren't nice to each other, and neither were the North or the South. They're alotta scars and lives lost fighting for what one thinks is right. I told Terry "right" is a bad word. She seemed to understand. Being right is not worth the cost. My kid sister is eleven years old and she's smarter than most of the people who rule the world.

She definitely got it. Too many people die in war. For what? Being Right? Dad hated our next-door neighbor. Mr. Russer died one day, unexpectedly. He had a heart attack. Upon his death, my dad completely changed his opinion about our neighbor. It was one of the few times I ever saw my dad cry. Terry asked me, "Why do people change after someone dies?" I couldn't answer her. I didn't know what to say.

"Terry, I don't know why death brings out the good in people. It just does. Look at Dad. He's helping out Mrs. Russer, fixing her car and stuff. Dad's not like that". She looked disappointed as she said, "I know".

Our education stopped when we heard mom and dad fighting about money, it wasn't the first time. Dad wasn't nice to mom; Mom started hiding dad's money. I couldn't figure out if she was doing it cause she was scared dad would leave her, or she felt that she earned it because of the horrible way she was treated. Either way, stealing is stealing.

The phone rang, it was for me. Mom answered it just to get away from Dad. "Kenny it's for you, It's Stephanie" I acted like she needed help with her homework and tried to be cool, "What's up?" She told me nothing and then everything. "I missed you and I wanted to hear your voice."

I couldn't tell her I missed her. But she was on my mind all weekend. "Wanna have lunch tomorrow after fourth period" I heard the smile in her voice as she said, yeah, that'd be nice. She asked me if I had fun going camping. I told her, yeah, but I couldn't tell the truth. I wanted to tell her about what me, Jimmy and Tony shared, but couldn't trust her. Or maybe I couldn't break the trust of the boys. It was really no different than Friday night. She wouldn't want me to tell them, so why should I tell her. I did need to get it out though. I wanted to trust someone with everything going through my head. Family, Friends, and Love are way too much to juggle in the head of a teenager.

Mom told me again as the phone rang. "It's for you. It's Jimmy."

CHAPTER THREE

"My Dad just died"
I felt bad about the silence; I couldn't believe what I heard. I told him, Tony and me will be there in a heartbeat. Running out the door, I told mom what just happened and didn't hear her answer. I ran to Tony's and really didn't give a shit about what his father thought, as I pounded on his front door.

"Where's Tony?" His father said he was upstairs. In a passion, I knew he wouldn't wanna fuck with; I made him come down here. "Look Jimmy's father just died, and we're his best friends, so whether you like it or not, Tony is coming with me. We gotta be there for him.". Tony's dad understood and yelled upstairs to get down here NOW. Tony ran down the stairs in his boxers and tank top. I told him what just happened.. He said, "We gotta be there for him."

We ran to his house and hugged our numb friend. He looked like he aged a year in a few hours and his mom aged quicker. His dad had a seizure watching TV, while Jimmy and his mom were upstairs. He died alone. Jimmy and his mom wore guilt. Tony asked if he was alright, Jimmy always tried to be fake strong in front of Tony. Jimmy broke down, "Why couldn't I just watch TV with my dad? He'd be alive now" Tony got semi-religious, "Jimmy don't do that to yourself, sometimes it's your time to go. There's nothing anyone can do to stop it". Tony hugged Jimmy till his tears stopped. Jimmy cried and cried, Tony refused to let him go. Tony seemed to welcome Jimmy into the pain fraternity, it was a club you'd never wanna join. Once you had to, you were in, whether you liked it or not.

Tony made sure Jimmy would go on, "So Kenny, me and you walkin to school when you come back?"' Jimmy wiped the last tear from his eye and said "Fuckin A right" I had to join something called a group hug. Friends held each other like we knew there were harder times to come, and we'd always be there for each other. You don't have to say it, you feel friendship.

We stayed with Jimmy. The ambulance came and took his Dad away. Jimmy ran to his mom as she completely lost it. Through all the tears raining, I heard my friend say to his mother, "I love you so much mom and I love my dad too" He held her tighter than the teddy bear he had as a kid. I sat there and watched pure love between a mother and her son. A friend of his mom's brought her a cup of tea. Jimmy let go and came back to us. I told him your mom is gonna really need you now. He told me, "I'm gonna need her too" Tony didn't forget, we'll be here for you. Jimmy grew up and said "yeah, I know" No more hugs, no more tears tonight. Just a strong handshake and a look straight in the eyes. That's all Jimmy wanted. He was tired, but I knew he wouldn't sleep.

Tony and I left and walked home. We didn't talk for the first few blocks. It wasn't awkward silence. We were overwhelmed. Tony finally broke the silence with passion, "What the fuck????? Can you believe that Kenny? That shit we saw, the ambulance taking Jimmy's Dad away. Whadda we do? "I had to answer Tony. "We be there for him, it's that simple. Tony, you know that I know about your hard times, we're friends so it's simple to me. We're just gonna be Jimmy's friend. That's all he wants," Tony told me I'm alright for a dumb guy. I told him he's one "F" away from the short bus. We laughed and he looked at his door. "Thanks Buddy. We gotta try to make Jimmy laugh tomorrow."

Tony went into his house, and I thought about needing Stephanie. By the time fourth period would arrive, everyone would know about Jimmy's dad. That kinda sucked, as I knew everyone would be checkin him out. He's just a kid, don't stare at him to make him feel bad. And, don't ever say, "If you need anything, just call me." Like someone would actually pick up the phone and say, "I need you".

I got back home. Both mom and dad were at the door waiting

for me. They were holding hands. I never saw that before. Terry was right behind them. "Mom said, "We're so sorry for your friend's loss" And Dad followed, by pulling me in, to my family, "We really are son" Terry came forward and I broke down. My family held me, all of them. Yeah, I was sad and scared about what happened to Jimmy and his dad, but it was the first time I felt part of a family. Mom and Dad were really good to me. I didn't care what made it happen, but I sensed it was a wake up call..

We hugged and cried, they even let Terry stay up late to let me talk about what happened. I had so many questions they couldn't answer. My Dad, My DAD, says, "Sometimes there are no answers". I never knew he had that in him, but he helped me a lot. Dad knew our neighbor and my friend's dad just died .I think he realized it was time to make some changes.

Before I went to bed, I decided to tell my family about Stephanie. They let me talk. "I met this girl in school, and I think I like her a lot. I know I do, cause I want her with me at the funeral, and mom, dad, terry; I want you there too. I need you, all of you" Dad led the way and said, "We'll be there" Mom's eyes looked like she got her man back. I got off the couch, the only couch I've ever known, went to hug my parents. "C'mon Terry, it's way past our bedtime and we can't be late to school tomorrow. We made our way upstairs and headed to our rooms.

I rested my head on the pillow, looked at the clock and tomorrow was already today. There was gonna be alotta tomorrows becoming todays. It happens too fast. This was my first. In the last week, I grew up more than I wanted to. Yeah, it was fun to be with Steph again. I hate that losses brings gains. Mom and Dad woulda never been together again if Jimmy's dad didn't die. I should be thankful for the change. Maybe I am, my night with Steph and getting high with my friends, but Jimmy's dad dying affected me in a way I never knew change could. I saw Jimmy hug his mom, tight, and my parents seemed to find each other again. Who knows, maybe things around here ain't gonna be so dark anymore.

Yeah, the sun came to rise and it was time for school again. I got dressed and filled my knapsack with all the homework I didn't do. Mom handed me a fresh glass of orange juice. I finished it quick. She stroked my hair, and told me to "be good today" as I made my way out the door. I knew what mom was sayin. It was about Jimmy, not my behavior in school.

Tony was outside waiting, "About Time". I knew he was bustin my balloons. We had to get to Jimmy's. Both of us didn't know what to do. "Whaddya say we say to him Kenny?" I didn't know. I figured it would just come out. Jimmy looked tired and, beaten, but happy to see his friends.

"What's up brother?" Tony never called him brother before but the message was clear. Last night Jimmy lost his Dad, this morning he gained two brothers. Jimmy told us he's decided he's gonna give his Dad's Eulogy. "Don't ask me, cause, yeah, I'm sure. "My mom and me talked all night and I asked her if I could do this. Mom never said no to me, so this was not the time to break the streak." " Ok Jimmy, All I ask is that you do your best"

I had to ask, "Are you sure you can do this? You ain't exactly tearing up English Class" He was the man of the house now, "Watch" that's all he said.

He changed the subject and asked Tony not to be tuggin on the tiger in the bathroom between classes cause he might lose it and need a place to go to be alone. Tony complied, "No problem." Jimmy busted out laughing, "I'm fuckin with you man." Finally, someone one-upped Tony.

We laughed our way to the school doors. I looked at Jimmy and told him to "be cool, don't let any of the assholes see the hurt." I asked him if he wanted me to look for a sympathy girlfriend Stunned and confused, he never thought about it. The smile we were looking for, "Yeah do it" He knew I was only kidding. But it put a thought in his head. He grew up a year or two in a day. How many girls can date the older boy who's the same age as you?

4th period was over too quickly, and I had to have lunch with Steph. I didn't wanna talk about the things I needed to talk about. We met in the cafeteria, got our ugly plastic trays and stood in line.

God love her, walking through the line she tells me she heard about Jimmy's dad. I acted like my old dad and said "yeah" That was it. She gave me a glare that would scare the devil, "Is that all you can say?" Frustrated, I asked her, "can we just get our food?" I learned what a cold shoulder was cause she quickly turned away from me and her right shoulder bumped up against the cold soft ice cream machine.

We both paid our dollar thirty- five for lunch, and I followed the cold girl to our table. I didn't want silence. I knew she was just caring. And I shut down like my dad. "Look I'm really sorry I shut you out in line." I released what happened last night, everything, about what me and my family shared. I went on to tell Steph how I told them about her. She kept listening and eating bad school fruit. I finally let her know the most important thing I said to my family. "Stephanie, I really like you and I didn't know how much till Jimmy's Dad died .I want you to come to the funeral with me."

There was a silence then a smile. She reached across the table for my hand and our eyes met. Eyes say much more than words, they thanked me, cared for me, and I saw what she was missing. Steph missed being needed. "Of course, I'll go with you and your family." I didn't care who saw. I stood up, held her and gave her a long sweet soft kiss in front of everyone. Teachers even stared in awe of our innocence and chemistry.

We left the cafeteria. I told her every boy and girl hates us now. Boys wanted to be me, and girls wanted to be her. Stephanie busted out laughing, with personality, as she said, "Fuckin A right" That's the first time I heard her curse. We were cool, the lunch I wanted, but didn't, was awesome. I know I like her. I didn't even finish my Hershey's box of chocolate milk.

I had three more classes. Each one, I went to the teacher first and let them know I didn't do my homework. They understood. Mr. Chidlow even asked if I knew anything about the funeral. I told him yeah; Jimmy is giving the eulogy. He didn't expect that, but his reaction was all about Jimmy and how concerned he was for one of his students. "Kenny, this school is a community, and a community is nothing different than a Family, it's just bigger. So, I need you to tell me about the details of the funeral" "I promise you I will Mr. Chidlow."

I knew not to tell Jimmy.

Tony, me, and Jimmy walked home after school and the first words outa Jimmy's mouth were, "Did you find me the sympathy girl?" I cracked up and told him, maybe, but she's a big-un, so I didn't wanna tell her how upset you are. "All day at school and the best you could do is find just one????.. Why do I even have friends?? The one thing I wanted, and you try to hook me up with Fanny?" The three of us couldn't stop laughing. Jimmy wasn't being strong. He was just being with his friends. I guess Tony and me gave him all the strength he needed.

Tony decides it's his turn to break balloons. "Hey Studley, I heard you kissed that Stephanie girl in the cafeteria. Rumor has it, you stopped time" Leave it to him. Jimmy wanted to know everything, and Tony kept pushing the right buttons... Jimmy wanted to know if she had a friend "yeah". "Really? What's her name? "Fanny". Jimmy sunk in a laughing way. Tony told him she was gonna be his first kiss whether he liked it or not. Laughing got louder as Jimmy said, "you don't think I have the guts, do you?" "Sympathy love can get you at least to second base" While we all laughed, Jimmy remembered Fanny was big in all the good places too.

It was another one of those tomorrows already becoming to-days. A few days passed in a blur. I remember telling Mr. Chidlow where and when the funeral was. And today was the funeral. Stephanie called me in the morning saying her father was taking her to the church; she made me promise to save two seats next to me, one for her and one for her dad. Jimmy and his mom were in the front row so they had no idea what was happening behind them.

The entire eighth grade showed up, not just the kids, but also their families, moms, dads' brothers and sisters. Tony 's father was even there in his Sunday best. Teachers, they were no different. They did the same. Husbands, wives, and children filled the pews.

I knew Mr. Chidlow made this happen, but how? How did he make all these people show up? What did he say to them? I knew he'd never tell me and I knew to thank him later.

The mahogany coffin sat right in front of the altar. Father O'brien said all the things priests say during a traditional funeral. There was nothing traditional about my friend Jimmy. Father invited Jimmy up to give his dad's eulogy. He walked up to the altar, got to the podium, and fumbled for his piece of paper. He finally looked at the congregation.

Of course, he expected family and a few friends. His eyes saw the whole eighth grade there to support him and honor his father. His first words weren't planned, "Mom, turn around and look. My whole class and their families are here to honor dad!!!" There was a little bit of laughter as Jimmy's mom turned her head. Once the laughter subsided, Jimmy spoke into the mic and said, well here goes. He exhaled twice and began his eulogy.

TRIBUTE

"I never told my dad I loved him and I don't remember if he ever told me. I'm sure he did, but kids aren't the best at listening. Dad didn't have to say he loved me, He showed me and my mom every day. Words mean a lot less than actions and his actions? words can't describe them. He made sure my mom and I had everything we needed. I went to his job a few times and I believe he did the same for his co-workers. He never said it, but he taught me, it's not important to hear thank you if you're doing the right thing. The thanks are in what you're doing. I know, I didn't thank my dad enough, he didn't care. He breathed the old saying; it's better to give than receive.

My dad loved to take me two places, fishing and baseball games... high school games, an hour away. Jimmy looked at his mom and she whispered, "yes he did'. When we went fishing, he made sure I understood it's not important if we catch anything. He taught me there's always another day. We're not giving up; we'll just come back. And every time, he'd bring up my mom. Dad would always ask; you're being good to your mom right? I'd tell him yeah. And mom, I hope I have been, and I will always do my best for you"

. Both Jimmy and his mom teared up. Jimmy left the podium for a second, but before he left, he said he'd be right back. He walked to his mother and hugged her again, like the night his father died. Everyone watched knowing they'd never forget what they were seeing.

Jimmy returned to the mic, "Okay, Dad took me to these baseball games, an hour away. He didn't like the pro teams. They seemed to do it for the money, and he loved seeing the worst kid on the high school team get a base hit at the right time. In high school every kid plays, if they don't, then the coach is just bad. My dad always told me, your team is only as good as the worst kid. Make him good and your team is great. I have a feeling he did that at his job too.

I'd always ask my dad, though, the high school games are only seven innings, not nine, like the big leagues. He answered, everything you can see in nine, you see in seven. And now, it's the first time I ever disagreed with my dad. He died in the seventh inning of his life, and God I wish we coulda been together for nine. Dad, I love you"

Jimmy rocked our world, everyone's. Steph and I held hands the whole time, but we were alone in listening to Jimmy. The whole church was. Stunned by his words, the Priest sensed it and let us all have time to appreciate what Jimmy just said. I looked across the aisle at Tony and he pumped his fist knowing our buddy nailed it. Mr. Chidlow was seated near the back of the church with his family. He was nobody's fool. He wanted to watch the community. Father O'brien broke the traditional service. After the long silence, his voice changed. It overflowed with heart and compassion, as he asked us all to go in peace.

Row by row, we all made our way outside the church. Everyone stood in front of the steps making small talk. The toughest part of the day was soon to come. We made our way to the car caravan leading to the cemetery. Car doors slamming gently echoed in finality. It's a hard sound to hear. Doors slamming and burials have a lot in common.

Everyone gathered around Jimmy's Dad's final resting place and put on their strongest emotion. Parents looked at the hole in the ground, thinking it could be them. Teenagers and classmates looked at Jimmy wondering how they could grow up without a parent. The young kids didn't understand what they were watching, They knew to be on their best behavior.

Father O'brien said a prayer and the saddest parade of roses began. One by one, everybody walked to the coffin and placed their rose . Jimmy and his mom were last. They placed their flowers together. His mom whispered in his ear, and He took a few steps back. Mrs. Fortunato wanted one last private moment with her husband. Her heartfelt eyes, shoulders and legs showed how much she missed her pillar of strength. She couldn't leave the coffin. People sensed it was time to go, enough witnessing, and the caravan made its way to the after party. Later, Jimmy told me he watched his mom have her private "remember when" talk. He learned too late, he didn't live in a house, he lived in a home. He just couldn't see it till today.

Cars found Jimmy's house and his block sold out quick. Every block around his house filled up. Neighbors welcomed strangers to park in their driveway. They all waited patiently for Jimmy and his mom to get back to their home. Upon their arrival, the sound of car doors opening was a lot better than hearing them slam shut. It was kinda like a sunrise with noise. Families made their way to Jimmy's house with trays of food. Jimmy's mom was the perfect homemaker, but she was overwhelmed by the community's kindness.

My mom, dad, sister, Stephanie and her father finally got in the house. Mom and Dad made small talk with Steph's Dad. Her Dad looked like he felt outa place, or maybe he finally found a good place. Either way, he seemed a little awkward. My dad got a few beers in Mr. Demarino and everything was good. But Dad didn't leave mom's side. After a joke or two between the three of them, Dad threw his arm around mom's shoulder. Another thing I never saw before.

I asked Steph to follow me. She didn't ask where, we held hands and made our way to Mr. Childlow. I stepped forward and introduced myself to his Mrs. and two daughters, Elizabeth and Ashley. "Mrs. Childlow, my name is Kenny Mancuso and your husband is one of my teachers." "Nice to meet you Kenny"

"And this is my friend Stephanie, I want her to be my girlfriend, but I don't know if I'm old enough to have one of those" She laughed, and Stephanie slapped me in a playful way as she said, "Nice to meet all of you, Elizabeth and Ashley, you have beautiful dresses." The kids shied up.

I spoke up. "Your Dad means a lot to me" I went to hug him and whispered I'd never forget what he did. He gave me a two pat hug and a proud smile. "Steph, I'm hungry. Let's go look at the food. Mr. Chidlow, you're the best" he raised his hand to give me a high five and said, "So are you".

Stephanie pulled me aside as we walked away and asked what that was all about. I didn't know how to answer. That trust thing popped up again. I believed my teacher wouldn't want anyone to know how he called every family in the eighth grade and got them to come here today. I didn't want my girl to feel shut out. Whaddya do? You bullshit. "Steph, he's my favorite teacher" I can't wait till I feel close enough to trust her. It's gonna take a long time though, I hope she'll understand.

Tony had his arm around Jimmy's shoulder; He forced Jimmy's head to look at Fanny. From an eye sight away, you could tell Tony was trying to give his friend the confidence to talk to a girl. Fanny knew they were talking about her. She looked anxious and hopeful.

Fanny had shoulder length curly hair that framed her face. Cute dimples, soft innocent skin, and glasses that hid her midnight blue eyes, she was a little taller than Jimmy. Her Black dress fell just below her knees but failed to hide her big bosoms.

Nothing could hide them, and she knew it. All the boys in school just stared. She didn't feel comfortable with the speechless attention. So, when Jimmy walked up to her and said hi, it was pretty special.

Fanny fumbled for words and told Jimmy how sorry she was about his Dad. She went on to tell him how much she liked his eulogy. Jimmy noticed Fanny's glass was empty and asked her if she wanted to go with him and get more soda. I looked across the room at Tony and he had a face full of pride for his friend. He caught my look, as I gave him the unspoken "you da man"

I turned to Steph, and she saw everything. But nobody saw Jimmy and Fanny disappear. Me and my girl wondered where they went and what they were doing. I said to Steph," They probably ran down to the closest elementary school and tried to break in" Her laughing smile followed a swift slap on my arm. It felt nice to not be the new couple. I hoped Jimmy and Fanny hooked up. All he had to do was kiss her, and I knew there was no way she'd reject him.

They thought they were being so cool, entering the house from different entrances. Busted... they had the same excited, relieved, happy smile. I went to say something, and Steph slapped me again before I could say a word. She was my balance. But Tony was Tony, "Jimmy where you been?" "Getting a breath of fresh air." Tony, with a "don't even try to bullshit me", smile, said, "Really? I gotta get me some of that kind of fresh air.".And he walked right outside. We all knew we'd talk about it on the walk to school tomorrow.

Families started to leave, this was the tough part. As the crowd dwindled to a select few,. Tony made his dad stay; Stephanie's dad did too. For my family, It was an easy thing to do. Tony's dad helped clean , Steph's dad joined in. My family, Steph, and Tony tried to distract Jimmy's mom from the loneliness she was about to feel as soon as all of us were gone. I wasn't worried about Jimmy, he had me and Tony, but his mom had nobody. Havin nobody must really suck. Mom sensed it, and brought up the name of a new coffee shop in town. "Let's go there on Thursday" Jimmy's mom just nodded ok. "It's my treat, I'll be here at 11:30 to pick you up" Mom knew not to use the "if you need anything, call me" line. Days later, Mom told me she had a nice cup of coffee with Mrs. Fortunato and they're going to try to meet every week. .

It was a long day, really long, all funerals are. My family got in the car and made our way home. Nobody talked much. Our emotional tanks were empty and only sleep would re-fuel them. We found the way to our bedrooms. All of us said our goodnights and even threw in a few I love yous. Not exactly Walton Mountain, but the thought was there. We were just tired of being strong all day. I grabbed the phone and shut the door to my bedroom.

I called Stephanie and she picked up on the first ring. I wanted to talk to her, but didn't know what to say. The way she says "hi" melts me, breaks down a lot of the walls. I couldn't say "hi" half as good as she did, but I always tried. It musta sounded nice cause she said she wanted to call me tonight too. We had chemistry, great chemistry. I wanted to trust her, but I knew it wasn't her I couldn't trust. It was me. I didn't feel safe enough with Stephanie to tell her everything. Before Jimmy's Dad died, Dad never talked, so it was hard for me. I really liked her, so I knew I had to try.

"So, whaddya think about today?"

"It was a beautiful day. Jimmy's eulogy was so special, and I'll never forget it cause you didn't let go of my hand. Kenny, I haven't been to a funeral before and didn't wanna tell you. But you held my hand, you never let go."

"Well, you didn't let go of mine either." I had to change the subject quickly.

"Hey did Fanny call you? I'm dying to know what happened when they went outside."

Steph put me in check. "Baby, I know you never said a word about when we first kissed. Cause if you did, I woulda kicked you in your pride and joy"

I couldn't stop laughing. I never heard it called that. "Trust me, Jimmy's gonna talk tomorrow on the way to school. Me and Tony made this happen"

As a girl would say, "Please don't spread this all around school"

"Stephanie, what my friends and I talk about goes no further. It's just the way we are"

. "So why didn't you tell them about me?"

I hated how smart she was. She was trying to get me to say

something about her. And it worked. "You're different" She continued to push me,

"What's different mean?"

"Different means I like you a lot, so would you stop with the fuckin questions?" I heard a little bit of laughing as she told me "I like you a lot too."

I told her I'd see her tomorrow and hung up the phone. Why aren't days after funerals holidays? I was spent and had to wake up and be strong today for my friend. And, every day, till he was okay. I forced myself to fall asleep to get ready for tomorrow. My last thought was about Mr. Childlow. You don't get paid for that. I held my pillow and wondered how many families appreciated what he did. I know my family got closer but funerals and honeymoons, Both have feelings that can't last forever. It's a lot easier to say the honeymoon's over than the funeral.

Morning sunrise came and it was time go to school. The worst thing about hormones is they make you stink if you don't shower every day. Every morning ten minutes were stolen from me just so I wouldn't smell. If I smelled Stephanie would be grossed out. The shower water beaded down on me like a hot summer rain. I washed all the important parts and then, hung out under the rain. I relaxed and thought about nothing but the water, until Jimmy and Fanny came into my head. The shower quickly ended. My clothes and knapsack were ready for school. I ran downstairs, chugged my O.J. and made it to Tony's house.

Tony was outside waitin. He gave me the macho hug,

"Hey Brother, you alright? Let's go find out if Jimmy touched the fun bags" "You think he did? I say he pussed out"

"Jimmy heard you when you were talking about symph sex, remember??, he kept askin you. I'm bettin he brushed da balloons."

"Ok Tony, you work it though. You'll get it outa him. And if he says he did, tell him you don't believe him. Make Jimmy give details"

Tony called me crazy but knew I was right. Besides, it'd make for a good walk to school and distract Jimmy from the first day of "getting back to normal."

Jimmy left his house with his tough guy face. Me and Tony had smiles. Tony hugged him again, "Hey brother did you tap da balloons yesterday, or what?' Tony knew exactly what he was doing. He didn't care about what happened between Jimmy and Fanny. He cared about life going on without his dad.

Jimmy was on the defensive right away, He thought he'd be smart and say, "that's none of your fuckin business"

Tony wouldn't back down, "Kenny he was too scared to do anything." Peer pressure always wins.

"Fuck, we made out for a while and yeah I went to second. With Fanny's set what guy wouldn't try. "They were really big and felt like soft mounds of dough" Jimmy had us. You couldn't make that one up. What made him think of fresh bread at a time like that.?

We were right outside school when the bell rang telling us first period began in five minutes. Tony stopped with the jokes. "Jimmy, We're you're friends" Jimmy tried to speak and Tony told him, "Shut the fuck up. I'm trying to tell you something. We've never gone through what you've gone through in the last week. I don't know what's goin through your head, but I do know one thing. We all go through our own private hell. And I've been lucky enough to have you and Kenny to share mine. So, you gotta know you can say anything to us. We're brothers and don't ever forget it. And one more thing, we're still gonna give you a wedgie"

School days were winding down and summertime was almost here. It always seems like a summer sun hits the bushes and trees on the last day of school. Kids you didn't like all year, you got along with for a day. It's closure. J. T. and me, we knew we'd have fun all summer. School was the bond that brought Steph and I together. Now's it's gone. I liked her too much to see her in September. But we were cool all summer. Movies, roastin marshmallows, going to arcades, and walkin on the boardwalk, I hated that she'd always beat me in skeet ball. But she and me had fun all summer long. Kissing on the Boardwalk till it was time to go home.

The sun set and I went home. Dad had a few cheap beers in him. Music played in the background. After I got a soda, he calls me to the table and. asks me," you know who this is?" I had no idea. Dad told me it was some guy named Bruce. I think he was Dad's Boss. The song was about some screen door slammin, a dress wavin, and a vision dancin. He loved the song. Trying to get closer to my dad, I asked, "what's the name of the song." From the time I sat down, he never looked up, Dad's head rose, with a weathered warm look, he said, "Thunder Road".

Growing up in Verona, I heard Dad's boss on the radio every day. Droppin my head on the pillow, I got why Dad liked the song. Mom and Dad's marriage had alotta Thunder, and neither one was to blame. But Thunder can take a lot outa anybody. I know he'd never admit it, but my mom was the vision he saw dancin across the porch. I hope he can see himself back to the vision.

Before I fell asleep, I checked on Terry. One knock and she let me in. I sat Indian style by her bed and asked her if she was okay. A meek yeah didn't cut it. "Terry, what are you thinking?' ...

"I don't know"

.. "Yeah, you do, just tell me "

She opened, "I know it's been awhile but the funeral scared me" "

"What did?"

" The whole thing, Kenny, it was soo nice but so hard."

I couldn't explain to my sister, something I couldn't explain to myself. The best I could say was," You're right"..." It's hard, but what you saw at the church?, the heart, beauty, everything will stay with you. Don't be scared of it, Remember it. Cherish it. Someday when you have a friend that needs a friend, you'll be there. Cause that's what the funeral was all about.. My sister gave an innocent tired look, I stood up, kissed her on her forehead and told her, "good-night, Terry, I love you" By the time I got my words out, she was asleep.

CHAPTER FOUR

Triple date night was here. There's something bizarre about a date night where the parents are the other couples. The doorbell rang and Terry ran to answer it. It was Steph, her dad, and his trophy girlfriend, Monica. Dad didn't ask. He just went to the fridge and grabbed two cans of his best beer and handed one to Mr. Demarino. Mom graciously took their coats and asked Monica if she wanted a glass of wine. Putting her arm trustingly on Stephanie's shoulder Mom said, "I'll let Kenny learn some manners and get you something to drink." Her voice got softer as she leaned to Steph and said, "Ask him for something he has to make for you, like ice tea" Girls will be Girls and mom was being a girl with Stephanie.

As mom walked by to get Miss Monica her glass of wine, she told me to ask my guest if she wanted something to drink. I sounded fake but it made mom happy as I asked my girl if she was thirsty. She confidently chimed, "yes, I would. Can you make me some iced tea please? two sugars and a little bit of lemon" I wasn't ready for this and turned to tell mom to make it but she was consumed in first time meeting talk. Lost, I forced myself into the kitchen and heard my kid sister yell. I want some too, just like Stephanie's.

I turned around to give a glaring look at Terry and out of the corner of my eyes, I saw Mom and Steph exchanging sorority smiles at my expense. I rose to the challenge though. I mean how hard can it be to make iced tea.? I threw some tea bags in a glass pitcher and filled it with cold water. Nothing happened. I figured I didn't use enough tea. So, I went back to the cubbard , got the rest of the tea bags, about fifty of them and dumped them in the cold water. Still, nothing happened!!!!. Stephanie yelled to see if everything was alright and then my sister piled on,, "hurry up. I'm thirsty" I used to love that kid, but she was testing me tonight!

Mom finally felt I had enough and came in the kitchen to check on me. "Oh Kenny, honey, what did you do????" "Duh mom, I was trying to make iced tea, but the tea bags aren't working. They must be broken" As only moms can say, "let me show you how" She quickly filled a big pot with water and boiled it. Once it was boiling, she put a few of the tea bags I used and dumped them in the hot water. Mom tossed the others away. She tried to make me feel important as she turned off the burner, handed me a wood spoon and told me to stir the pot.

While I was "making the tea" mom filled the pitcher up with lots of ice and placed a strainer over the top of the pitcher. I had no idea what she had in mind. She took the spoon from my hand, picked up the pot and poured it into the waiting cold pitcher of ice, allowing for the bags to fall into the strainer. She asked me to get two tall glasses and fill them with ice. Mom poured the tea and dropped two lumps of sugar and a lemon slice in each glass. A quick stir and she said, "here, now take these out to Stephanie and your sister"

Terry drank almost half of hers right away. Stephanie smiled, said thank you and asked me what took me so long. I told her the tea bags were broken so my mom had to fix them. Stephanie and Miss Monica gave a knowing look at each other that seemed to say," "Men!!" Mom came out of the kitchen and asked Monica if she'd like to see the rest of the house. They took their short tour and passed the men watching the knick game on TV. Terry asked Steph if she wanted to see her room and they took off too.

Left standing there alone, I made my way over to the "boys" and asked the score of the game. We made guy talk and dad ribbed me about makin the iced tea, "Ya didn't see me crushin any grapes in the kitchen, did ya??? "Steph's dad got the joke and the two bumped cans in a quick man toast. Dad heard an empty echo, got up to get two more beers before the girls came back from their tour. He always seemed to steal beers when mom was in another room. I didn't wanna embarrass him, but I felt like saying, "what? You don't think mom can do the math? All she has to do is look in the fridge and see how many are left"

Mom called us all to the table and I asked what's for dinner. She confidently answered," Gorgonzola Cheese Salad and shrimp scampi" Fish Friday. Mom brought out the big bowl of salad. It had a pyramid of the cheese grated on top. Monica commented on how good it looked and mom told her she got the recipe from this restaurant in Connecticut, just over the New York border. Monica piped in," you mean Manero's?" Mom nodded as she was mixing the salad. They both went on to mutually brag about the place. Everyone agreed the garlic bread and salad were the best in the tri state area. People would wait an hour in the cold to get a table. They went on, joking about how strong the garlic was, didn't make it the best place to go for first date night. But it was the place to have a baby!! There was a sign in the place that said, "If your baby is born here, they will eat free at the restaurant for life" The sign sold alotta steaks, but there was never a baby born there. So Manero's made out like bandits.

Dad changed the subject and asked Mr. Demarino if he heard about the two seniors who got arrested for smoking pot outside Verona High. Nervous tension rocked me as dad asked me if I knew the kids. I continued shoving salad in my mouth. He went on, "Why do kids smoke that crap anyway?" I wanted to say, dad, you're poundin beers like it's water and there's gonna be a drought any minute. What's the difference? It was a stupid one so I kept my true feelings to myself. His answer woulda been cause one's legal and one's not. I sheepishly answered his question," Don't ask me, I don't know why" Dad fired back that he better never catch me smoking that garbage. Monica's face was hiding, she knew a thing or two about a "jimmy cough"

I wanted to end the drug talk, so I thought I'd fight back and ask about sex. After that, rock n roll would bring us all together. I waited for the perfect silence to come and then asked my Dad, " How do you know what size condoms to buy and how many sizes are there?. Is it like shoes?" Bingo!!!! All sorts of pieces of silverware dropped, sounding like a drum solo at a Who concert. Dad raised his voice and reminded me my kid sister was here.

I was ready for his "reminder." Dad, she's twelve and takes the bus to school. Don't let her fool you. I bet she knows all the words that rhyme with condom. I love my kid sister, she insisted, "Kenny you're wrong!!!! Now, the word rubber? There's blubber, flubber, clubber, nubber, chubber" With uncontrollable laughter, Mom and Monica begged Terry to Stop!!!! They must've remembered their own bus rides to school as kids. Dad finally relented but was curious to know why I asked in the first place. I told him cause when mom takes me grocery shopping, about once a month we go down that aisle and mom gets something, I don't even know what it is. The people who are shopping for condoms stand there for a while reading all the boxes. It looks like they're looking for their size.

Mr. Demarino glared at Steph. She responded, "Dad, I know what you're thinking, don't worry!!! Kenny's just messing with you and his dad. He's like that, ya know. I love that he always makes me laugh. His sense of humor is my favorite thing about him" That's my girl lovin her boy!! She's right," yeah, we're one"

Mom started serving the scampi. Dad poured the wine in our fancy glasses. Big Italian dinners in Verona always lasted for hours. We loved our good food, good friends, and good conversation. This was no different. Stephanie changed the conversation as she asked Terry who was her favorite group She answered, "The Beatles" Monica told us it was hers too. She asked Terry about her favorite song. Terry told the table her favorite was "Help" Mom told her baby, "You have good taste, honey. It's mine too. My sister told mom she already knew cause she plays it all the time when she's housecleaning. Steph couldn't contain herself as she blurted, "Isn't Ringo soooo cute?" Four girls agreeing, you don't see that every day. I couldn't be jealous. You can't compete with a Beatle for a girl's heart. And, besides, Steph would just flirt right in front of me with the first bowl cut guy she saw, just to get under my skin. I guess I should be happy they didn't start oohin and aahin over Davy too.

Dad was a little quiet. He was too busy sneakin peeks at Monica's trophies. Mom caught him in mid peek. She gave him a priceless look. It was easy to read and brought Dad right back to reality. Her eyes shouted, yeah, like you have a shot with her and even if you did, you could never keep up with her. Dad's eyes reluctantly answered, "I know but I can dream, can't I" Maybe mom and dad's marriage was better than I thought. They definitely understood and accepted each other.for better or worse, as the saying goes. Triple dating was a lot better than I thought it'd be and everyone at the table probably agreed.

Mom got up and started clearing the table. Playing the role of the perfect guest, Monica quickly helped mom out. I could hear them sharing a conversation about me and Steph. Monica asked mom, "don't they make a cute couple? You should be really proud of the way you and your husband raised your son. Kenny's a great kid" Mom smiled as she said "Aww thanks, But we didn't do it all on our own, Kenny raised himself a little too" Monica didn't understand what mom was telling her. She thought mom was being humble. I knew exactly what mom was thinking. She was talking about the rough times in her marriage and felt guilty about neglecting Terry and me. As kids we didn't care, we just ignored their bullshit and pretended it wasn't happening.

Monica started to make the cappuccino and set the mugs on the table for the adults. She teased my sister and asked her if she wanted a cup too. She wasn't a natural, but it was easy to see Monica was trying to fit in. I think she liked tonight. It musta been a nice change from the meat market bar where she and Steph's dad hung out on Friday nights. I think she was even a little envious of mom and dad. This was a first for me. I never met anyone who wanted to trade places with my mom and dad.

Mom was busy in the kitchen whipping up one of her trademark desserts, Ice cream cake roll. Sweet white lard was rolled up in chocolate cake. A well- rounded scoop of vanilla ice cream sat on top smothered in chocolate sauce and whip cream. Fat food protocol demanded a cherry on top. It was better than dessert should be allowed. With coffee and cake, the conversation slowed, and I just got lost in seeing the candles reflect in Steph's eyes. It was a make out moment and the threat of parents catching us made it even hotter. The thought, not the candle.

She dove headfirst into the forbidden fruit. "Kenny, do you have the pages of the textbook we're supposed to study for the history final" I'm slow. I didn't get it, which actually fit my personality. Steph gasped with frustration and asked me where my books are. I told her in my room. "Where's your room? I'll find the book" Mom and Monica laughed and said men can never find anything. I, sheepishly, took her to my room where she attacked me as soon as we got there. I swear I'll be ninety and never be bored by her kiss. It's like adolescent viagra, there's a reason it's not made. It would be a weapon of mass destruction.

Steph's dad yelled upstairs it was time to go. She guessed he wanted to take Monica to their bar. In mid kiss, she knees me right in my little man of La Mancha and buckles my knees. She walked away with a girlie giggle. So, everyone could hear, she told me to hurry up. I hobbled my way down the stairs. My kid sister opens her big mouth and asks me why I'm walkin funny. Steph turned that screw and asked, "Yeah Kenny, why are you walking funny? Did you stub your big toe again?'" I fought back. "Yeah, it hurts bad when you stub the big one"

We all gathered at the front door and the adults wanted to see how me and my girl would say goodnight. Broadway didn't have a bigger stage. I just went to her, kissed her on the cheek, gave her a friendship hug, and said goodnight. Playing her role perfectly, Steph took the stage. With a face that was far more innocent than her years, she shyly wished me a good night, and told me she hopes my toe gets better. I had to wonder if Juliet made Romeo stub his big toe. We fooled them all. The 'rents thought we were cute.

Summer vacation didn't come quick enough for me, Steph, Jimmy or Tony. Me and my girl couldn't wait to hang out at the shore on warm nights makin s'mores by the fire. Every couple made some stupid excuse to steal some make out time. We all knew everybody was lying but nobody would bust another couple. It was kinda fun seeing who could come up with the stupidest excuse. Ours was we had to go check on Terry, I forgot Fanny's kid sister and Terry went to the movies. It was fun in a weird kinda way. kids' actin like old married couples. Singles weren't invited and if they stopped by, they left real quick cause they felt like pathetic losers who couldn't find anyone to like them.

Tony didn't care. He waited up on the boardwalk in his muscle shirt showing off his natural dark tan. The loser girls would stroll by Tony, and he'd pick up a few every night and take them to the make out Mecca under the boardwalk. He didn't take names or numbers, just a little bit of their innocence. They didn't care either. Somehow, they felt less like a loser kissing a guy they knew their mom and dad would hate. Tony loved being the guy that the dad would fear, and the mom would be forced to remember...Every girl in the world had a Tony they'd never forget. Good Girls never forget the bad boys and the good guys never remember the bad girls.

Summer gave us "da fellas" nights too. With no homework, we could get outa hand and not worry about what time we woke. If we were up by the time Bob Barker told us spray our pests, it was all-good. We'd smoke alotta pot at the shore and talk about everything. One night, each of us was all alone in our high. listening to the sounds of the waves crashin on the sand. I'd close my eyes and try to guess when a big wave would come crashing. There wasn't a pattern or rhythm, but you could listen to the splashin serenade for hours.

Jimmy broke the silence. "My dad came in my room last night"

Tony and me thought Jimmy hit the pipe too hard. "What?"

"Yeah, I'm not kiddin, he did. He just left here too. He doesn't like me getting high but he likes hangin out with us and seein me happy."

Tony responded, "You gotta be fuckin crazy. There ain't no such thing as ghosts" Jimmy got all defensive and told us his dad ain't no ghost; he's an angel now. It'd only been two months since his dad died, so anything he wanted to say, me and Tony would listen. I told Jimmy to go on and tell us about last night.

"You know I can't talk about this stuff with Fanny, right?" We nodded. So he went on. "The first time it happened, it really freaked me out. There I was grabbin my pillow, open my eyes and see Dad standin there. He told me it was okay and not to be scared. Dad asked if I was being good to mom and Fanny. He knew Fanny liked me at the party, yeah, he was there too. We talked for hours. I asked him what it's like in heaven and he said he couldn't say much... member privilege He said it was all I thought and more. A smile came across his face, "only high school baseball games, no pro." He cried telling me how much he liked my eulogy. Dad couldn't contain how proud he was as he reached in his pocket and showed me a copy of my tribute to him. "It's the first thing they give you when you get to heaven"

Tony looked jealous listening to Jimmy. He was scared it would take his dad to die for him to love Tony. Fear quickly brought disappointment as he realized there was no way "Da Man" was letting his dad on the shuttle bus to Heaven's country club.

Tony finished his daydream dilemma and continued listening to Jimmy. who went on to say how his dad would wait till I was asleep and then go to mom's room. He said he couldn't talk to mom, that's a heaven rule. But she could feel him and he felt her too. The boss upstairs says it's what a couple feels about each other is way more important than the words they speak. Sometimes words can be mean and there's no mean people in heaven. His dad, being dead, seemed to get a lot closer to his mom. I guess sometimes people learn too late. Jimmy told us they have a curfew in heaven and it's sunrise. His dad stayed with his wife till the last possible second, before he had to be back.

After his dad taught him about heaven's rules, Jimmy became a lot nicer to Fanny. He learned on his own to be affectionate. Fanny didn't know how to accept his changes. She thought she wasn't good enough to have a boy treat her nice. So, she never had to worry about what she'd do if someone did. Girls always think it's easier to be with the bad boy. They know they're better than them. But, the nice boy scares them. It's like they feel they have to be on their best behavior. It's a wasted competition. Besides, the nice guy would like the real girl who hung out with the bad boy. At least she'd be herself. Fanny got a little nervous about being herself as Jimmy was changing. She felt she wasn't gonna ever do better than Jimmy, so she better not fuck it up. She was alright, Jimmy liked her and that's all that mattered.

This was my favorite summer. But I say that every year. Each summer is different. Last year was fun playing capture the flag and catching fireflies. This summer it was making out and smoking pot. The one constant of every summer was the amusement park on the shore. Labor Day was the official end of summer but for me, it was standin on the boardwalk and watching the sun sink just above the Ferris wheel. Catching the memory was always unexpected. It usually happened on a Wednesday or Thursday about 5:30. We'd all tell ourselves we'd still come back on the weekends once school started, But, we never did.

Summer was my favorite season. It was a great school vacation. I don't know who named the seasons, but they sure did a good job. You definitely Fall into September. There's that short sadness when you realize the summer is over. You Fall alright, right into Winter. The only thing good about Winter is Christmas. Thanksgiving got the short end of the stick. It got lost between the two seasons. Besides, We only got two days of school off and I didn't like turkey. Christmas had cool songs and how could you not like Santa Claus. Everybody got into the Christmas spirit. The Spirit meant people were nice to people for a few weeks. Once it's over you crash and winter haunts you with darkness. Sure, you can go sleigh riding a few days, but shivering your ass off sucked. So Spring would stubbornly nudge winter aside and everybody blossomed, just like the flowers.

Daydreaming on the boardwalk was awesome until I looked at the sun. It had fallen between the spokes in the Ferris wheel. Time to catch the bus back home and get a window seat so I could do some world watchin.. This year was gonna be different. It was high school. I went from being the big guy at a small school to a freshman punk at a big school. I didn't like being a punk. Punks get their asses kicked. I had more important things than my ass to worry about...Losing Steph.

I didn't sleep well the night before school started. Yeah, Steph and me were one, but in high school, she could easily get a better "one". Or maybe some senior would get her and my life would be shattered to pieces. No one could appreciate what I was thinking. I didn't wanna hear that you never forget your first love crap. And Rod Stewart had to remind me ten times a day about the first cut being the deepest.

CHAPTER FIVE

Morning arrived, I chugged my orange juice and headed out the door to meet Tony and Jimmy. It took a little longer to walk to Verona High. And Jimmy and me had a nervous shake to our voice. Tony picked up on it and busted our balls. " Ain't nobody gonna kick your ass and if someone tries to take your girl, let em. It only means they're worthless bitches. Fuck em if they wanna dump you. Anyway, the only thing you gotta worry about is getting caught cheatin on them. There's alotta ready babes in high school". Tony told it like it is, no pullin punches. Jimmy and me felt a little better or at least that's what we showed Tony.

We got to the school. Holy shit, Verona High is fuckin huge. The noise made it seem even bigger. It took ten minutes just to find my homeroom. But, what a ten minutes it was. There were hot girls everywhere, and some were even checkin me out. You gotta be cool and act like you've seen her lust look before.

I sat next to this hot girl in home room. The hottest thing about her was she had no idea how hot she was. Today, I was a little late to homeroom, so I couldn't say a word to her. I promised myself I'd never be late for homeroom again. Classes went by in a blur. Each subject had hotter girls than the last one. And the walks to your next class between periods, I never knew there was this many good looking girls in the world. It was like my own little beauty contest and I was gonna take my time deciding who was "Miss Verona" . Has there ever been a tie in a beauty contest? Well, I guess there's a first time for everything. I made the rules, after all, the pageant was only in my head.

I couldn't wait till school got out and me, Tony and Jimmy could talk about the first day. We didn't talk about names, just their bodies. Big balloons were everywhere especially on the older girls. They carried them around much better. Since they were older, they understood the power of their "treasure chests" Not only did the like us staring, they liked it even more catching us and makin us speak stupid dumb real quick. "Little boy can't talk, you sure you're in the right school.? Usually, you guys take the short bus." Sometimes I had to get a little spunky right back at them or I'd lose their respect. "Bendover, I'll give you a short bus!!!" Tony and Jimmy cracked up as Tony said, "Kenny you ain't got stones, them are some big boulders you're carryin around in that package of yours." New School., same great time walkin and talkin our way home.

Steph called after dinner. I made my mom lie and say I was at Jimmy's. Fifteen minutes later, mom came upstairs to put some laundry away. She stopped by my room to ask if everything was alright between Steph and me. I gave her a hesitant, "Yeah". She accepted me at my word but gently spoke, "I'm here if you ever wanna talk. I think Stephanie is a great girl for you and I'd hate to see anything happen between the two of you." "I hear ya mom" I didn't know how I felt about her meddling. I know she meant well, but she boxed me in at a time I needed space. Now I had to worry about Steph and mom if it didn't work out between us. After the first day of high school, I didn't see how Steph and me could make it.

The first week was just like the first day. Getting used to a whole new world, I didn't take Steph's calls. She called Friday night, and my mom made me talk to her. I got to the phone and heard this attitude. I was in no mood. "What's goin on Kenny?" I gave her a defensive, "nothing" She saw right through my bullshit. "Nothin huh? I see you in the hall yesterday and you wave at me like I was nothing. Just tell me, we still "One" or not." There was awkward silence. "Kenny, please just tell me if we're one or not." I had to say something. "I don't know" She started crying and told me to let her know when I decide. And, she hung up. . It was only a few seconds, but I found myself spiraling out of control at the thought of us not being together anymore. Thank God the weekend was here. I wanted to be alone to figure out what I just did. I barely slept as I felt emotionally paralyzed lying in my bed.

Morning came, me and Tony. got a slice of pizza for lunch. I had to talk to somebody and knew Tony would be straight with me. We met at Vincenzo's around one and sat down at the table in the corner with the red and white-checkered tablecloth. He knew something was wrong." Aren't you getting tired carryin around that heavy heart?" I got right to the point. "I think I broke up with Steph last night" He couldn't believe what he heard, "you gotta be fuckin kiddin me right?" I took a bite of my pie and said, "no I'm not" with a mouthful of pizza. He asked what happened and I told him, I didn't think she and me would last through high school, so I thought it was best to cut it now. He backed me up, "wait, whaddya mean you think you broke up with her last night. You either did or you didn't" "well then, I didn't"

I knew Tony would set me straight, but he showed another side. "Kenny, this is pretty easy. You gotta listen to your heart, not your head. Your heart can't lie to you. Look, I can't tell you what to do cause I gotta be me and you gotta be you, but just listen to it and you'll find your answer" "I gotta be me?" who are you? Sammy Davis Jr." Tony cracked me up, "look, you can call me a ginnie, a whop, anything but a muleyon. Don't tell anybody but I think Ol Sammy can sing and if he's okay with Frank, he's okay with me" "Yeah, I guess I "got to be there" Tony liked Sammy and I thought Michael was the best. Tony was alotta help. So was the pizza. But Vincenzo's aint right unless you finish with a cherry Italian ice. Lunch wasn't even over and already, my heart was knockin on my chest telling me to listen.

We finished our ices and made our way back home. Tony told me not to sweat it and I'll know what to do when I know what to do. Ya gotta to love his pot thoughts. Who else could come up with words that made no sense, but made all the sense in the world? Once home, I went to my room to have a "come to Jesus" talk. Time to find the Rolling Stones, and my headphones. "Wild Horses" was my favorite song. Lying on my bed, staring at the ceiling, I began. "What the fuck did I do?? Why did I do it? I got real pissed and knew why. I did it because I didn't wanna lose her. If anybody was getting dumped, it was going to be her, not me. I couldn't take being dumped. She was the most important thing in my life. I forgot I was the most important thing in hers." My life with Steph flashed before my eyes. Walking her home from school, our first kiss, our sleepover, the funeral, hanging out at the shore and makin out. She wasn't a part of my life. She was my life, and I was hers. I didn't know how I was gonna fix this or even if she'd let me. I had to try though.

The next week sucked. Tony and Jimmy tried to snap me outa my funk but realized there was nothing they could say or do. It was gonna take time, my time. On Thursdays I had fifth period free. I went to my locker to get a few books. Rounding the corner, I saw this huge senior at Steph's locker. He had his hand over her head and it rested on the wall of lockers. She looked trapped and had to listen to this big jerk. Just cause he wore his Blue wool jacket with the leather sleeves, he thought every new girl wanted the football star.

Tony saw everything, walked right up to the guy and told him to leave the girl alone. "Keep on walkin punk boy. You aint gonna do anything about it." You never challenged Tony. He steps right up in the guy's face and asked the guy what he called him? "I said punk boy and you aint gonna do anything.

Tony got even closer, "I'm not huh?" At that point Tony looked him square in the eyes and grabbed the guy's tool bag and started squeezing real hard, until the guy dropped to the floor and was crying in pain. "A punk just kicked your ass and you didn't do shit" To humiliate the guy more, Tony spit on him while he was down on the ground. "Now, get up and get the fuck outa here before I get pissed. And don't you ever even think about talking to this girl again".

The guy could barely stand up, much less walk, as he made his way down the hall. "Hi my name is Tony. I'm one of Kenny's best friends. Are you okay" Steph answered him," I know who you are, we never met but Kenny talks... I mean talked about you all the time. I remember you from the funeral. And thank you, I'm okay. That guy was an idiot"

Tony wasn't big on long hellos. "Well, it was nice meeting ya" and he walked away.

Steph was always polite. It took her a second to yell, "it was nice meetin you too" Tony turned his head and smiled at her. then started shaking his head like he didn't understand girls.

We got out of school and walked home. Naturally, Tony wanted to tell us about the ass kicking he gave to a senior. He started,"Wild day today"

I bumped in, "I know I saw the whole thing"

Tony looked confused, "You did?" Jimmy had no idea what we were talking about and wanted to know more.

"I saw you kick that guy's ass today when he was talking to Steph"

Tony turned modest, "Man, he was nothing, I saw in his eyes nobody ever challenged him, so I knew he'd do nothing but cry like a baby" Jimmy was completely lost but decided to shut up and listen. Tony continued, "But that wasn't the wild thing. This teacher, Mr. Bishotti saw what I did and called me into his office. I thought I was in big trouble"

Jimmy was catchin on, "Tony, you're the only guy I know that could get kicked out of school in less than two weeks" "That's not what happened you idiot, so shut up and listen"

"Mr. Bishotti was waiting for me. He told me to sit down and asked if I wanted a soda or anything. I said no thank you, figuring I'd score points for being polite" Mr. Bishotti saw the fear in Tony's eyes and Tony knew if he got kicked out, his father would kick the livin shit outa him.

The teacher spoke up, " I saw your little stunt today and while I don't like what you did, I do respect the courage you showed standing up to the senior and protecting the girl. By the way that senior is on my football team and he's the toughest guy in the school or was.

"Son, you have a decision to make. I can kick you out for

fighting, or you can be on the football field at 3pm tomorrow ready to practice."

Tony hesitated and stuttered, "But I never played football and I ain't interested" Mr. Bishotti's hard demeanor came out. "Did you hear me? I never asked you if you played or wanted to. I said you got a choice to make. I'll leave the room for five minutes and when I come back, you give me your answer. No Bullshit, no negotiation"

Tony couldn't believe a teacher cursed. He liked it though. He knew there was no decision to make. Mr. Bishotti returned. "Sir I'll be on the field at 3, but don't expect me to like it."

"I really don't care if you like it or not. And my name isn't Sir, It's Mr. Bishotti in school and Coach on the field. Don't forget it. Now get outa here. I don't wanna see your face till 3 tomorrow"

Tony found habits hard to break, "Thank you Si.., I mean Mr. Bishotti.

Tony asked us, "Can you believe that shit? He let me go."

Jimmy caught on, "I have a feeling he didn't. You'll see"

I thought this was gonna be good for Tony. I was the book worm, Jimmy liked makin gadgets. And Tony liked getting in fights.

Once home, I had to face the music. Sitting on my bed, I dialed the phone for ten minutes and stopped in mid dial every time. What was I gonna say? I always pick the best times to go stupid. I remembered what Tony said about my heart. Since my head was in stupid mode, I figured the best thing to do was let my heart do the talking.

It rang twice and she answered. My heart exploded at the sound of her voice. I didn't even say it was me calling, I just let it out. "I'm Sorr.."

She stopped me in the middle of the word. "No, don't be. You don't have to be. "I shot back, "We're gonna fight now about me saying I'm sorry?"

She responded, "No. Calling already tells me you are"

I had to explain. "Please, Steph let me talk" She didn't stop me. "I was stupid. I did what I did cause I thought you were gonna dump me for some better guy. I couldn't take it. So I felt if I dumped you, it wouldn't hurt me. I was wrong. It hurt like shit. I thought about all the times we shared and realized ain't no other guy or girl is gonna break us up. The only ones who can do that is us"

Steph put on a hillbilly southern accent, "Yo momma didn't raise no fool boy" We shared a few mushy I miss yous and She had a question." So are we one? With all the conviction of a preacher in my voice, "Fuckin A Right. And Steph, baby, I saw you checkin out Tony's ass"

She didn't deny it as she turned that knife. "Hell yeah I did. He's got a cute ass and what's that big bump in the front of his tight jeans?" She did it again, getting me all speechless and frustrated. "Awwww baby you know I love your bump in your outa style jeans"

That's my girl. It felt really good to have her back. I wanted to get brownie points. "Steph I "L" you " She didn't know what the hell "L" meant so she asked. I told her, "Like, Love, Lust or all of the above."

Her smile came through. "I can live with that. I "L" you too"

. I got all excited, "Really? You lust me???"

She had me, "That's for me to know and you to find out.. See ya tomorrow" and she hung up with me thinking and stunned. I was right. Wild horses couldn't drag me away from her.

Sure enough, the next day, Tony was on that field at 3 o'clock. He was alone, but he wasn't leaving. After ten minutes, some old fat. used to be jock guy comes walkin toward Tony. Tony thought the whistle and the hat made the guy look like he thought he was important. He wasn't. One short whistle blow like Tony was a dog, "Come with me. Coach says I gotta put you in equipment" Our buddy didn't like the equipment, but he saw right away the pain he could put on somebody.

The first week was tough. Coach Bishotti never said a word to him. Tony got in fights every practice and the coaches had to drag him off his victims. They tried to teach him right, but Tony refused to listen. One practice Coach Bishotti had enough of watching Tony's antics. This time, he stepped in and dragged Tony off the other kid so hard Tony went flying to the ground. His coach stopped practice and called him out." Get up!!!! NOW!!!! I'M SICK AND TIRED OF YOUR BULLSHIT. So stop actin like a loser cause I know you're not. YOU HEAR ME? YOU'RE NOT A LOSER! You better listen to what my coaches are trying to teach you. I don't care if you kick every kid's ass on this team, but you're gonna do it within the rules of the game. If you don't, we can go right back to option one. You remember right????"

Tony didn't wanna get kicked out. Until now, the only ones who knew Tony wasn't a loser was me and Jimmy. Losers don't do what he did to protect Steph and his coach saw it. We talked about it on the walk home. I had to throw in my two cents." Ya know Tony, I know you're not askin me, but it sounds like this coach really doesn't care about what you do on the field. I think he's looking out for you. I've heard about coaches that go nuts when you make a mistake. He hasn't. The only thing he's yelled at you for is fighting and you know you can't do that on the field" Tony sheepishly agreed.

Jimmy wanted to know, "Well do you like it out there?" Tony answered quick and then slowed down. "No, but... I do like the hitting part. It gives me a rush like I've never known. When the play starts, thoughts of my dad get me in a rage and I pretend the other guy is my father, and I hit the shit outa him. It works cause you can't hit your dad. That ain't right" We couldn't believe it, "You serious Tony about what you're thinkin out there?" "Hell yeah!!! I'd be getting my ass kicked if I didn't"

Midway through the season, all the coaches met to review each kid. Coach Bishotti asked about "The freshman kid, Tony" His defensive coach, Coach Pacelli was the first to give his opinion. "You really wanna know?" Bishotti told him to go on. "He's the best kid on the team or, at least the defense. "Other coaches chimed in and agreed. "You don't coach this kid. You just tell him to go get the kid with the ball. He can't be stopped" The offensive coach put in his words," We've tried everything to stop him, and he goes through my guys like they're not there. And another thing, if we need a tough yard? He's getting the ball."

Coach Bishotti shared his thoughts with his coaches. "I don't care what you say. He's not starting. He's a freshman and that isn't fair to him or the seniors. He'll play but only a little. You guys decide when though. Key plays are fine but how's the kid he's replacing gonna feel? And I don't need his parents beating on my door asking why their kid got taken out.

By the way, what do we know about Tony?" A coach answered, "not a whole lot. He doesn't participate in class; he hangs around with two friends and the girls love him. I know he's tryin hard in practice cause he's always the last kid in the showers. Coach Bishotti had his thoughts about why but kept them to himself. "What about his parents?" Another coach answered. "His mother left when he was seven. Nobody knows where she went and the father is known as the town drunk" Coach was starting to see the picture, clearer than he wanted to.

Tony filled fall afternoons for Steph, Jimmy, Fanny and me.. We learned to tailgate when we didn't even have a car. We all kicked in a few bucks and bought one of those cheap Hibachis. Just the four of us, and the idea caught on and by our rival game we had over two hundred people doing the same thing in the lot. Two things I'll never forget. The steam coming out of our red plaid thermos filled with hot chocolate. The other was Steph in her bright white wool hat and matching scarf. Damn, she could make the cold look hot.

At the game nobody knew what we were watching, But when Tony played, the four of us would stand up and yell his name as loud as we could,. One time Coach Bishotti turned around and gave us an approving smile. The game would end and half the time we didn't even know who won. Once Coach was done talking to his team, we met Tony on the field. The first year, me and Jimmy rode Tony about him sittin on the bench. "He was dead tired, but still fired back. "Hey I scored, didn't I? And why don't you come out to the field on Monday at 3pm. I'll show you the bench"

Fanny was the biggest football fan out of the four of us. Her dad played for some Italian guy at Penn State. She asked Tony what it was like out there. Tony answered, "There ain't nobody tough, but it's sooo fast. It's like a huge fight. People coming at you from everywhere, it's a rush. I think I like it.. I love the sounds of people hitting people"

We made it through our freshman year a little older, a little smarter and a little more "mature" Puberty came and went, and we were different. Steph and Fanny were girls becoming women and the guys were sproutin hair around their package. There was always one late bloomer and he used to hide in the shower after gym. Naturally, the guy with the swingin chain took the shower next to him: making the boy feel even meeker Nobody made fun of him. He heard the snickering but it was only in his head. And, people wonder why some kids hate gym.

CHAPTER SIX

Sophomore year wasn't much different than freshman. We began to learn who we were. Getting an identity was both good and bad. The other kids would describe you as the tough kid or the smart guy. And Girl's identities were determined by their looks, the hot girl or the girl with the big rack. It doesn't matter who you really are, your classmates decided for you. Every kid fought with their parents and said, "you don't know me. You don't know who I am" Mom or Dad knew more about us than the kids in school. But we chose to take out on them what was being put on us. I wondered how long it would take for my identity to become mine, not theirs.

Tony became someone to watch on Verona's football team. When the summer started, me and Jimmy didn't think he'd play again. He did his time for the crime. But Coach Bishotti stayed in touch with Tony and they got together all summer long. At first we thought it was pretty pathetic this Coach was recruiting Tony to play again. We were wrong. He'd invite Tony out to eat, go to movies, play air hockey at the arcade. You know, kids' stuff.

We'd bust Tony's balls about what this guy was doing to get him back on his team. Tony defended him, "We haven't talked about football once. We check out the moms and daughters walking on the boardwalk. He'd crack me up when Coach said, "I'll pretend I'm your dad, Let's see if we can pick them up. Bishotti bet me he could get the mom's number before I could get the daughter's and he'd always win. I never picked up a girl. They always came to me. So, I had no idea what to say to them. He would bust my chops, watching me fumble my words. From then on, I'm callin you "Stuttering Tony", S.T. for short."

Tony kept talking about his coach. "We had awesome air hockey games and sometimes we'd bullshit about nothing for hours." Jimmy didn't believe him, "And you're trying to tell me he never once brought up football???? " " Tony surprised himself listening to his own answer, "No, never, not even one time" Jimmy continued to press him, "Then why the fuck are you playing???" Tony thought about it for a little bit. He didn't want to admit to his friends or even himself, he thought his coach was pretty cool. More importantly, he didn't wanna think about another adult letting him down or deserting him. He finished his thought and had a confused look on his face as he answered Jimmy, "I don't know."

On Saturday afternoons in the fall, Tony knew exactly what to do on the field. He got better every week and made some hits that the crowd would hear and cheer. Coach would be the first to greet him as he came off the field, "Way to go S.T.!!! That's S.T. Power!!! S.T.P.!!!" It took a lot to make Tony smile, especially on the football field, damn, if Coach couldn't get him to crack one. But Tony could get a smile or two outa his coach too. Kids asked him, "Why does he call you S.T.?" Tony would look at Coach out of the corner of his eye and say, "I'd tell ya , but then I'd have to hit ya"

Even the crowd would chant "S.T.P.... S.T.P." Tony didn't listen and he didn't care. The reason he played never changed. One day on the walk home, I had to ride him, "So Tony, if you started getting along with your dad, would you, all of a sudden, suck at football.? That fucker always had a comeback, "No, I'd just hate you instead"

As the season had a few games left, college recruiters would come to see the older kids. Tony saw them talking to Coach and pointing to him. Coach never brought it up and he didn't wanna know anyway. In the Hoboken game, he made 18 tackles, took out two players and, oh yeah, scored twice. They ended up winning 41-8.

Steph and me loved going to Friday night dances and grinding to Freebird. We never did "it" but started getting pretty hot and heavy. When we made out, I'd always push her hand toward my magic wand. It took some time, but she finally got the nerve to reach inside my pants and see exactly what was going on. Well, she didn't actually "see" it was more like feeling around like a blind woman looking for a light switch. Somehow, she convinced herself if she didn't see it, she was still a "good girl" I didn't really care what she was doin in there, .it felt real good., Thinking about her hand felt better in my head. It was much better than what she was doing.

When it was my turn, I was pathetic. I reached inside her pants and started feeling around like someone trying to get the last cookie in the bottom of the cookie jar. I never knew how different boys and girls were. Our stuff is right there at the edge of the zippered gateway. I reached around her little slice of heaven for two months before I realized I wasn't even close to the good part. It was a lot further south. She was too innocent and shy to tell me I was way off. She let me find out on my own. What a waste of two months!!!!.

It wasn't a race, but I think Jimmy and Fanny started doing "it" in tenth. We'd double date together. At parties, they would disappear sometimes five and six times a night and return the same way every time. Jimmy would have his shirt tail hanging out and Fanny would always be adjusting her clothes Each time she came back, she'd ask the same question, "Can I borrow a cigarette?"

Steph and I hid our own anxieties. We were curious to know if they were screwin, but didn't wanna ask. Cause they'd put the same question to us and we didn't wanna say we weren't, when they were. They might not like us anymore. I also didn't need Tony and Jimmy giving me shit. They thought I was fuckin Steph so let em think what they want. Growin up, I never thought, out of the three of us, I'd be the last virgin. I figured Jimmy wouldn't get laid till he was in his late thirties, so I had plenty of time.

On April 23rd, I celebrated my Declaration of Independence. I got my driver's license. Dad was pretty cool. He let me use the car to cruise the streets with Steph. On Friday nights we'd drive around for hours looking for people to look at us. It wasn't the nicest car on the block, but how can you not like an old Mustang Convertible.? It had an AM radio with the dial tuner and the five big black buttons you could push for your favorite stations. Dad had an eight track with Iron Butterfly's "In-a-Gadda-Davita" in the glove box. I never knew Dad liked acid rock..Steph and me didn't know how to use it so we left it alone.

The Friday night after school let out , I borrowed the car and took Steph to our first make out spot behind the elementary school. She reached over and gave my stick shift a long playful squeeze as she said, "awwww , my baby's romantic"

Being a guy, I shot back, "you can have romance in my pants!!!!"

She quickly removed her hand and slapped me hard on my arm, "You had to ruin it, didn't ya??"

Steph pulled back and told me, "We gotta talk"

"Awww Shit. You dumpin me a minute after you were rubbin me??

"No, Silly. I wanna talk about something with you"

"OK honey. I'm listening"

"Baby, All my life, I lived in this shit town. Dad never took me on Vacation. He'd get a sitter and go away with some whore. The furthest I've ever been is the White Castle on the edge of town. I wanna go away for the summer and get a job at the shore"

I asked, "Seaside Heights?? That's over an hour away"

A smile brightened up her face, " Fuckin A right . Isn't that awesome?"

Sometimes carin about your girl really sucks. Puttin her needs first is the right thing to do, but she's gonna leave me for the whole summer. This sucked. With a sad look on my face, she ran her hands through my hair , " Baby, no. Don't be sad., I need you to do this with me."

I thought about it for a little bit. "How are we gonna get there? Whaddya expect me to do there all day?" "

Get a job!!! That's what I wanna do. I want my own money. And Honey? You figure out how we can get there, I promise you I'll make Little Kenny very very happy" That's all I needed to hear.

It was getting late, and we drove her home. She gave me a nice soft kiss, "Don't forget what I said"

How could I!!!! I woke up Saturday morning and joined dad in the back yard. Summers at our house officially began when Dad planted the tomato plants. I asked if I could help. He looked at me like I was crazy. "Son, you're either nuts or you want something. Which one is it?

I returned the joke. "Dad, if I went crazy, don't ya think I'd be the last to know?" Dad got right to the point. "Alright, kid. Out with it. Whaddya want?"

"You promise not to get mad?"

Dad was losing his patience, "I'm gonna get mad if you don't tell me. Wait a second... you better not tell me you got Stephanie in trouble"

"WHAT????" I didn't understand and the look on my face was in sync with my confusion. Dad was happy I wasn't gonna call him Grandpa anytime soon. "C'mon kid talk, I'm listening"

"Ok, Dad. I wanna get a job this summer with Steph down the shore at Seaside Heights"

"If you wanna get a job, I don't care where you work"

He wasn't getting it. "Dad, I'm not done. I need to borrow your car"

"Whoa. How do you expect me to get to work??? "We both stood there and looked at each other. I think Dad remembered young love with mom. "Ok, son. You can have it for two weeks, no more, no less"

Huh? The summer was over two months long. "But Dad" He stopped me. "I can make it less than two weeks. Wanna go for one?"

I shut up and spent the rest of the weekend trying to figure out how to make Steph happy. After all, her makin me happy was all the inspiration needed. I called Sunday night and told her I had good news and bad news. Excitement busted through the phone, "Tell me, tell me baby"

I started, "My dad's letting me use his car for" ...

She cut right in with her fake southern accent, "I knew you could do it baby!!!! That's my man being a man!!!!!"

I had to bring her back to reality. "You didn't let me finish. He's letting me use it for two weeks"

Panicked disappointment filled the phone, "Oh". After a long silence, Excitement returned as she came up with the answer. "Baby, we can do it. Tomorrow, we go to Seaside and not leave till we get jobs. We tell them we can start right away. And that gives us two weeks to save our money and buy a cheap car. If we can each make two hundred a week, that gives us plenty"

The stubborn man in me came out. "Steph, I can't let you do that. Your money is yours"

She thought I was being ridiculous, "Oh, just shut up!!!! We've been together for over three years and all we ever do is say" we're one" It's just words and bullshit. We can do this and be one. I really wanna do this baby, for me and for us" I could never let her down when it was about her, so I went along.

I woke up early the next morning, took Dad to work, and picked up Steph at 8am. We took our time, got lost once and arrived at 9:30. The boardwalk opened at ten. We decided it would be a good idea to split up and look on our own. We'd meet back here under the big Arcade sign at 4pm, just in time to pick up my dad at 5:30. I swear I walked in every game booth and store in the state of New Jersey, and nothing!!!! It was about three o'clock when I turned around and headed back feeling like a loser. There was alotta commotion at the ring toss on the milk bottle booth, and I heard this kid tell the boss to go fuck himself. You never said that on the boardwalk. The boss fired him immediately.

I jumped at the chance and spoke up, "Sir, I'm a hard worker and I'll do a good job" He liked I called him sir, asked me my name and when I could start. I told him, tomorrow morning, whatever time you tell me. I chose my words carefully, and he knew when he would tell me what to do, I'd do it.

He spoke up, "Be here at 9:30 tomorrow morning and if you're one minute late, don't show up".

I couldn't control my excitement and went to shake his hand. "Thank you, sir. I promise you won't be sorry."

He warned me, "I better not be, See ya tomorrow."

I forgot one thing, "Sir, how much will I make an hour?"

He wondered when I was gonna ask, "five dollars an hour plus tips, the nicer you are to the customers, the more tips you make. That punk I just fired, never got tipped cause he wasn't nice"

"I'll do a good job sir"

Halfway to heaven, I had some strut in my step as I made my way to meet Steph.

I stopped in the ice cream restaurant to get a quick drink of water. Slurping from the fountain, I heard a recognizable voice. "Can I help you?" And there she was, in her dorky red and white striped apron with the nerdy ice cream hat. She still looked good, though. Steph beat me to it. She already had a job. She told her boss her ride was here and asked if she could leave. He seemed like a nice old man and said, "See you tomorrow morning. You did a very good job for your first day"

On the boardwalk, she couldn't control herself, "I did it, I fuckin did it, all by myself!!!! Any luck baby?"

I acted all sad, started shaking my head and looked up with a growing smile, "I did too!!!" She jumped on me, wrapped her arms and legs around me,

"Oh baby, I knew we could." And we made out right there with the sunset fallin as fast as we were fallin in love.

At the car, I faked an attitude, "You gonna tell me how much or what?" "Huh?oh , five an hour plus tips, so tomorrow I'm showin more leg and cleavage"

I had to bring her back to reality, "Steph, honey, Fanny has cleavage. You have just enough to make a guy wanna see more. You ain't never gonna strangle me with those"

She fired back, "you'd love it if I tried" With the windows down, we held hands the whole way home as the summer air filled the car. Steph put her head back and took a nap. Her hair blew all over the place and she looked more peaceful than I've ever seen her. Serenity looks beautiful on my girl.

She woke up at the exit for Verona. I dropped her off and gave her a "working couple" kiss. Short and obligatory. Dad was waiting at the gate as I pulled up at 5:25. I told him I gotta job and he was proud of me. He asked about Steph and I told him she did too. Dad was happy for both of us. "Ya know, your mother and me got our first summer jobs at Wildwood. I pumped gas at the corner Gulf Station and your mom worked the counter at IHOP"

"Really Dad? IHOP has been around that long?"

Dad took a fake "I oughta" swing at me, "Yes, son. We had electricity back then too. Your mom ever heard you, she'd send you straight to your room. If you know what's good for ya, you never make a girl feel old. Besides, why do you think we go to IHOP after church?" I guess mom's weekly walk down memory lane did her some good.

Summer dinners were always light. Tonight, we had chicken and corn on the cob, both grilled. The butter seemed to melt differently on grilled corn. With the steam rising, the corn glistened with the melting butter. Add fresh black pepper and you were good to go. I love the sound of a good peppermill. Mom always made us use these dorky looking corn holders, so we didn't get messy and wipe our hands on our jeans. Mom worked too hard keeping house, so messin up our pants was a big no-no. She hated doin laundry. The big treat was sun baked iced tea. We couldn't get enough of it. Mom asked if I had any luck getting a job. I told her I did, but she saw I looked real tired so it was okay with her I didn't say much. Even Terry saw I was tired. Before dessert, I asked to be excused to go to bed. And my head hit the pillow real quick.

Morning came and ten hours of sleep weren't enough. Still tired, I remembered not to be a minute late. I dropped off Dad, and on my way to pick up Steph, began to appreciate and understand what my dad's life was like. This was only my second day and it was already getting old. Dad's been doin this for twenty years. I understood why dad would come home and wanna be alone. Mom wanted to share the day, but dad didn't wanna share the hell. Mom had her own, but she felt left out of dad's heaven. Raising kids makes you miss life in the real world. Mom or Dad's worlds weren't what the other pictured them The neighbor's garden always looks much better than yours.

Two honks of the horn and Steph came right out. Bouncing down the small flight of stairs, She looked good, fresh, and happy. How can she look so rested? Wasn't she tired? I forgot Steph got a little more sleep than me. Windblown highway sleeping can do that to you. It's awesome random noise. that puts you out. "Good morning baby!!!!" I got a special girl. Girls aren't exactly the best morning people.

We learned a lot about morning radio. More talking, less music. Mom would kill me if she knew we listened to Howard Stern. I never understood adults thinking he was a horrible influence on kids. It was just radio fantasy, good for laughs. Besides, the grown-ups who were critical of shock jocks' jokes, ended up being a far more dangerous influence than some guy on the idiot box. Priests, Principals,

And Politicians were the worst... or at least they were to Howard. One day, he talked a guy off a bridge who wanted to take the suicide swan dive. Everybody said bad shit about Howard, but I'll tell ya what. Not one of the three "P" s coulda saved the guy's life. So maybe the bad guy on the radio wasn't so bad.

Steph got real embarrassed listening to some of the wacko stuff. We both did, thank God the windows were open to drown out the uncomfortable silence. One of us would finally ask the other, "can you believe this? It's the funniest thing I ever heard. And you know he's telling the truth. You can't make this up"

Listening to the radio would become part of our daily routine.

Work went a little easier and faster today. I got my first tip from a grandmother treating her grandson to a fun day on the boardwalk. He won a Giant Panda bear which was almost as big as him. Next to the kid was a college couple. She gave her boyfriend a mean look and said, "why can't you be like him???" She was nice to the boy and gave him a few love taps on his head and a few of tender cheek pinches were thrown in. Grandma's face was beaming. That's what fun on the boardwalk is all about. The nice old lady slipped me a dollar as they were walkin away. My boss saw the whole thing. "Keep it up kid. I didn't get my first tip for two weeks"

My shift ended; Steph was waiting for her highway haven. She was out like a light by the first exit. It was alright with me. I liked doin my daydream drivin. It made the trip go faster. I found a jazz station on the radio and loved it. It was calm, and relaxing. Music without words was really good. I began to recognize the songs but never knew the band, didn't care. You never had to stop in mid thought to remember to sing the best part cause there wasn't any. The whole song was good. Exit 155 came just as the song ended and Steph woke up. She yawned in the cutest way as her arms stretched out her whole body.

I got the working couple kiss as she got outa the car and made her way to the front door. I hit every light on the way to pick up Dad. He was a little pissed at me. For being a few minutes late, he made me drop him off at Harry's, a regular guy's dive bar, where the working man meets to bitch about the job he couldn't leave fast enough. I guess it was just a reason to chug back a few beers and hang out with bar friends. Dad never introduced a bar buddy to mom. Mom hated Harry's and the cryin in your beer bullshit stories. Cause Dad made the buck, he thought he could blow off some steam anytime he wanted.

Walked in the door and yelled "I'm home" In the kitchen, there was this girl I didn't recognize from behind, she had on white short shorts and a summer red tube top She had the nicest ass I've ever seen. She turned around, and, oh shit, it was my sister Terry. Where did my baby sister go??? We hadn't hung out a lot lately and guys don't pay attention to the changes girls go through. I swear, overnight, she went from a cute loveable little girl to a teenage bombshell the boys at the high school couldn't wait to get their hands on.

It freaked me out knowing she was going to Verona High in a few months. Terry saw the weird look on my face and asked me, "Are you okay Kenny?"

"Yeah, I'm ok. It's just that you grew up overnight and it looks like we're not gonna have "sittin Indian style" talks anymore. No more helping you with your homework" "

"Awww , you'll always be my big brother and a girl always needs one of those" She gave me a thankful hug which I halfheartedly returned. The dirty thought was still in my head, and I didn't feel right about touching her, even if it was in a family way.

Mom came in the kitchen and asked where Dad was, I told her he was down the street at Harry's. Mom got that annoyed look on her face. She told us to sit down for dinner. It hit me; mom always used to say Dad was working late when he was really at the bar. When we were younger, she looked tired wearing that strong front. . I understood, but I felt like I was in the middle. Mom hated when Dad couldn't sit down for dinner with us. But, Dad, needed some time to forget the hell of his boring working life. Mom wouldn't understand. There was a lotta moms in the neighborhood who didn't understand either. They would bond talking about the Phil Donahue show. Mom whipped up a nice salad and pulled the chicken parm outa the oven. She slammed the oven door shut. Veal Parm was too expensive to eat. We only had it on special occasions.

Some nights mom would make me get Dad at Harry's. It was kinda fun goin in there. Dad's, bar friends were nice to me, "that's Frank's Boy" I got the weathered working man's hand mess up my hair. Only guys went in there, girls were scared. Except of course, the bar maid Bunny. All the married guys would flirt and hit on her, hopin to get a few minutes of heaven behind the dumpster. That was their fantasy, not hers. The men loved her cleavage. I didn't know what cleavage was, but with hers, any guy would be a fast learner. Dad's friends would tease me. They gave her a soup look, mmm ..mmm. good, then ask me what I'd do to that. As a young kid, I didn't know enough to answer. Didn't care what I would do to her, my fantasy was trying to think what she'd do to me. Sproutin a boner in a dive bar wasn't the best place to have little Kenny pop out and make an appearance.

Her boyfriend Fester treated me right. I never knew his real name but he looked exactly like the light bulb guy on The Addams Family. He sat at the end of the bar, hangin out and smoking his cigarette. Bunny's boyfriend was a plumber. We first met when I pinched out a lot more than normal and tried to hide it with almost a whole roll of paper. It was during the holidays and he came right over to the house. Dad always "knew somebody". He'd give me a hard time tellin the bar buddies how I blew up the shitter at Frank's house. I had to have a comeback, "hey give me a break, it was the day after Thanksgiving." You had to have balls no matter how old or young you were at Harry's.

As time went on, I knew I could talk to Fester about anything. One day I got the guts to ask him " Ya know, every time I come in here, at least ten guys are tryin to fuck your girlfriend. Doesn't that piss you off" "

He took a long drag of his cigarette, "No why would it?"

"Didn't you hear me??? Ten guys wanna sleep with your girl behind the fuckin dumpster"

Fester set me straight. "Everybody wants what someone else has. They think they can have the same thing. It ain't Bunny they want, they want their wives to be like Bunny. Anytime you got something good., it's gonna happen. It goes with the territory. I thought about it, and understood what he was sayin. Fester, though, had to be Fester. As Bunny was comin over to refill my coke, he says "Besides, Bunny loves my package too much, Dontcha baby"

She'd play right along, "Oh yeah baby, give it to me now" As she was bending over and sarcastically begging him to spank her ass like the bad girl she was. They had great chemistry in a good crude sorta way. School ain't the only place to get an education. Dad was done bangin the pleasure machines, no money left, . It was time to go. Me and Dad left.. We didn't talk much, but I liked walkin home from Harry's with my Dad.

The Chicken Parm hit the spot. After dinner, I spent some time with my not so baby sister. I felt bad about letting all those changes she was going through and me not being there to listen to her. I promised myself I'd never let this much time pass again. She was my baby sister, and that's the way I was always gonna see her. She'd get mad every time she went out and I'd tell her to "Be Careful" But she forgave me cause it was big brother love and in our family, she only had one big brother. We tease each other in front of people and tell each other, "You're my favorite sister" or you're my favorite brother"

We talked in her room as she was getting ready to go hang out at the mall. I asked her who she was going with, and Terry told me about a new girl named, Jenni. She was gonna be here in a half hour. "So, when you meet her, be nice." Terry made me promise not to mess with Jenni. I begged to tease her friend a little bit, but she shot me down. Mom yelled upstairs that Jenni was here.

Jenni just moved here from Pearl River. Her big blonde jersey hair didn't fit her shy demeanor. Terry didn't like the look, so she never thought they'd be friends. It sucked being the new kid and my little sister finally felt bad enough to talk to Jenni. Looks aren't everything and they began a friendship that would last their whole lives. Terry never had a best friend and neither did Jenni so they got along just fine on their own little island of misfit toys. They'd spend hours on the phone giggling about all the cute guys at the mall" Terry had a crush on Jenni's older brother, Billy, but would never tell her best friend. He was forbidden fruit, and everybody knows how good that tastes.

I told Jenni it was nice meetin her. They headed downstairs and I heard the giggling when my little sister said, " Ewwww, he's my brother!!!! And he already has a girlfriend" They had something in common. Both liked older men. I had one dirty thought and felt all guilty like I was cheating on Steph. It was just a "I wonder" fantasy, I wasn't serious and guys my age have "I wonder" thoughts a hundred times a day. When Farrah's poster came out, there was a whole lotta "wondering" going on in every neighborhood.

I quickly fell into my work routine Went to my room, put on my headphones and listened to music till I fell asleep. In between songs, I'd hear mom and dad fight cause he got home too late. Soon enough, the next song would start and I didn't have to listen to their bullshit. It seemed pretty stupid to me. Dad wasn't gonna change and mom yellin only made it worse. Dad was definitely wrong, but who wants to hear shit the minute they walk in the house. There were alotta worse things he could do. Havin a love affair with a poker machine was his crime. He wasn't breakin one of the big ten, so he felt it was okay.

Work got a lot easier and by the end of the first week, I felt like I'd been there for months and even had a few regulars who'd try their luck every day at the same time. Steph had the same with her ice cream lovers. People are such creatures of habit, but I don't understand why. Are they worried about being bored or are they just boring? Rainy days must throw them into a depression. And the end of summer must cause a bad state of withdrawal. Maybe they're just lonely and we become the friends they don't have. They were nice people, harmless, and great tippers. You could depend on it for lunch money everyday

Steph was pretty cool when I told, okay I asked, if I could hang out with Jimmy and Tony Friday night. "If you don't, I will. I'm sick of seeing you every day" She was messin with me. As soon as the sunset we were out the door and hitched to the lake. We threw down our sleepin bags and Jimmy, boasted, "I rolled a real big fatty. Let's get fuckin kooky stoned" Jimmy loved his pot. "Tony, you turned our boy into a Rasta mon" Tony had to bust Jimmy's balloons like he did when we were younger. Jimmy was firin it up as Tony asked, "Hey Jimmy when you get high with Fanny, does she like kooky kinky sex?" Jimmy lost it and still had his "Jimmy cough" "Nah, She wants to, but I ain't that kinda guy" Me and Tony said, in concert, "Bullshit" Tony kept it goin, "C'mon don't bullshit us. Whaddya make her dress up as? A maid, nurse, she's a teacher, you're the boy who had to stay after school?" Jimmy wouldn't let Tony win., "Nah, that shit is old. I like her to be my babysitter" We laughed all night. No deep shit. Just fun. We were stoned out of our minds when Tony started singin, "I gotta be me" It became our anthem.

I stayed in Saturday night. Mom and Dad went to some pool party. Terry told me Jenni and her brother was comin over to hang out. "Be nice to him. He's really nice but he hasn't made any friends here." Jenni had a two-quart bottle of coke under her arm but didn't look like coke was in it. The big rumor was the country was gonna change to the metric system like the rest of the world. Nobody believed it and how much was in a liter? Seemed like too much math to me. The girls went to the kitchen, got ice and did some more giggling.

Jenni's brother stood there and thought he should introduce himself. " Hi, My name's Billy, Billy Ruben" Exaggerating, the last vowel, I said" I'm Kenny Mancuso" Two things were real clear. He wasn't Italian and he wasn't Catholic either. Verona was an Italian neighborhood. Those people lived on the other side of town. It was like two different continents. Neither one would hang out in the other neighborhood. What the fuck was he doin here? Didn't his Dad know what he was putting his kids through?.

I had to be fake nice and bullshit with Billy. Ya do anything to make girlfriends and little sisters happy. We talked about the Yankees. How bad could he be if he was a Yankee fan? Besides, a lotta his people lived out on the island, so most were Met fans. Reggie and Billy Martin had us talking. Billy thought Reggie was a chump and one day Martin was gonna kick his ass right in front of Nettles, Chambliss and Thurman. We got along a lot better than I ever thought we would.

By the end of the night, I had to ask, I didn't give a shit. "What the fu" he stopped me, "Why do we live in an Italian neighborhood? Is that what you wanna know? "

"Well, yeah, is your dad nuts?" "Nah, actually he's pretty smart. We move around a lot, and we live wherever we like the house. The neighborhood don't matter. It's toughened me up. Have people tried to kick my ass just cause I'm Jewish? Fuck yeah, but ya gotta fight back. My dad always told me the world ain't all Jews, so you better get used to it. The shit don't bother me. I don't care. Jenni gets a little sad sometimes but she's a young girl who wants everyone to like her." I started to understand, "Really? You don't get pissed when someone calls you a Jew" "Not at all, besides I'm not a Jew, I'm Jewish. Jews are the ones who go to synagogue all the time. I think if my family went in there, they'd kick us out" Billy was growing on me. "You mind if I ask you something?" "No problem" "Do you get pissed when someone calls you a ginnie" "Fuck no, sometimes I take it as a compliment, and sometimes I don't care" "See that's what I don't understand about us. Jewish people wanna be treated just like anybody else, but when people do, they get all sensitive. If you don't get upset at me callin you a ginnie or a catholic, I shouldn't get pissed at you callin me Jewish. Am I makin sense here?'

"Yeah, gotta say you are, you fuckin Jewish bastard" He told me to, "Shut up and go make some pizza, you fuckin whop" "Heeeeeeyyyyy you can call me a ginnie, but a whop gets me all upset" We had a good laugh and I asked him what kind of pizza he liked cause I was gonna place an order. "Sausage and Pepperoni"

I messed with Jenni, givin her "older man" looks, and she returned the glance with flash of fantasy. Billy didn't have the stones to ask me anything about Terry. But he was lovin her short jean cutoffs with the holes that made you think you were seein her underwear, but it was just the inside of the pockets. He couldn't get enough of seein her halter-top either. What the hell was my baby sister doin wearin a halter-top? Didn't she know how guys stare? She better never kiss a guy or wait at least until she's married for a year.

They both left a few minutes before mom and dad got home. Terry cleaned up real quick and stumbled up the stairs and got in bed just as the front door opened.

They asked where Terry was, and I told them she was tired and went to bed about an hour ago. Mom told Dad to be quiet goin upstairs so he wouldn't wake her. Dad had to check on his baby. He opened the door, saw her sleepin. He got a whiff of alcohol coming from the room but convinced himself it was he who smelled. I guess dad had one too many at the pool party.

After we got home from Church, Steph left an answer on the answering machine. This machine was awesome. It had a tiny cassette and somehow it would rewind to the greeting message every time the phone rang. You could set it to pick up at one ring or four. One meant you didn't wanna talk to anybody. Four meant you could decide if you wanted to be home. Who comes up with this stuff???

Steph wanted to get together and look at car ads in the paper. Dad was parked in front of the TV watching the Yankees and the Sox. He'd always say he'll know he made it to heaven when he turns

on the TV and the Yankees and Boston play every day. Babe wearin the B, pitchin against Joe D. Eck facin The Mick, yeah that's heaven to me too. Reggie was up with the bases packed. I told Dad I was borrowin the car. He shooed me away, didn't care what I said.

Steph's Dad answered the door and invited me to watch the game. When the Sox were in town; everybody knew what "the game" was. We watched a little, Reggie ended up hittin a double off the wall, clearing the bases and givin the Pinstripes an early three run lead. No lead was ever safe when these two played. Steph came downstairs with the paper, "Get your keys, we're takin a ride" Steph's Dad quickly saw who the boss of us was. "You better go now, or she'll ground you"

"Mr. Demarino, I never feel grounded with your daughter" He got what I was saying and smiled about the compliment I gave his little girl.

We got in the car, and she told me where to go. Four towns over, we pulled up to this house with a white '62 VW Bug parked in the driveway. Steph wanted to know, "So, do you like it?" It looked like a nice enough house to me. Was her Dad planning on moving? Why didn't she say a word to me? "Yeah, it's a nice house. Whaddya tryin to tell me?' "No, Stupid, I mean the car." I liked feeling relieved a lot more than the car, but the car was fine.

The owner came out to meet us and asked us if we wanted to take it for a test drive. He handed me the keys and we got it. I looked around the inside, four speed, clutch, manual A/C (roll down windows), AM Radio, just two knobs, no buttons. Radio's gotta go. It started right up. I didn't wanna tell Steph I never drove a car with a clutch before, so this was gonna be a trip. Put it in reverse, popped the clutch too quick, and the car conked out. "This clutch is different than the one I'm used to" Take two- I let it out slowly, giving it gas as well. We made it out of the driveway!!!!. The house was on a side street, so I had two blocks to learn before it was real. Pressure makes diamonds! I passed the test. It seemed easy enough to drive and VWs are good on gas and easy to fix. "So Baby, how much?" Steph played the role of used car salesman, "400.00" The price was right, but the job didn't fit my girl. She was a much better buyer than seller. Steph confidently told the guy we'd take it and pay for it when we picked it up on Friday. She knew it was payday and we'd have 800.00. Four hundred for the car and a few bucks to get it registered. After we got it ,we decided to celebrate and, have a fun night at the shore.

CHAPTER SEVEN

Wednesday night, we had our car, so, me and Steph stayed at the shore, had a nice dinner and went for a walk on the boardwalk. Dinner was good as we gave up being the working part of the working couple. I missed her and missed us too. We struggled to get back the chemistry we had. Holding hands, walking down the boardwalk, the music blared from the cheap outdoor speakers. I got all touchy feely when, Carole king's version of "Will you still Love me tomorrow" played. I pulled her into me, and we made out like we used to. The kiss felt like it lasted forever.

From the day we met, I fell in love with her eyes and been in love with them ever since. The eyes are supposed to be the keys to the soul and she's got great soul. My eyes told a different story. She saw my pain and made me talk. I fuckin hate when she does that shit. "Tell me what's wrong baby" I looked everywhere but her. Then she starts with the bitchy, "look at me!!!!! Talk" I felt like an idiot. "it's like the song says, you gonna love me tomorrow? . Steph, I love you", it was the first time I ever said it. Not exactly the right moment. . " I just want us to be happy forever. I know my parents always try to get it back, but it left them a long, long time ago and now it's too late. . I never wanna feel about you the way my dad feels about my mom."

I could tell she was startin to get pissed, real pissed. I never saw this side of her. "Fuck you and your tomorrows too. That's all you ever think about. And all you're doin is wastin today. I take the time to know I love you every minute we're together. Fuck Tomorrows. I hate them, every fuckin one of them."

"Do you remember the first night we spent together?" I gave

her an unsure nod and a yeah, but had no idea why she was asking now, four years later. She went on, "What did I ask you when I was in your arms??" I didn't remember. "Lemme fuckin remind you" Steph cursed a lot when she was pissed. "I asked you if you thought your parents loved each other. I let you answer and then told you about my dad and Monica. You've never ever, ever asked me about my mother. You selfish bastard!!!" She was right, I never did. "I never knew my mother; she died while delivering me. Live with that one.!!! I never had a today or a fuckin tomorrow with her. Dad can't talk about it, so I don't know anything., the color of her eyes, hair, do I look like her? Do I remind my dad of her and he won't tell me?"" She started to cry and her tears fell like waterfalls. I hugged her and wouldn't let go, telling her I was so sorry, I never knew.

She pushed me away, told me to stop. She had to go, go somewhere. She ran away from me and onto the beach. Stunned I just stood there before I helplessly tried to follow her. I looked for Steph all night., hoping that she was okay and hoping I could find the right words.

The morning sun rose to welcome the empty boardwalk and the seagulls celebrating a new day. I spotted Steph sitting alone on one of the boardwalk benches. Tears were still falling but they were more like a slow dripping leak. I stood in front of her and let her talk. My favorite word came out of her mouth, "Hi" I took it in and gave her a "Hi" back. "I cried all night, I had to. I'm sorry baby, you're not the only one who's never asked about my mother. Nobody has. Until last night I never told anybody either. How can you tell somebody that.? I didn't even want to tell myself'" A few weeks ago, I found out what happened when I called the hospital. I made up a story, so they thought I was old enough to get the information. I hung up and felt numb. I couldn't think, feel, talk, anything. I sat there for two hours doing nothing. When you told me you loved me, it just had to come out. I couldn't stop it. And baby, I feel real lucky it was you, cause I love you sooo much." We kissed and the chemistry was back, but much, much stronger. I understood why she believed today was far more important than tomorrow. My Steph, she's always right.

She wiped away the last tear and her spunky personality came back. "Oh shit, your parents are gonna kill you. You gotta call them now!!!" I would, but what about her dad? She told me, he's never worried when I'm with you. So, I'll call but he won't be mad." Parents hate getting woken up to a collect call from their kid.

Mom picked up and before she said a word, I told her I had to spend the night with Steph. She took it the wrong way, "No mom, it's not what you think. But everything is okay now and I'll tell you about it tonight" I told Steph, "my mother is happy you're okay. I'm not the only one in my house who loves you. Ya know." Steph called her dad, had the quick conversation, everything was fine.

I decided to push the envelope. On Friday night, I was coming over. Me and Steph were gonna talk to her dad. I'd start, but we'd both ask him anything we wanted about her mom. "Will you call him and tell him you're coming over?" "Hell yeah. So, start thinking about everything you wanna ask him cause this is gonna happen . His girl can wait"

Her fake southern accent came out, "Sugah-plum. I just get a tingling in my heart when you act like a May-on"

Back at her, "Frankly, my dear I don't give a shit…. I'll take care of everything, don't worry"

Fuck, it was time to walk down the boardwalk and go to work… it's gonna be a long day. The minutes couldn't pass quick enough and each hour lasted a lifetime. My boss wondered why I was so tired and my regulars told me I looked horrible. One asked, "Rough Night?" I felt worn out as I gave them a meek, "Yeah" Five O'clock finally showed up at my booth and I went to pick up Steph.

She looked as tired as I was and couldn't wait for her routine highway nap. We didn't need to talk about last night; it became a part of us. I gave her a gentle concerned look as I asked if she was Okay. She gave me an "everything is gonna be fine" nod. She reached for my hand and held it the whole drive home. I finally understood what being one was all about. She hurt, I hurt. But we were gonna be better for it.

I gave her a simple kiss and a lingering squeeze of her hand.

"See ya tomorrow baby. Go get some sleep" She slowly walked to her door and turned around to blow me a kiss. I always thought blowing kisses was stupid, but this was the best one ever.

I got home and Dad was at Harry's. Terry was spending the night at Jenni's. I needed mom. She always cared about her kids, but I didn't appreciate it. I never wanted to trouble her, so I wouldn't ever say what I was really thinking. Tonight, it had to change. Mom was upstairs when she heard the door close. She came down to ask me if I was okay. I really didn't know if I was... When I didn't answer, she asked me if Steph was ok. "Mom, can we sit down and talk? I really need to talk to you"

"Of course Kenny" And we took our spots on opposite sides of the couch. I couldn't look at her. I concentrated on feeling my words.

"Mom, do you remember about four years ago when I stayed at Jimmy's one night and then I "forgot" I was going camping with Tony and Jimmy the next night" Mom looked real confused and had no idea why I was bringing this up now. ."Well I lied. I never went to Jimmy's. I spent the night at Steph's house when her dad was away. I'm really sorry. I know I shouldn't have lied but I didn't know how to tell you. Besides, you and Dad weren't getting along so I figured you had enough to deal with. Nothin happened mom, honest" I looked up and saw her disappointment. I had to hug her and tell her I was sorry again. Mom could tell I was worn out and had something on my mind, so she didn't get upset. She was more concerned about me than some stupid lesson I should learn about lying. Mom held me and spoke "while it's not okay to lie, it just means we aren't ready to tell the truth. That's why people lie to themselves. Sometimes the truth can be really scary"

"Oh mom, you have no idea how true that is" She knew I learned a truth lesson last night.

"Mom, how come I can't care about Steph? Last night I told her

I loved her, but I don't know how to care. I mean, I can do the easy things like the car and the shore job. But that's just because I wanna make her happy. It's all bullshit, mom"

"Kenny, I'm lost. I've always thought you cared about Stephanie. I'm proud of how you treat her."

I didn't deserve her praise. "Mom, really, I'm telling you, it's all bullshit"

"Are you telling me you don't care about her?"

"No!!! You're not getting it. I care for her, but I don't care about her. I told you. I don't know how, and it sucks"

When it came to raw emotion, mom let the bad language slide. "Kenny, honey, you're trying to tell me something and I don't understand. I can't help you unless I'm clear about what you're trying to say"

"Mom, me and Steph have been together for four years and I thought we were close. We can talk about everything. I can't lie, but mom, we've talked about you and Dad a lot. About your marriage, about the way you feel about each other, the way you treat each other. Mom, I hope you're not upset when I say this, but I don't want me and Steph to be like you and Dad"

Mom was right. The truth can be really scary and now it was staring right in her face .She knew this day would come, but how can anyone be ready for it. With a worried looked she asked, "does your sister know yet?"

"Yeah, mom. We've known for years. Look we know you're both doing the best you can, and we've never walked in your shoes. We know it's hard, but we love you both."

I hoped mom wouldn't feel guilty, yet she did. She used her hands to cover her face. I let her alone until she started to cry. She said she was soo sorry and I told her she had nothing to be sorry about. Sometimes marriages just go bad and when they do, it's too late to do anything about it. Mom was sorry cause she felt responsible for letting it go bad.

I had to get Mom out of her darkness. "Mom, I'm only seventeen. Please don't be sorry. It's no one's fault. Besides, I can't take two women I love putting on the waterworks in one day"

"Two? Oh my god is Stephanie okay???"

"Yeah. she is now."

Mom looked relieved. "I'm sorry honey. I interrupted you. Please go on"

"Thanks Mom. Well, ever since me and Steph have been together, it was always about me, talking about you and dad, Jimmy's Dad funeral, you know... things like that. When I told you I didn't know how to care about her, I meant I never asked her about her life and how she's grown up" I stopped and took a deep breath, "Steph's mom died delivering her" Mom was shocked and hurt for her fantasy teenage daughter in law. "I never asked her about her mother in all the time we've been together. She called me a selfish bastard. Steph was right. I was.

It never even entered my mind. All I did was look at Steph and was happy she's, my girlfriend. Like I said, I didn't know how to care about her" Mom pulled me in to be hugged. Teenage boys don't cry or at least they didn't in front of anybody. But, Mom isn't just anybody, she's my mom. I shed a few tears.

I got myself together and told Mom I was calling Steph's Dad tonight to tell him me and Steph needed to talk. We were gonna ask anything Steph wanted to know about her mother and he was gonna tell us whether he liked it or not. Mom felt the need to make a point, "Seems like you learned how to care about Steph last night. Kenny, Men three times your age never learn what you just learned. And they miss out on what love is all about, caring for and about each other"

"Thanks mom, now what's for dinner?"

We had meatloaf. I love everything about it but it's name. It sounds like a food you'd give someone you didn't like. If you got sick, people would always ask you, "What'd ya have... Meatloaf?" Somehow tuna fish got a pass. That stuff stunk like something died. Mom and I made small talk while she ate her meager salad. God Bless Her!!! She still worried about her figure. I would never call mom old. We're Italian. We love fat food. Pizza, lasagna, Rigatoni, Manicotti never made Jane Fonda's good food list.

I finished dinner and excused myself to make the call. I thanked mom for dinner with a hug and a kiss. "Wish me luck Mom. Don't ask me what I'm gonna say, cause I have no idea" Mom never asked for much. Tonight she got a lot closer to her son and that was all the thanks she needed.

I found the cordless and called Steph's house. She knew I was calling so she let her father pick up. "Mr. Demarino, Hi, it's Kenny. Do ya have a second?"

"For you? I got all night. Whaddya need?"

"If you're free tomorrow night, I'd like to come over and me and your daughter wanna talk to you for a little bit."

"Okay, ya makin me worried here, everything alright?"

"It will be after we talk to you. See ya at 7:30 Mr. Demarino" And the easy part was done. I hung up the phone and tried to figure out how I was gonna begin. I remembered what Tony said, "Listen to your heart and everything will be fine"

Work was boring and I was distracted thinking about tonight. At the end of the day, I picked up my check and met Steph outside the ice cream shop. I could tell she was nervous about tonight. Fantasizing and wondering about her mom was different than what the truth could hold. Steph told me she was thinking about backing out. "Maybe I'll like the mom in my dreams a lot more" I knew she was just scared. If I "cared" about her, I couldn't let her back out. She'd always wonder, and it would slowly take over every thought she had. Her mom would always be there, and it would tear us apart cause she would blame me for letting her take the easy way out.

"Steph, we gotta get our shit together about tonight. I figured I'd start and then turn it over to you. You have to ask the questions. I'll hold your hand and be right by your side the whole time.. If you need to cry, use me as your towel."

"Thanks Kenny, I couldn't do this without you and I'm really sorry I went off on you"

" Baby, baby, baby, stop your shit. There's nothing to be sorry about. Now lie back and take your nap. You're beautiful when you sleep" Steph relaxed and pushed her windblown hair away from her face and fell softly asleep. I woke Steph in front of her house and loved her for a minute "See ya in a few baby"

I got home and ran into Dad. Mom told him what we talked about last night. I thought I was in trouble as Dad asked me if I had time to go for a quick walk around the neighborhood. Outside we went and he started, "So ya nervous about tonight, son?"

"Yeah, a little. I'm scared cause I don't know how this will all go down"

He put his fatherly arm around me, "Yeah, I understand. It ain't easy talking to your girlfriend's father about the important stuff. No matter how much he likes you, you're not family. But, Kid, there are a few things you should know. First, I'm really proud of what you're doing for Stephanie I'd tell you why, but there's too many reasons and you'd end up missing tonight.

"Kenny, if you're old enough to do this, then you're old enough to learn a little more about life. From the day a kid is born, they expect their moms and dads to be perfect. We can't be. We're human, we're parents. Kids, well they're growing up, so they can make mistakes. Nobody realizes the world is backwards. You're the perfect ones, not us. And that's how we see you. Sometimes we yell and scream cause we don't want you to make the same mistakes we made. As parents, we make you feel bad, cause we did too. I'm not makin excuses, son. I love your mother and I know I don't always show it, but I do my best, and sometimes my best sucks. So tonight, when you're sitting there with Mr. Demarino, remember he did his best for his daughter, whether it was right or wrong. C'mon, Let's go back home. "

"Thanks Dad and while you may not be the best dad in the world, you're the best Dad to me"

I skipped Dinner and got to Steph's right at 7:30. Mr. Demarino answered the door, got me a soda and asked me to sit down. Steph was upstairs. I always wondered what girls did up there while they were makin the guy wait and talk to the parents. She finally made her way down and took a seat next to me. I asked her if she was okay. She nodded and I said, "Then, let's do it!"

I started, "Mr. D., I know Steph told you we spent the other night at the shore, but she didn't tell you why. We're okay now, actually better than okay. We had this big fight. "

He looked surprised, "you two fought? Really?"

"Yeah we did, and it was pretty ugly. Your Daughter's been keeping something inside for a long time and it just came out. I'll let her tell you about it. Go ahead baby" I gave her a soft supportive kiss on the cheek and took her hand.

"Dad, I didn't know how to do this, so I thought I'd write you a letter. I'd like to read it to you now.

Dear Dad,

Ever since I was a little girl, you've taken care of me. You were always there, to change my diaper, take me to school, buy me dolls, put a band aid on my boo-boos and hold me till I'd stop crying. I wasn't different than any other little girl. I thought we were gonna get married. As I got older, I dreamed about you walking me down the aisle in my beautiful wedding dress. You've never complained or yelled at me even if I got my brand-new dress dirty playing outside with the boys." Mr. Demarino's eyes slowly began to tear up.

"I refused to complain. You gave me your life. I didn't want to upset you, so I couldn't bring myself to ask about my mother. You gave me enough love for two parents. All I know is she died when I was real young. Well, there's been some things that have been on my mind, and I need to ask you for the answers. I did some checking and I now know she died giving birth to me. I hope you can understand. I love you, your daughter Stephanie Anne."

Mr. Demarino, covered his face for a few seconds and then ran his hands through his hair. Wiping away a few tears, he answered, "I knew this day would come and always thought I'd be ready for it. I planned to tell you sometime before you got married, but I can't say no to my little baby girl. So anything you want to know, ask away."

Ok Dad, just tell me about her. You know, what did she look like, where'd she live. What were her parents like. Stuff like that."

"Okay honey, Her maiden name was Julie Stefano. She had dark hair like yours, but with a fifty's flair. She loved wearing the clothes like on Happy Days. Your mom really loved clothes. Her favorite color was white cause it matched her smile. And it really did. Your mom knew what made her look good. I'd tease her about all the different shades of white she wore. She grew up in a railroad apartment on Ferry Street in Newark. Her mom and dad were fresh off the boat from Italy. Her father worked as a ship builder and mom would work weekends in the corner bakery. Your Grandma could really cook. She made the best gravy.

They wanted a better life for their daughter, so they moved out to Verona when your mom was going into the eighth grade. That's when we met." Me and Steph gave a quick ironic stare at each other. "I had the biggest crush on her. She was the shy new kid and I acted like I was being nice. New kids need friends. We ended up goin steady all through high school. That's what we called it back then. Our Senior prom was everything a high school kid could ask for. Time went on forever when we slow danced to a song called, "Earth Angel" They don't write songs like that anymore. Hold on, I'll be back in a second."

Mr. Demarino ran upstairs, and I asked my girl if she was cool. "Yeah baby, I'm in a fog. I never heard my Dad talk like this. He's told me so much. I feel like my mom's here with me"

"Steph, she is. She's been waitin for this day as long as you have" I thought about Jimmy and his angel. I guess, tonight, I began to believe in them too. Steph looked happier than I've ever seen her.

Mr. D. came back carrying an old book. It was a scrapbook about her mom. Stephanie, anything you want to know about your mother is in this book. I wanna give this to you. Steph said she couldn't accept it. She wanted it to be a part of both of them. They agreed to keep it on the lower shelf of the coffee table.

She snuggled up next to me and shared all the pictures. It was her mother from the time she was a little girl to her wedding picture. Steph wore a never-ending smile. She was definitely her mother's daughter. Her dad looked on and seemed relieved this day was over. I felt pretty lucky as you always look at the mother to see if your girlfriend is gonna look hot when she gets older. Steph was fixed on the wedding picture. In some ways she was meeting her dad tonight too. Steph found a note beside the picture and asked her Dad if she could read it. "Of course, you can, your mom was a great lady. I can brag about her till you fall asleep." Steph slipped her hand under the clear vinyl page that protected the pics. She opened the note and began to read it.

Julie Anne,

Tonight, you agreed to marry me and I'm the happiest man in the world. I promise you we will have a life, where every dream you had as a little girl, will come true. From the time we met, I couldn't wait for this day. I thought Love at first sight just happened in stupid romance novels, but you've made all my hopes and wishes come true. You are everything love is.

With all my love, all my life,

Joey

"Dad, that's beautiful. I had no idea you were romantic. Oh, you gave me her middle name!!"

"I didn't. Your mom did. It was her grandmother's name. And you're right, I'm not romantic. After your mom died, I couldn't be. I knew I'd never find love, pure love again. And I don't want to. This one time, it was more than I can ask for.

Stephanie, honey, I know you always thought I dated bimbos, but you never knew why. There's never gonna be another Julie for me, so why should I even look. It's a waste of hope and time. Do you really think I could be close to Monica? Do you think I wanna be? No way. She's just a band-aid on the scar of my loneliness. It's not fair to her, but she has the same reasons for being with me. When adults get older, their biggest fear is being alone. It may sound bad to you, but anybody is better than nobody"

Steph was conflicted. She was so proud her Dad could love, but ashamed he thought his daughter would let him live alone. "Dad don't talk like that. You took care of me, I'll take care of you. So don't worry about being alone. "Steph got up and gave her dad a "Jimmy " hug.; the pure kind like Jimmy gave his mother.

"Dad, I know this is hard for you, but I have one more question. What happened the day I was born, I mean, how did she die?"

Her father started to cry but he gathered himself. "I was in the operating room, Your mom made me be there! Everything was going fine. The Doctors realized you were a stubborn little girl and they had to do a C-Section. You came out crying and looked like the miracle you are. As they were cleaning you up, to give to your mom, she started to hemorrhage, It got bad quick and I held you in my arms by your mother's side. She was starting to lose consciousness and it took every ounce of strength she had, to reach out and caress your head. Her last words were I love you so much. I don't know if she was saying it to me or you., but I'm pretty sure it was to both of us."

Mr. Demarino was drained. Steph was too. She got her answers tonight. I knew it'd be years before she could understand and appreciate everything she heard. She felt like the luckiest girl in the world, but it still hurt. Mr. D, well, he looked pretty rough too. He got out of his chair and said, "Kids, I'm goin to the bar to get good and drunk, and when I do, I'm gonna put fifty cents in the juke box and listen to Earth Angel."

"Have fun Dad and call me if you need me to drive you home" "Stephanie, don't worry. I'm walkin, it'll do me a lotta good." We both got up and Steph led the way. She gave him a big Daddy-Daughter hug. After it was over, he called me in and hugged me. "Thanks Kenny, thanks for lovin my daughter. It means a lot to me and even more to her. See ya later"

The door shut and my girl led me back to the couch. She took me and we made out for an hour straight. She stopped to take a breath and said, "Baby, I'm ready.. I wanna, you know." "You sure?" "Yeah, I always wanted it to be special and be with someone I loved."

She took me upstairs to her bedroom and we slowly undressed each other. She was perfect, far better than I deserved. Under the covers and wrapped within each other,. both of us felt nervous, wanting to please each other, when we didn't know how. We finally figured out how to do it, you know, what went where. The first time wasn't all it was cracked up to be. Me and Steph felt bad for the other, but that didn't last long. She promised me we'd get better. Two minutes later, I was ready to try again. We tried for hours, and I think by the fourth time, we got the hang of it. Me and Steph spent the rest of the summer doin it every day and everywhere. I'll tell ya one thing, she did like adventure. She was determined to get me to say no and I was determined not to. Being stubborn can have its advantages.

August came and summer raced to its end. Me and Steph continued to get closer. Spendin most of the time at the shore, I felt a little outa touch with Tony and Jimmy, But they understood. Jimmy hung out at home, helping his mom do all the yard work, he didn't have time to do, once school started. Fanny helped Mrs. Fortunato with all the housework. They got close and his mom taught Fanny how to make all the foods Jimmy liked. Fanny and Jimmy liked playin house together. Once his mom went to bed, they liked playin their own game of truth or dare. They shared a lot more dares than truths.

CHAPTER EIGHT

Tony liked hangin out on the streets. He liked money too, not a lot, just enough so his dad wouldn't make him pay rent. Tossin pies at Vinchenzo's gave him money and girls. Alcohol started to kick his dad's ass so he didn't have the strength to beat Tony anymore. Words took the place of punches, and he began to hate his son. Tony wouldn't admit it, but it really hurt him. How could he be a fuck up if he could graduate high school.

Coach Biscotti and Tony hung out a lot this summer. He wanted the best for Tony and Tony didn't like it. He couldn't stand more thoughts of failure in his life. Then, his father would be right and it would crush him. One night Tony and Coach really got into it..

Coach said, "Ya know Tony, there's a hundred colleges that want you, I get calls about you every day. College can give you a life you never dreamed of "

Tony got real pissed, "Dreamed of? You wanna talk about dreams? Are you fuckin kiddin me?

Coach wouldn't back down, "No I aint kiddin you. I think you're scared, scared of being a failure. I never thought fear would kick your ass"

"Coach, you don't know what the fuck you're talking about. I've been told I'm a failure every day of my life. Failure don't scare me, it bores me"

"Then what's the problem Tony. Don't bullshit me. Tell me"

Tony gave a one-word answer, "Disappointment"

"Whaddya talking about? Goin to college is a disappointment to you?"

"You don't get it Coach!!!. Look when you were my age, what did you wanna be?"

"I wanted to be a Psychologist and help kids with their hell"

"Okay, ya see, there was a day you had to give up your dream. Maybe you weren't smart enough. Maybe you didn't have the money. Who knows? Who cares? But that day, your dream died. And it really sucked. I know you still wish it coulda happened. Me? I don't want that shit. I can't live with the disappointment. I know it aint much, but I can put in my time working down on the docks. I'll be just fine"

"It doesn't have to be that way Tony"

"Coach, look in the mirror and tell yourself the same thing"

With Coach challenging Tony to an arm-wrestling match., They ended the night makin peace. Loser had to buy the Italian ices.

Coach Bishotti hated to admit it. He even hated to think it, but he knew Tony was right. He never wanted to be a teacher. He had to be, to pay the bills. Coaching was his way of helpin kids. Bishotti cared about Tony as much as Jimmy and me. He thought Tony was a kid that life was screwin and didn't think it was fair. At school, Coach saw rich spoiled kids bitch and complain about their fathers not buying them a new car. He wanted them to trade places with Tony for one day. Tony never complained about nothin.

Practice started up before school did. For Tony, it was his last year of kickin everybody's ass on the team. He told Jimmy and me about this freshman punk. He said he was either gonna make him quit, cry or break his leg". Jimmy busted Tony's balls, "oh big tough guy, kickin a freshman's ass. You're a real bad ass!!" Tony laughed a little and said, "Yeah, Ain't I????" Even though he still didn't like his teammates, they voted him as the only captain. Maybe they were scared of pissin him off. Besides, they all knew Tony wasn't listenin to any kid.

I applied to Princeton, just for laughs, Georgetown, Bucknell, NYU and Rutgers. I wanted to stay near Jersey so I could be close to Steph. Rutgers was my best shot. Steph wanted to be a cosmetologist, so she worked part time at the local beauty parlor. Jimmy, he was planning on goin to New Jersey Institute of Technology to learn how to make computers. He tried to convince Tony and me that one day every house would have a computer. Encyclopedias would go out of business. Tony told him he better ease up smoking all that pot cause it was makin him crazy. Fanny wanted to go to the University of Makin Jimmy Happy. I think she was already accepted.

Some days Jimmy and me would hang out on the bleachers watchin Tony's football practice. It was about three days before the first game and Tony knocked the crap outa this kid and then fell to the ground screaming in pain. "Coach, Coach, I'm hurt. I think I broke my dick" Coach Pacelli yelled for someone to get a splint. Tony couldn't take it., "Coach, this fuckin hurts. I feel like I wanna die" A kid reminded Coach Pacelli, they didn't make splints for that part of the body. Pacelli was losin it, "Then get a tongue depressor and some tape. Hurry!!!" There was one thing Italians never did and that was touch another man's package. So Coach Bishotti asked for volunteers. A chorus of silence ran through the practice. Coach yelled alittle louder, he sure wasn't doin it. "This is your Captain for Christ's sake" Bishotti saw Jimmy and me and called us over. "Tony says he broke his dick and we need someone to put it in a splint. An ambulance is on the way" Jimmy stepped up to the plate and got the tape and tongue depressor. He knelt beside Tony, asked him if he was okay. Tony nodded between deep breaths. Jimmy musta known something about broken bones cause he started feeling Tony's leg and askin him how it felt? Tony got confused. "How does what feel? Jimmy looked him square in the eyes and said, "that Ben-Gay I put in your jock asshole!!!!. That's for all the wedgies you ever gave me" Tony turned red and Jimmy stated runnin as fast as he could "When I catch you, I'm gonna kill you, you fucker!!!!" I couldn't hold it in any longer. I started laughin till I almost pissed myself. Tony, well he told me to shut the fuck up and asked Bishotti if he could go take a quick shower. Coach made him be back within fifteen minutes. As Tony was leavin, he turned and said to his team, "if I hear one of you laughin, I swear I'm gonna hit you so hard your momma is gonna have to pick out an oak box for ya" They waited for the Gym door to close behind him. Then they all started crackin up. The door quickly busted open, "I heard that!!!!" Even Tony had to smile a little bit as he was adjustin his jock.

Tony made it back to practice and Jimmy was nowhere to be found. Tony and me walked home. Billy the Jew spotted us and asked to talk to me for a second. He gotta kick outa his nickname and gave it right back, callin me Kenny the Whop. I liked my name too. I told him it made me sound like a Mafia hit man. Anyway, he asked me about my summer and working at the shore. He didn't come up to me to ask me about my summer, especially when I saw him a few weeks ago. Enough Bullshit. "So what's up Billy? Whaddya want?" He got a little nervous. "Ummm, well I wanted you to know me and Terry have gone out a few times. I think she's pretty cool and I like her a lot. I didn't wanna do this behind your back, so I guess I'm askin for your blessin." Thinking about it for a second. My sister was growin up and I could be an asshole by standin in the way. "Billy, if my sister's happy, I'm happy. But, if I ever hear you mistreat her, we ain't friends, I'm your worst enemy and if you're my worst enemy, you're his too." Tony backed me up and looked like a rabid dog looking for something to kill. He had to bust Billy's balls. "Hey, your sister's name is Jenni right" Billy nodded. "She's fuckin hot. You mind if I throw her some of my sweet Italian sausage?" Billy passed the Tony test. He didn't bust ya balloons unless he thought you were alright. .

I knew mom wasn't home yet. She went shoppin with Jimmy's mother. I thought it was pretty cool they still hung out together. I had some time to kill so I stopped by Harry's to tell Fester, I finally did it with Steph. He was the only one I could brag to. Fester shook my hand and told Bunny to get the man a nice cold bottle of Bud. I was only seventeen, but Bunny let me slide. We toasted by knockin bottles and then he starts with the ball buster examination. "Ok, Kenny. Tell the truth, how long did ya beg for? I told him I didn't. She did. Bunny joined in. "Baby you must be one hunk of man meat. I hope she's not vegetarian". I had the perfect line, "Well she aint anymore!!!" The two of them lost it. Fester took the lead back. ",

Don't lie to me cause I'll know. How long did ya last? One pump or two? "I got ballsy, "that's none of your fuckin business" Like the perfect duet, they both said, "then it's one" I turned redder than the bud label. Fester eased up, "Kenny, no sweat, you're just a busy guy" "I told him, "I know, I rushed to do it again two minutes later"

We all had our laughs; Fester got a little serious sayin he was happy for me and I'd never forget it. He knew Steph and me worked the summer at the shore. Fester was like an older brother. Bunny was listenin, comes over and says, "We'd like to double date with you and your girlfriend one night. I figured Steph would be up for it so I said, "yeah, but let me check with her for a good date" "See that, honey? He checks with his girlfriend before he commits them" Bunny loved givin her man a hard time.

The bar door opened, and it was Dad. I thought I was busted but he was cool. And Fester, that prick, says" hey, did ya boy tell ya he's a man now? He got laid the other night" Now I knew I was in trouble. I'm starin at Dad, waitin for him to say something. "Bunny, Get my man a beer" Fester starts up again, "Oh Frank, you won the pool, yeah it was one and done" "That's my son, makin me proud" At Harry's, Dad treated me like an adult. I liked it. I didn't go in there a lot.. Bein the Proud Papa at Harry's made Dad feel pretty good. I finished my beer and gave him a man hug as I said; "I'll see ya later." Fester gave me the handshake and Bunny gave me a big hug with her rack starin me in the face. What a way to go out.

I got home and mom pulled in with a pepperoni pie. I yelled upstairs for Terry to come down. Mom asked how I liked being a senior, and my sister spoke up, "yeah, how's it feel to be the big man?" I told them it felt no different than last year, but the ninth graders seemed really young and scared. I woofed down three pieces and Terry watched her figure so she only had one. It was a quick dinner. Homework followed.

Terry and me went upstairs. I gave her a second to settle down and then knocked on her door. "Do ya have a minute?" My sister missed the times, so she quickly shut her book, "of course I do for you, big brother" I didn't want to sound like I was pissed but I guess it came out that way. "Why didn't you tell me about you and Billy?" There was a deafening silence. Surprised, with her mouth open, she started. "I don't know. It just kinda happened. We started to have fun together. Ya know, Kenny, ya never know when you meet a guy if you're gonna start goin out with him. Like I said, it just happens. You have to know what I'm talking about. You didn't tell me or mom and dad about Steph until Jimmy's dad died." I hated to admit it but she was right. It still hurt. I always thought she'd come to me and we'd talk about this stuff.

She saw my hurt. "Kenny, it's different now, we're both grown up. While we might need each other less, there will always be times when we need each other more. And you're my brother, I can't think of anyone I could depend on more. Kenny, I'm not sayin I'm gonna marry Billy, but when I do get married? The night before, I want you to promise me you'll sit on the floor beside my bed, just like you did when we were young kids, and we'll laugh and cry till the sun rises. Can you promise me that?"

Girls are so much smarter than boys. "Yeah, I promise. Oh, Billy passed the Tony test. He asked Billy if he would be mad if he slept with Jenni." "You mean Tony likes Jenni???" "No, Terry, it was a joke!!! But he did say she was hot. Now don't go telling your friend. She'll get all hot and bothered" Terry told me about Tony's reputation in school. "It's so funny, all the guys are terrified of him, and even some girls are. The other girls think he's sooo cute. Why are they scared of Tony? He's such a teddy bear" I had to set her straight. "That's only cause you know him and he's been nice to you ever since he was your biggest customer at your lemonade stand" "Kenny, I wish Tony did like Jenni. She seems to get all the losers liking her" "Lil Sister, that aint gonna happen. Tony don't date"

Tonight was Verona High's first game. We had a car so tailgating became part of our ritual. I decided to be nice and invite Terry and Billy. Terry was the boss. She said yes, but we had to invite Jenni too. Steph and Fanny sensed Jenni felt like a third wheel and went out of their way to make her feel part of the group. Steph, my baby, challenges the boys to a touch football game in the parking lot. Now the girls had no idea how to play so me, Jimmy and Billy thought it'd be funny as shit. We forgot about one small detail. It was touch football. There was nooo way I was touchin any girl on their team except Steph. She'd kick my ass if I did. Jimmy and Billy had the same problem. The girls beat the hell outa us. They took our pride. But it was all-good, after the game Jenni felt comfortable. She'd much rather hang out and have fun with friends then go to the game on a date with a loser.

We cleaned up our mess and left a little early to get good seats. Back row of the stands were the best. We saw about twenty college coaches sitting together to look at Tony. There's something about those lights shining down on the field that charged the atmosphere. The grass looked greener; the yard lines seemed white as freshly fallen snow, and the end zone felt like the garden of Eden.

The team was getting ready with last minute coaching about each player's responsibilities. Before, every game, there were two traditions. The captain would speak and the head coach gave his pep talk. Coach Pacelli asked Tony if he wanted to say anything. Tony didn't even stand up."Yeah, Do your fuckin job and we'll win" Short and sweet, but sooo true.

Coach Bishotti began, "Seniors, for most of you this will be your last season playing football. No more I'll get em next year, no more I'll try harder, If you don't leave it all out there on the field, you'll regret it for the rest of your lives. I promise you. When you first started playing football here at Verona, it was your dream to make Varsity. When you made Varsity, it was your dream to start. When you start, it's your dream to go undefeated. We have the players to make that dream come true. But it ain't gonna be easy. They'll be times when you question if it's worth it. Well, I can tell you, it is. You'll be 80yrs old and someone will ask you if you were a part of that undefeated team, and that's a dream come true." Looking right at Tony, he went on, "When you're out there, and you hurt so bad you can't go on? don't give up on your dream. It's not worth the price and it will haunt you for years to come. So, we got Trenton, an inner-city team who has no reason to play except to kick your spoiled asses. They have no respect for you. Let's go out there and make the dream of a lifetime begin tonight!!! Bring it all in. On the count of three, yell Dream"

They busted out of the locker room and took the field for calisthenics. Tony took his spot in the last row near the punk freshman kid. He watched Tony like he was his hero, but didn't dare say a word to him. Before the coin toss, coach called them in for one last talk. They all raised one hand in the air and yelled dream at the top of their lungs. As the only Captain, Tony made his way to the middle of the field

Trenton had five big black Captains. They looked real mean and each outweighed Tony by at least fifty pounds. They knew all about Tony and gave him the respect he deserved. He refused to return the favor. This was Jenni's first game and she looked a little worried for Tony. "He looks so small compared to them." Fanny the football expert let her know, "Size doesn't matter" Trenton won the toss and took the ball.

On the first play, Tony set the tone for the game and the season. He busted through the line and knocked the running back unconscious. You could hear the violence. People in the stands were concerned about the injured player but couldn't believe how hard Tony hit him. Coach Bishotti thought back to the first practice he ever had with Tony; the one where he did everything wrong. He realized Tony had come so far in such a short time. He knew it was hatred for his dad that made Tony play, but he was playing by the rules, and that's all Coach could ask for.

Back in the huddle, Tony went off on his teammates. He had his back to Trenton, but his team could see their players. "Listen to me, look in their eyes now, they're scared shitless. You wanna win? Kick the shit outa them while they're down. Hit them so hard they'll never forget you, and then remind them they wont. Make these bastards cry. If you cant do that, get the fuck off the field and turn in your equipment"

Tony was all business. He did what captains are supposed to do, make every player better. It was like the first meeting with Coach.

He gave his teammates two choices, kick ass or quit. Like Tony, they all chose option one. Verona cruised to a 47-0 win. Tony took the second half off. Even the freshman punk kid got in and made a few tackles. When he came off the field, he looked for Tony's approval. But, Tony gave him a look that said, Get the fuck outa my face punk"

Tony and Coach renewed their tradition and shared a few laughs on the field after the game. The mob of college recruiters quickly made their way to the two of them. Tony got serious, "Coach, I ain't interested. You hear me? I'll say it again. I ain't interested in talking to any of them. Respect what I'm sayin and keep them away from me. I'm goin to be with my friends now" Coach went along with Tony's wishes. He had to say something, "Tony?" Tony was already annoyed, "What????" Bishotti finished his thought. "I just wanted to say ya played a good game tonight and I'm really proud of you" Tony was stunned as he said, "Thanks Coach" No one ever told Tony they were proud of him so when he came up to us, he looked kinda dazed. Jimmy asked him if he was alright, and Tony shook it off. All of us gave our props to him for the way he played. Jenni looked star struck. Steph stole a quick peek at his ass. Fanny loved the hit. And Billy, said, "you're not a bad player for a ginnie" Tony was practically family to me and Terry, so we didn't wanna go givin him a big head.

He hit the showers. We all went back to the car for some after game tailgating. A few cars were left. They were probaly coaches. A cop car cruised the lot and busted our balls. We weren't doin anything wrong. They always pull that crap. He stopped and told us we better be gone the next time he comes back. Why do they gotta be that way? It's bullshit. Fanny and Jimmy walked home. They cut through the woods to have their after game delight. The rest of us piled in the bug and drove back to my house. Jenni was sleepin over and the three of them hung out watchin Chiller Theater.

I asked Steph if she was tired. She wasn't. "Steph, I wanna take you to meet a friend of mine" We parked across the street from Harry's, and she freaked. "Harry's? Are you fuckin kiddin me? I can't go in there. I don't even have a fake ID." I let her go off for a bit. With a sneaky smile, I looked at her, "So ya wanna go in or are ya scared?" She always had the perfect answer. "Baby, with you by my side, there ain't nothin to be scared of."

We made our way in. I hate Harry's front door. It slams closed and the noise turns everybody's head to see you on stage. Everybody had the same look. "Who's that hot little girl with Frank's boy?" Bunny's working hard but quick to get a dig in. "Kenny honey, you here for another love lesson by the dumpster?" She knew how I felt about "love on the dumpster". I hated it. Me and Steph found Fester sittin in his usual stool at the end of the bar. I introduced them and Fester was nice for all of two minutes. He asked Steph to go out back and help him take care of a "man matter" My girl caught on quick. Bust his balls hard. "I'd love to Fester but it looks like you have an innie where you're supposed to have an outie. I've never been good at treasure hunts. When ya finally find it, you real-ize it wasn't worth your time" Ouch. Even Bunny had to tease her man and said, "Kenny, you got all you can handle with her. "Yeah I do and I love handling all of her , if ya know what I'm sayin." Steph was in.

Bunny got us two sippin beers and we stayed for about an hour. Fester and Bunny were really nice. They accepted us as a couple, not a couple of kids. Bunny took the lead and told Steph they'd love to take us out one night. She accepted. Fester, being Fester, says, "Good Baby, we'll take them out, get em good and drunk Then take them back to our place and play swap. Steph will wake up in the morning not knowin where she is and think she slept twenty years when she opens her eyes and thinks I'm Kenny" Steph is crackin up. "Fuckin A right. And after a night with me, I'll age ya twenty years. You'll be thinking you're talking dirty when you say to Bunny, "Who's ya Granddaddy!!!!" I love my girl. She can spar with anybody.

We said our good byes and Fester and Bunny got serious and both were nice to Steph. I thanked them and we said, "See ya later"

"That was fun baby. Thanks for takin me there"

"I knew you'd like them"

"You're right. I do. They're a great couple. and Funnnnnny!! Wow"

Yeah, I don't do it a lot but I like hangin out with them. It's different than kids our age"

"It is different Kenny, but in a good way. We do different things. Look, what couple our age would do what we did last summer?"

"I know. We're cool as shit"

She let out her cute laugh

"Baby, the only problem tonight was I couldn't get the Addams Family song outa my head. Oh my God. He does remind me of Fester!!!"

We pulled up to her house and I asked if we could fool around. I wanted to bend her over the garbage can. It wasn't a dumpster, but it'd do.

"Fuck what is it with you and Fester and sex by the dumpster"

"We like sex to be really dirty"

With a wicked smile she tells me, "Guys are sooo bad"

We shared our soft kiss goodnight. I like how we kissed at the end of the night. It kept us fresh. Walking backwards to the car, I loved looking at her and never grew tired of the vision. She was hot the first day we met, she's even hotter now, and she'll be even hotter twenty years from now. Yeah, she was the only girl I've even been with, but why would I want more. If I did, the girl would be less and make me want Steph more. I learned that a few years ago and I'm never gonna forget it. Friday nights should never end.

But they do and Saturday night was the boys night out. Tony wanted to get outa town and hang out by the docks. Havin a car really opened up our world. All sorts of shit went down there. People watchin was cheap and cool. It was like watchin a dozen movies goin on at the same time.

Jimmy was in the back rollin a joint. I didn't feel like getting high; didn't wanna miss any of the movies. Jimmy lights up and passes it to Tony. He tells Jimmy, "No fuckin way. I'm not smoking that shit durin football" Me and Jimmy couldn't believe what we were hearin. The stunned looks made Tony explain. "Look, I promised myself. Besides Bishotti's been pretty good to me, and if I got arrested now, I'd feel like I let him down and embarrassed him. I don't wanna do that"

Jimmy still wasn't sure, "You serious Tony?" "Fuck yeah, I am. Last night, Bishotti told me he was proud of me and I know he wasn't talking about the way I played. What adult has ever been proud of my ass? None. Nobody."

"But, last night, you're not gonna believe what happened. I gotta show ya"

Tony reaches into his jacket and pulls out these envelops. "There's over fifteen thousand dollars in these" Jimmy put the joint out, "Where the fuck did you get all that money?" "All those coaches watching the game last night thought they were being cool hiding them in different parts of my locker. I'll tell ya what. Some schools like me a lot more than others. Ya can tell by the weight. It freaked me out cause in one night I made more than my dad makes in six months" Enough of this bullshit. I had to speak up. "Tony, you didn't tell him, did you?" "No Fuckin way. I'm not that stupid" "Well then you gotta return it to your Coach. You spend that money, and they'll own you. Trust me, it'll come out and no matter how much you spend, it won't be worth it. Plus, you just said you don't wanna embarrass Bishotti. This would crush him. Give it back Tony. I'll take you to his house tomorrow. Coach will know what to do." "But, Kenny, it's fifteen thousand dollars!!!" "It just means fifteen thousand problems Tony" He came around, it was the right thing to do. We went to Bishotti's the next day.

When Dad had tickets to the Giant game, we always went to nine am mass. Priorities, ya know. IHOP was packed but we lucked out and got a table. Mom and Terry got fruit and coffee. Terry did her best, livin on the fruit. Her best wasn't good enough as she'd always steal bites from my bacon and cheese omelet. Dad got a large stack to soak up the beer he'd be drinkin at the game. He kept looking at his watch and mom was annoyed. Sunday breakfast and dinner have always been family time. It wasn't askin much to pretend you wanted to be here. I think mom realized in the blink of an eye me and Terry would be grown up and outa the house. She savored every minute we were together. Maybe Dad did too. Who knows. He kept most things inside. Mom made small talk, askin me how Steph was and Terry about school. My sister wasn't ready to tell mom and dad about Billy. And after church, it wasn't exactly the best time to say you're datin a Jewish guy. Dad had the check figured out in his head. He gave the waitress twenty-seven bucks and told her to keep the change. Me and Terry gave Dad our traditional thank you hugs.

We got home at eleven am. and I called Tony to tell him I was on my way. Growin up in Jersey, the Giants ruled the northern part of the state. Philly owned the southern part. All the chores you had to do were finished by the pre-game show. Kick off time was one. We talked on the ride about how we thought Coach would take our news. If Tony had no idea, neither did I. This hot looking brunette in a Phil Simms jersey met our knock on the door. There's something about a girl in a football jersey that makes her look really sexy. She yelled, "Honey, two kids are here askin to see you"

"Hey Tony, Kenny, Come on in. This is Julie" We all said our hellos and Tony asked if we could talk to Coach in private. He brought us down to his basement where he watched game film. Tony seemed a little jealous. "Coach you never told me you watch film. How come you never invited me?" "Kenny, is this the Tony I know and love? The one who never wanted to learn anything or listen to anybody about football?" I had to laugh a little. "Yes Mr. Bishotti. I believe it is" "Ok fellas, what can I do for you?" Tony reached into his pocket and handed the envelops to his coach. Bishotti looked annoyed. "Shit, I knew this was coming. It's not gonna stop Tony, no matter what I say. Ya see, I'm just a high school coach in their eyes. You're a big-time college player. All I can do is send these back to the school's Athletic Director with a letter. I'll let you read the letter before I send it. Plan on eating your lunch in my office tomorrow. And Tony? Ya did the right thing here. This is what I was talking about on Friday night. Ya made me proud of you." "Thanks Coach. And you know I'm not goin to college, so this is my last year playin football and I gotta show you and myself I've learned something." "Tony, you've shown me more about learning than I ever dreamed of" "Well, then Coach. Maybe I gotta show myself" "Come on guys, let's get upstairs and watch the game. Julie made some great Lasagna"

I was a witness. I always knew Tony was intense, but his coach did something to him. I was overloaded on energy just watching what was between them. I think Tony felt okay about being good at something. But, this was his last year. I worried about what he'd feel when he was done playin football. Me and Jimmy were goin to college, so he'd lose his passion and his two best friends. Ain't no passion working at the docks. Only pain.

"So, Coach, don't lie to me. Who's this Julie chick? Do ya like her?"

"Hey, You two be nice to her. She's alright. Nothin serious. Besides, she makes great Lasagna."

"Tony felt real comfortable with his coach, "I bet that's not all she makes nice for ya!!!"

Coach had to dig right back. "Maybe if you could learn how to talk to a girl, you'd find someone as good as Julie. Stuttering Tony"

We all laughed and Julie felt like she was missing something. She spoke up.

"What's so funny?"

Tony fessed up and told her, "Coach wants to teach me how I should speak to a girl." Julie stole the spotlight. "Sounds like the blind leadin the blind to me!!!"

She was in and it broke the "stale meeting someone new" feeling. Julie brought us our lasagna with a nice fresh piece of Italian bread and put a big pitcher of iced tea on the coffee table. She asked if Phil McConkey scored yet. Phil was a Navy man. My mom always said there's something about a man in uniform. Bavarro was the tough soul and McConkey was the heart of the team. Simms and L.T. Nothing more you had to say about them. The Giants were playin the Cowboys and Emmitt was tough to stop. Tony actually watched the whole game. He focused in on L.T. watching every move he made. Tony was learning and the best player in the world was teaching him. L.T. and S.T. played the game the same way.

One game was enough. We said our thank yous and headed out the door. Tony wanted to cruise the neighborhood. He wouldn't say it; he just didn't wanna go home. Tony never thought of his coach as the dad he always wanted. He liked Bishotti and the special relationship between them. Four years ago, Tony was nothing to anybody but me and Jimmy. Bishotti opened the door and accepted Tony for who he was. He never tried to change him; Coach let Tony do the changing on his own. And I think if Tony never changed, Bishotti would still accept him.

I had to be home for dinner. I dropped Tony off. He walked in the door of Hell's house, as he liked to call it. His dad was passed out with half a beer in his hand and the other half all over his shirt. Empties were everywhere and it smelled like his dad peed himself. There were two Swanson Salisbury Steak TV dinners in the freezer. Typical Sunday dinner at the Matellis. This was the life of a man who worked at the docks. I can't believe Tony wants this.

Fanny would help Mrs. Fortunato make an early dinner. Cleaning and cooking, Jimmy had it maid. He hung out at home learning about this guy named Gates. Supposedly, he was ahead of his time thinking about computers. Radio Shack sold computers. They were real expensive and didn't seem to do anything more than a three ring binder. Typing took longer than writing so computers seemed like a waste of time to me. Since Jimmy's dad died, the house didn't change much. Fanny brought some love and warmth to it. Mrs. Fortunato appreciated what Fanny did for both. Jimmy seemed to take it for granted. That's not meant in a bad way. He knew he had it good, he just didn't know how good. Great food, Great sex, Great love, Great understanding. What more could ya want??? Jimmy had it all.

After I dropped Tony off, I decided to surprise Steph and stop by. Mr. Demarino always made me feel welcome. Stable love brings that family feeling. Steph was busy makin Sausage, sweet, and peppers. The smell streamed throughout the house. Yelling from the kitchen, I heard, "Come here baby. Gimme my kiss and taste this sauce I'm makin" I love it. Kiss first, taste second. Damn, she even looked good in an apron with her hair bun style. Whoever invented the bun should be shot!!! Had the kiss, tasted the sauce, got the dig, "Nice hair" I went back to hanging out with her dad for a few minutes. He asked about mom and dad. I gave the typical, "Fine" Then came the school and college questions. "School's good and Rutgers is my first choice. I ain't stupid. I don't wanna be far away from Steph." He teased me, "Now there's a good answer for the Rutgers interview. Kenny, why do you want to attend Rutgers? Sir, The reason I want to go here is I don't wanna be far from my girl-friend" Steph was listening from the kitchen and returned the hair dig. "Dad, don't let him lie to you. The only reason he's not goin far away is because he doesn't trust leaving me alone in town with Tony Matelli" Her dad sided with me, "I think Tony, oops I mean Kenny, has nothing to worry about, I'll watch out for ya!!!" I looked at my watch and had to get home for dinner. I went back in the kitchen to hug and kiss the cook. "I love ya baby, see ya tomorrow."

A great weekend ended with a special Sunday dinner. Mom made her special salad. With the Parmesan Italian Dressing, draped all over the freshly cut chilled tomatoes and iceberg lettuce. There was other stuff, I didn't wanna know what it was, but it tasted good. The main event was Veal Marsala and linguine in clam sauce. Dad looked tired from the game and the meal did him good. I knew he was gonna fall asleep before the clock started ticking on Sixty Minutes. It was Terry's turn to do the dishes and let mom enjoy her cappuccino.

I asked to be excused to do homework and fill out some college applications. They're so stupid. Do they really care that I didn't join the chess club? And Volunteer activities? That's a joke. Not only do we have to pay alotta money, they wanna see if we'll work for free.

Since we weren't allowed to drive to school till the spring se-mester, me, Tony and Jimmy only had a few more months of walk-ing. Where'd the time go? It seemed like yesterday Tony was braggin about how he could tug the tiger. Now, girlfriends, colleges, jobs dominated our lives. It wasn't a bad thing. In a few years, we'd have barbecues and the three of us would bullshit till the sunrise or the beer and pot wore out; whichever came first. Wives and girlfriends knew they would take a backseat to our friendship.

I was getting sick of school at the wrong time. I guess I was a bad influence on Jimmy. We thought we were a lot smarter than our teachers. That's not sayin much. Who isn't smarter than a high school teacher? We did have to get our shit together. The S.A.T.S were in two weeks. Tony didn't care. He did whatever homework he could and got some girl to do the rest. Tony may not have learned about history, but he sure could make some with the girl.

Verona High's football team was rolling, and Tony got better, stronger and smarter with each game. Coach outsmarted the recruiters and taped the names on each kid's locker. Tony had two. A real one had S.T. taped and the fake one had Matelli. The fake locker had some clothes and pictures of girls. Thousands of dollars were placed in there every week. Coach returned every single penny.

After each game. we all went on the field and congratulated Tony. Me and Jimmy would give him a high five. Jimmy always threw in a "Ya kicked ass tonight brother" Fanny would show off her football knowledge saying something only Tony would understand. Steph brushed off the dirt from his ass. We all laughed, and Tony shook his head and smiled. Terry always gave him a big hug and Billy uttered a simple "good game, Tony" Jenni stood on the edge of us and never said a word. Tony would never admit it, but he really appreciated his small, but select fan club. It was one of the few times I saw him have a genuine smile.

In late October, the season was growing shorter than the days. Tony enjoyed the sunset fading walk home alone. Bruised, achy, and sore, he took his time to smell the burning leaves and brisk chill of a fall afternoon. He spotted Jenni walking about a block ahead of him. Tony quickened his pace and walked stride for stride with Jenni.

The silence was deafening. He finally got the nerve to ask, "Hey, How come you never talk to me?" Jenni shyly stood her ground. "I don't know how you were raised, but I thought the guy was supposed to talk to the girl first" Tony played the game. "Hi I'm Tony Matelli"

Hi Tony, my name is Jenni Ruben. Nice to meet you! There, was that so hard? Tony had to fire back. "For me or for you?" Jenni smiled, answering, "Both."

"You're really good at football"

"Eh, it's just a game. It don't mean nothing."

"What does nothing mean?" Jenni wanted to know.

He was put on the spot. "Not much, I guess. What means something to you.?"

Jenni played her cards close to her heart "I dunno. Maybe being with someone I like. But I haven't been lucky enough to find anybody. Guys just want one thing. You're no different."

Tony got a little pissed. "You don't even know me. How the fuck do you know what I want?"

"I see girls throw themselves at you. You don't exactly fight them off."

"You're wrong!! Don't believe everything you hear or see. I could care less about those girls. And I definitely don't wanna be with them. You ever hear of me going out with anybody?"

"Jenni thought about it, No I haven't."

You're gonna think I'm bullshittin, but this is the longest I ever talked to a girl"

"Why me?" She had some great questions.

"Why you askin so many questions?"

"I hear ya"

The walk ended in front of Jenni's house. Tony didn't realize he walked so far.

"Jenni, you goin to the game on Friday night?"

"Are you askin or askin me out?""

"Just askin.

"Ok, I'm just telling, yeah. I'll be there. Good Luck." "I'll see ya tomorrow"

"Yeah, I'll see you too Tony."

He walked away feeling something. He kept it to himself. Me or Jimmy would never believe Tony liked any girl, so he didn't dare mention it to us. Besides, what would he say? He didn't even know what to say to himself. He wasn't gonna change though. So what!! He had one good conversation with a girl. She did distract him a little bit. He was either growing up or growing soft. Time would tell.

Game day was here, and the tailgate crew got busy planning their Friday night. School spirit ran through the halls. Verona High's football team was good, and pride was clear. Even the teachers mentioned it at the beginning of each class. "Big Game tonight. If we win, no homework for the weekend!!" Steph wore her school colors, and the blue and white bands decorated her beautiful hair. She loved white.

Jimmy and Fanny were fired up. She felt good giving the scouting report on Morristown High. Her Dad was a big football fan. If he saw a touch game in the park, he'd stop and watch. Billy was full of shit acting like it was first date night STILL with Terry. The thought was in the right place. But you can't bullshit a guy. Terry learned all about it from me. She didn't care. Ya take it when you can get it. Jenni was the perfect tag-a-long as she got the girls to bond. It was pretty normal in high school. Even if you were a couple, the guys hung out with the guys and the girls did the same. Me and Steph would steal some "I'm thinking about you" looks.

Each game started the same. Tony walking to the middle of the field to meet four or five guys who thought they were tougher than Tony. He refused to shake hands or even acknowledge the other Captains. Tony loved the gamble of the coin toss more than he liked football. "Tails" He was three for three. Coach believed in routine. He gave his last-minute motivation and Verona joined their hands high and counted one, two, three, "Dream" was starting to be a reality.

Verona loved getting the ball to start the second half. It allowed Tony to inflict his first play pain on the other team. His teammates started to catch on. They all knew the first play set the tone. Tony was all about no bullshit and big-time intimidation. Three and out, Verona got the ball. The crowd roared as they knew Morristown was done. Tony jogged off the field and gave a quick stare that only Jenni saw.

The games started to get tougher, but so did Tony. The scores weren't much different. Usually, they won by two or three touchdowns. Coach Bishotti showed mercy on the other team and never let Tony play more than three quarters. As long as Tony didn't sign with a college, all the recruiters still posted with their envelops. The punk kid got a little more playing time. He wanted Tony to give him a little respect, but that just wasn't gonna happen.

Homecoming was here and the losers didn't want to go the dance with another loser. Me and Steph laughed at who was gonna be the loser king and queen. It had to be two people who weren't goin out and both had to look miserable being together. Extra credit for the couples who were gonna fool around despite their self-inflicted misery.

Billy and Terry spent the night dancing. My little sister looked nice in her dress which she and mom spent hours picking out. It had to be perfect. She liked being one of the few tenth graders invited. I began to see Billy was pretty good to my sister. Steph told me I could learn a thing or two from Billy. I love her. Only Steph could say one thing and knew I would know she meant the opposite. The music turned to slow dancing. I led her to the middle of the floor to dance. The "kiss and hug" music was Chicago's "Color My World" We looked in each other's eyes and sang every word to each other. It was the kind of thing a couple with history did. The song ended with a make out moment. I took her hand and left the floor. It was my turn to get the dig in. " So, baby, we still one?" Steph fired back. "You really want me to answer? I thought we left your "insecurity blanket" on the beach" I'm done climbin that mountain. . With a bent elbow and fist pointed up, I said," Fuckin-A Right we did!!! She struck again as she whispered in my ear what she wanted to do with me in homeroom, right on her desk. Steph made it clear. She wanted to "educate me" I had a feeling it was class participation. Off we went to learn about temperature. It got real hot between us.

Jimmy and Fanny were either outside making Fanny need an "after something" cigarette or munchin out at the food buffet. "Exercise" can really work up an appetite. We all met by the juice bowl and talked about things couples talk about. We'd try to guess how many losers would ask Jenni to dance in the next ten minutes. She showed a little spunk saying, one would be too many. Steph won the bet. Eleven guys were sent packing with their tail between their legs.

Tony took his spot. His back rested on the wall and one leg was bent in the cool position. Every so often he'd rub a muscle that ached from the game. Single girls practically stood in line for a chance at one night love. He wouldn't dare be seen leavin with any loser. The shore was different. He didn't know them, and they didn't know him. Summertime one night didn't matter. I realized Tony and Jenni had a lot in common. With her innocent school girl eyes,. She only looked at Tony. Jenni would never say a word to him. If she did, she was just another loser. Besides, Tony wasn't interested in schoolgirls. Dock daughters were more his type. They didn't want much and were happy with less.

Tony went to the soda bar and filled a glass of ice. Doing his best impersonation of a nice guy, he asked Jenni, "What kind do you want?"

She was stunned he was talking to her. "I'll take a diet coke. What are you havin?"

Tony answered with a sarcastic look, "I'm an un-cola kinda guy"

After his walk with Jenni, this was supposed to be easier, but it wasn't. Both stood there tryin to find the words that wouldn't sound stupid. Tony remembered Coach Bishotti teasing him about his shyness and here it was staring him in his own reflection. Why couldn't he talk to her like a normal guy? It was the first time he ever thought about havin a mom and askin her for help. After all, his Dad wasn't exactly the greatest role model.

Jenni wasn't helping the silence. She went through all the thoughts a girl in high school thinks. He didn't mean to, but Tony was takin shots at her self-esteem. A girl can only think, "What's wrong with me? Why won't he talk to me? Does he think I'm ugly? She was smart enough to know it wasn't her and it wasn't him either. Both were stuck in neutral. Jenni decided to be his friend and forfeited the expectations a relationship can bring. She learned to be patient with Tony. Friendships don't happen overnight. She refilled his soda. He thanked her. Jenni took baby steps, "No problem" And she walked away from Tony. He seemed confused in a good way. No girl ever walked away from Tony. I guess there's a first time for everything.

"I'm outa here" He called it a night and walked home alone. He walked in "hell house", as he liked to call it and saw his dad passed out with an empty bottle of Vodka on the floor. His Dad was getting worse each day. Tony began to realize his father couldn't go on the way he was going. He knew his father's abuse made him fucked up in so many ways. He felt peace in the karma gods rightin a wrong, but he wondered if it was better to forgive his father. Till today, it seemed so easy for Tony to blame his dad for a miserable future.

Me and Steph decided to cap off the night at Harry's. Bunny greeted me with a big booby hug. Not to be outdone, Fester hugged Steph with his strong plumber hands grabbin her ass.. We got our beers and joined Fester at the end of the bar. He knew about Homecoming and told me he played football at Verona High. Being the smallest kid on the line taught him not to take shit from anybody. We talked about homecoming, and he heard we kicked ass tonight. This guy came over and joined the conversation.

"Hey, your friend Tony is the best player I've seen in years." I tried to act like an adult while Bunny was showing her new earrings to Steph. "Yeah, he's not bad!!! I can't tell him he's good. Ya never want a friend getting a big head"

Who is this guy? Fester bailed me out. "Kenny, this is Fanny's Dad. We played on the same team together. He went on to become a football star at Penn State. And I stayed back here flushin toilets" We had a good laugh. Mr. Ferino used to come here when he was seventeen too. "Bunny's mother was the bartender back then. Fester, remember the night we came here and you met Bunny for the first time?" Fester smiled at the memory and Bunny came over and gave him a big pucker up kiss. Mr. Ferino gave him shit. "Yeah, he made me stay here till four o'clock in the morning so he could walk Bunny outside and wipe the ten inches of snow off her car. I froze my balls off waitin for him to get the guts to kiss her. Little did I know, ten years later, they'd still find love behind the dumpster. It sounds like it should be a Neil Diamond song, "Love Behind the Dumpster""

Me and Steph were tired, so we called it a night and said our good byes. Broken Bar promises were made. Bunny reminded us that we had to get together for our double date.. It was pretty cool meetin Mr. Ferino and hearin about how long Bunny and Fester had been together. They didn't need a clock to tell them it was time to get married. They chose not to. Why fuck up a good thing with a stupid piece of paper? I was a little surprised by the pride Fester and Ferino showed playin football for Verona. I knew I didn't have the ability to play, but I did have the heart. It's one of those little regrets you drag through life. Steph told me, "You can't have everything, but you can have everything that's important to you"

We got to the car and Steph gave me a nice hug and sweet kiss. With her in my arms, I did have everything. She always knew when I needed to laugh, when I needed love, and when I needed to talk. "Thanks for giving me an unforgettable homecoming Baby" She melted my core, "Yeah, it was unforgettable Steph.. But it's no different than any time we're together." We made out for a lifetime in a moment. No sex, just an innocent passionate breathless kiss. Four years and each kiss was as good as the first. And that's everything to us.

I woke up Saturday morning and mom made my favorite. French toast with perfectly melted butter and a pool of log cabin filled the top slice. Four slices were perfect, enough so I wanted more but not enough to get me sick. With Winter around the corner, Dad was out getting new tires and brakes for the car that was getting too old. My car couldn't afford any new parts. Some kids spend everything they have on their Camaro. Why? So they could race them down main street? I was happy just getting anywhere I had to go.

Mom sat with me. She enjoyed the way I loved her cooking. With everything goin on in school, mom and I hadn't talked in a while. I wondered how her and dad were getting along. I was old enough to ask, so I did. Mom appreciated my concern. "We're getting along alright. Not good, not bad. I can't speak for your father, but I'm startin to realize the house is gonna be empty soon. It goes so fast. You were my baby boy wrapped in your favorite blue blanket. Whenever you cried, I gave it to you, and you stopped. Dad passed out cigars for the first year of your life. He was such a proud papa. I never saw him happier than the times you and Terry were babies. And You!! Whenever Terry cried, you'd stand by her basinet and gently pat her head till she stopped crying"

"Mom, I can't believe you remember when Dad was teaching me how to ride my bike. I fell and skinned my knee really bad. You ran outside with the Johnson's band-aid box and covered my cut with the biggest one in the box. After I stopped crying, Dad asked me if I wanted to try again. There was something about the way he said it. I got back on. And I haven't fell since. Even when me, Tony, and Jimmy pretended we were Evel Knievel. But, mom, we got off the track. How are you two getting along.

"Kenny, We're fine. I do my thing and he does his. It seems to work. I guess we got tired of the fighting. It's not perfect, but I think we accept each other. We'd both be miserable apart. Besides, do you really think your dad could live alone? No!! He needs me and I like being needed."

"Who doesn't Mom!!"

Jimmy called me after breakfast. N.J.I.T called his mom yesterday and told her to look in the mail this week. He thought it was an early acceptance letter. I knew he was right. Schools don't call you for bad news. He was all fired up. This wacko computer making dream was starting to come together. He wanted me to get high and then he was gonna get some real good lovin from Fanny. She promised him a big surprise if he got in. And he was dyin to know what it was. I was happy for him; not just cause of college. They were the perfect couple, well perfect for each other. Jimmy never had to climb the mountain I did. His was different. Finding happiness after his dad died wasn't exactly easy. And Fanny stood by his side the whole time. She gave him everything he needed and more importantly, everything he wanted. I told him I'd fire one up after he got the letter. Jimmy said, "Fuck it. I'll hit the bong in my closet and then do some wild ass Fanny Fuckin!!!" Gotta admit "Fanny Fuckin" had a nice ring to it. I let him hang up and have fun.

The phone rang again, and it was Tony askin me if I wanted to go get a slice. I knew something was botherin him. We met and I didn't fuck around. "So what's up Tony? Why are we here? Tony took a deep breath and started to talk.

"Kenny, you know I ain't a jock asshole. I never cared if we won a stupid fuckin football game. You already know why I played and what I got out of it" I gave him a few listening nods to encourage him to go on. And he did. "Well this Friday night we play Florham Park, our rival. For the first time ever I wanna win. I really do Kenny. And it scares the fuck outa me. I mean, Bishotti deserves it. I don't talk about it much but he's done so fuckin much for me. I wanna give him this. Ya know Florham is pretty fuckin good. They only lost to Pearl River, who I'm thinking we'll meet in the state champion-ship. I've never wanted anything and if I did, it only lead to disap-pointment. I figured I got two friends and that's enough for me. I gotta do this. I gotta win. I don't wanna hear some bullshit "ya had a good season" crap if we lose.

"That's pretty cool Tony. And you're right about Bishotti. It'd be easy to say you've just grown up cause you've grown older. But that's not true. I know this guy did a lot for you. I never told you but when we were freshman, Bishotti called me into his office one day. He wanted to know about you and your dad. I told him the truth. He was too smart, and you were too. He knew if he tried to be the dad you never had, you'd see right through it. I'll never forget it. He said to me. "I don't give a fuck how he plays football. Your friend's been screwed over. And I think he's a good kid. I wanna make a dif-ference in his life." "And Tony, I think he has. Think about it, Tony. In four years did he teach you one thing about football? No!! I really don't know what he taught you, but I know he taught ya something.

Me and Jimmy were always a little jealous. So Tony, you dumb fuck, just go out and win the game. It's really that simple."

"Thanks Kenny. You got time to get an ice?" "Tony, you know better. It ain't lunch at Vinchenzo's without a scoop of cherry." He asked about me and Steph and I said everything has been really good since the summer. I told him about our fight. He never knew Steph's hell. Tony felt pretty bad. "Kenny, that really musta sucked for her. All my life I never complained but I guess I felt sorry for myself. I'd never tell anybody cause I thought it showed I was weak. I'll never understand it. We all hide pain like it something we're ashamed of"

"Tony, man, what the hell is goin on? You're getting smarter. And what's with you talking to Jenni?. Don't bullshit me."

He tried, but I didn't push it. "Nothin Kenny. I talked to her once, last night. Big fuckin deal. She hangs out with you guys during the games. So, the least I could do is talk to her for two minutes. And don't even say it. I know, I know. I'm changing. But seriously, foot-ball ending is fuckin with my head. It's the only thing people ever thought I was good at and it's gonna be over in a few weeks"

"Tony, it doesn't have to be that way and I know you know what I'm talking about". .

Saturday night was date night and me and Steph went to the movies. She wanted to see Raiders of the lost Ark. The title didn't exactly capture my interest, but Steph did. It was awesome from the minute it started to the end. Trustin Steph with everything opened my eyes to new worlds every day. We held hands the whole movie and even found time to sneak in a few make-out moments. And she was a little clingy for the whole movie. A lotta clingy gets old quick. A little clingy is a good thing.

We got to the car and Steph wanted to take a drive to Seaside for some fall Beach walkin. With an anxious trembling voice, she asked me if I heard from any colleges yet. I knew Steph. She wasn't askin me to give me a Fanny style of congratulations. I sensed something was wrong. "No Babe, no word yet."

She was fishin. "Is Rutgers still your first choice?"

"Steph you know it is!! Don't ya think I'd tell you if anything changed? What's goin on ? Why are you askin me this?" Steph tried to dodge the truth, but I wouldn't let her. "Honey, you always get shit outa me when I don't wanna talk. So, now the shoe's on the other foot. Talk!!!"

"Awww Fuck you Kenny Mancuso!!"

"First and last name? I must really be pissin you off"

"I'm scared alright?"

"Scared of me goin to college?"

"No, you dork. I'm scared of being left behind. You're gonna meet a whole new world and half of it's girls. C'mon Kenny. We're high school sweethearts. How many couples make it when they started goin out in high school? Look at your mom and Dad. Do you really think they made it? You know they feel stuck with each other"

I got pissed, real pissed.; pissed she believed that could happen to us. "Steph, Do you really think I would do that?? Let me tell ya something Do you have any idea why I wanna go to college?"

She answered meekly, " So you get a good job when you graduate"

"Wrong!!! The only reason I wanna go to college is to give us a better future and the only reason I wanna go to Rutgers is cause it's the closest school to you. Can't put those reasons on an application, but it's true. Baby, I ain't lying when I say you're my world. Deal with it. We're "One" remember?"

"Kenny, I trust you. I'm sorry. Nobody knows how special you are underneath all of those outa style clothes and if any college preppie girl figures it out, I will kick her ass the way a jealous Jersey girl can. You don't piss us off!!!"

I love her so much. She's got great spunk. She snuggled her head on my shoulder and we listened to the waves crash on the shore. Steph wanted to take a short nap and wake up to watch the sunrise. I ran to the car, got a blanket and a beach towel to use as a pillow. I got responsible and called mom and dad to let them know where I was. They didn't wanna worry, so a simple phone call got me brownie points. I returned to my girl, made pillows from sand, and covered it carefully with the towel. We snuggled under the blanket. She kissed me goodnight and was out in a few seconds. I'll never change. Watchin her breathe made me breathless.

Morning was gonna be here soon. I let her sleep as I gently caressed her body. I got lost in love desire. This wasn't gonna be sex. We made love at sunrise. And we were "One" at Six... in the morning..

I got home in time to miss church. Having the house to myself, I blared the stereo, pretending I was a rock star and Steph was the girl in the front row. The radio DJ fucked with my mind as he played "Scenes from an Italian Restaurant"; a song about high school love that didn't last. With the loud music playing, I didn't hear the front door open. Terry teased me." Still pretendin you're a rock star big brother?" I quickly turned the music down and ignored my sister. I asked dad what time the Giants were playin. "Four, they're playin Montana and the niners. Hopefully, LT didn't stay out all night" There were rumors all over Jersey that LT was a big time partier. Parcells only cared where he was on Sunday afternoons.

I went to my room and crashed for a few hours. The aroma of mom's homemade spaghetti sauce woke my sense of smell and the rest of me too. The crisp air, shorter days and Mom's special Sunday sauce were my favorite things about Fall. Summerall and Madden taught me football much better than Tony. He loved the violence; they loved the game. I liked them a lot. They seemed like they'd be friends when the game was over. Montana was Montana and the Giants took a beating.

Mom called us to the dinner table. A nice fresh salad was waiting. "Save room for the pasta and meatballs kids"

I got all excited. "Mom, you made your meatballs. What's the special occasion? Dad, you get a promotion??" He knew I was bustin his own set of meatballs. Terry chimed in. "Actually, I have announcement to make." She had the floor before we all hit it. "Me and Billy had sex last night and it was great"

Dad lost it and Mom stared at her daughter with the rage that only exists between a mother and a daughter. Dad fumed, "Where is he? I'll kill that bastard" Terry felt the joke went on long enough. "I'm kidding!!!! I just wanted to prove a point. You would never say that to Kenny. Dad you wouldn't even yell at Stephanie. And mom you wouldn't forbid her from seeing your son" Dad defended his reaction. "That's different. Kenny is a boy" Ut oh. Mom asked, "what does that have to do with anything Frank?" Terry spoke up again. "In biology class we were talking about the sexes and the different ways the world sees them. There are definitely double standards. For example, they'll never be a woman president. Dad countered," So what. They'll never be a black one either. What's your point?'. It's just the way the world is and there ain't no use in tryin to change it." Mom didn't like Dad's answer. Not only was he a male chauvinist pig, he was also a racist. Mom didn't care what happened in the world. She only cared about the world sittin at the dining room table. Ahhhh Sunday dinners were always family debate night, and we never knew what the topic would be or who the teams were. Sometimes it was me and mom against Dad and Terry, others it was the kids against the 'rents. In a weird way, it was good family fun.

Rival week began and the school was all fired up about Florham Park. Teachers always went light on the homework this week and they gave us fun assignments. Banners had to be made. There was a contest for the best noise maker. On Wednesday night, we had the bonfire, and the football team did a skit. As Captain, Tony had to participate. He had no choice. Julie, Coach's girlfriend made Tony and Bishotti's costumes. They dressed up as Cheerleaders with the biggest asses you ever saw. The crowd erupted in laughter. Both played the role with perfection. Rubbing asses together at the end of their cheer, cameras were flashing like a lightning storm. I knew times like this would never be forgotten. The night ended with everyone singing the Verona High Fight song.

On Thursday, the excitement of the week continued to spread through the school. In each class, we did something related to Verona High. In history class, the teacher taught us about the beginning of the rivalry as well as famous people who played in the game. Our current Mayor was a star quarterback in the early sixties.

Practice ended early and the team gathered on the bleachers to hear some words by the coaches and asked the captain if he'd like to say a few words to his team. Tony always declined, but today he stood up and faced the team. He asked the Freshman punk kid to come up to him.

"Hey, the walls are really thin in your house. Last night did ya hear me goin to town on ya sister?" Everyone laughed but the kid. The kid let out a rage that no one saw coming. He hit Tony with three brutal punches. Tony dropped to the ground and the kid didn't stop. He jumped on Matelli and continued to pound him. Screaming, "I'm sick and tired of your shit. You think you're so tough you don't know what the fuck tough is. And my name is Danny Pintauro. Say it, SAY IT NOW!!!; before I start whaling on you some more. The coaches rushed in and pulled them apart. Tony got up and shook Danny's hand. He hugged him and whispered in his ear. Next year, it's his team and he has to play the game with the anger and heart he just showed. He finished by saying, "And one more thing. I didn't even know you had a sister. I was just doin that to bring this out in you." Danny laughed a little and quietly thanked Tony." Danny took his seat in the first row of the bleachers and Tony began his speech.

"Since I became a member of this team, I didn't think of any of you as friends. I never said Hi to you in the halls or Malls. While I may've led by example, I treated all of you like shit. I'm sorry. I'm no different than all of you. This week was great, this year's been great and tomorrow we have a chance to prove this team is great. Nobody is going to give us this game. To win, every single one of us must play the game with the anger Danny just showed us. And I'm here to say Danny Pintauro can hit hard as shit when he's mad!!! I barely remembered my own name but there was no way I was gonna forget his!!" A little laughter eased the light moment, but Tony went on.

"We deserve this, our coaches do, families, girlfriends, and fans too. I don't believe in losing. Losing is for losers. They say shit like we tried our best. But Winners?, Winners always get the hot girl. So, let's win this game and remember it for the rest of our lives. One more thing. Thanks for letting me be your Captain and accepting me. I never let anyone know, but it really means a lot to me.

Practice over, speech over, and teammates came up to Tony huggin and thanking him. One by one, they approached Tony telling him, "We gonna win tomorrow"

Coach and Captain were the last ones the leave the field. Bishotti had a dumbfounded smile. Tony was annoyingly curious, "What????" Coach didn't wanna get all mushy. "Nothin!!!" Talk about a two word conversation that spoke volumes. Coach wanted to tell Tony how proud he was just to know him and Tony wanted to thank him for teaching him so much about himself and others. He knew Bishotti would be a phone call away years after Captain left Verona.

Coach put his arm around Tony, "C'mon, Let's get the fuck outa here"

"Hey Teachers aren't supposed to curse ya know. "

"Listen to you, Students aren't either. You got two options. I'd suspend ya right now but I think the principal would fire me"

Tony hit the showers and headed home. He needed to talk about everything going on in his head. Me and Jimmy were busy getting ready for tomorrow. It was gonna be the best tailgate party Verona ever had. He didn't show it, but Tony was still really nervous about the game tomorrow. He hated wanting anything. Wanting has always let him down. He wanted to win the game. He passed Jenni's house and stopped for a minute. Tony couldn't knock on the door. He'd feel stupid and wouldn't know what to say. So he stood there lookin at her house, pretending he could find the words. Just as Tony turned away, a window opened. It was Jenni.

"Hey Tony. Good Luck tomorrow. I'll be thinking bout you tonight and I know you're gonna make everyone important to you proud. See ya after the game"

As the window was shutting, He got the nerve to say, "Thanks Jenni. I'll be lookin for ya tomorrow."

Girls have so much power over boys. Tony was real fired up now. He couldn't understand his feelings for Jenni., After he'd make a great play, he'd look in the stands for her. Only the two of them knew. I guess Jenni was becoming important, cause he wanted her to be proud of him.

Steph was goin nuts shopping for anything that would make loud noises. She had a look and smile that reeked of excitement for the big game. Fanny and Terry caught Verona High fever too. Kids in a candy store, not really. Girls like to go shopping for anything. Billy, Jimmy and me went to the paint store. We were gonna get in trouble tonight. Me and my boys planned to paint the Verona "V" all over Florham Park's Buses. Jimmy, that sick bastard, wanted to break in their locker room and put Ben-Gay in all of their jocks... Hey, it stopped Tony, it could stop their whole team. As funny as it would be, I couldn't let him. We'd end up makin Verona High look pretty bad.

With our shopping done, the six of us piled in the Volkswagen. and dropped the girls off at Jimmy's house. Mrs. Fortunato had the cookies and hot chocolate waiting for them. She loved having the house filled with the fountains of youth. Fanny was practically a member of the family and Steph later told me she never realized how nice Fanny was until she saw the closeness of Mrs. Fortunato and Fanny. Jimmy's mom asked all the questions you would ask high school girls with boyfriends. College, jobs, proms and the big game, of course.

Before we began, Jimmy fired up a small joint. He figured our painting skills would be much better high. I don't know, there was something weird about getting high with my little sister's boyfriend. After the joint made the third trip around Billy read my mind. "Does this feel as weird to you as it does to me?" He had to say it while I was holding the last hit in. I busted out laughing and coughing. "Fuckin A right it does" Jimmy had no clue why we were laughing;. Single kid syndrome. My pal reached in his pocket and pulled out a piece of paper with all these typestyles. There had to be at least a hundred. The geek got it from one of his computer books. Jimmy gave each of us a third of a page. "Put a different style "V" on every bus. It'll be really cool. Billy wasn't the most artistic guy I ever met. "Yo man, I can't copy these." Jimmy fired back, "Look you stupid asshole, shut up and do your best." It took us about an hour to do all the buses. I still can't believe we didn't get caught.

I didn't sleep much. Steph called me at 7am. "Morning Baby. I'm gonna ask this sexy guy to lunch today and thought I should tell you first. " I wasn't even awake, "Okay baby" and hung up the phone My eyes went back to sleep only to be woken up by the nightmare I thought I just heard. The phone rang again. Steph is unbelievable. "Honey, I knew that'd wake you up. So can we have lunch today.? I wanna show you the outfit I'm wearin to the game." "Steph, No problem. Let's get a quick bite and squeeze in a "Love lunch" My baby, she's always up for it. I love that girl!

Lunch came and went quicker than lightning. Steph wanted to have "dessert" under the football bleachers. "C'mere Kenny. It'll be fun. We can watch the game tonight and remember us scorin earlier under the bleachers." She was a great lover in the way every guy dreams about. I swear, sometimes I could just watch her. She could be sultry in ways that are born out of pure fantasy. In my favorite mind fuck, she seduced me with her eyes and body. She wouldn't say a word, no talking, and touching her was forbidden. She'd finally put me out of my misery and attacked me in a fire of passion. She completely messed with my mind. I wouldn't be able to think about anything else today.

How could she know me that well? I was distracted about Tony's game tonight. I really wanted him to win. As kids, we'd joke around all the time, but I can't say I ever saw Tony happy. If he wins, he will be. Steph always knew Tony was one of my best friends, but I never shared with her his life at home. Love at lunch gave me a break from worryin about my brotha.

After school, Tony raced home to listen to some music before the team dinner. Tony liked some weird music. I knew he liked Sammy. He put on his headphones and listened to "The Impossible Dream" three times. When the last one ended, he took a long stare in the mirror. His reflection was ready.. He told his father he was going to the game. "Have Fun" That's all his Dad said. Four years and He didn't even know he played. He sure as shit never showed up at a game. The quick injection of anger only made Tony more ready to play.

The team gathered in the cafeteria. Coaches at one table. Starters at another, and the remaining players took up two tables. Coach went for the carb overload and had pasta for the team. Bishotti asked the players and coaches at each table join hands and say the Lord's Prayer. Afterwards, the atmosphere at each group of tables was different. The non-starters had light conversation. The coaches table echoed with confident experience. They all played in lots of big games. At the starters table, you could hear a pin drop. They were completely focused on the task at hand. As dinner ended, Coach asked them to line up in two lines, side by side. As a Team, they walked through the tailgate lot and the students erupted with support. The Band started playing our fight song. Coach Bishotti pulled out all the stops. Bunny and Fester even stopped by on the way to her shift. Fester had the "I'm a kid again" look all over his face. Mom and Dad, Mr. DeMarino and Monica, were gonna bring Mrs. Fortunato to the game before kickoff. Mrs. Fortunato asked Fanny's mom and dad to go as well. I think the whole town of Verona was shut down for the big game. My mom and Jimmy's never saw a football game.

The girls unloaded the car. Steph had on her white ear warmers matching her turtleneck covered by a Verona Jersey. I only paid attention to Steph's uniform for games, but tonight, Jenni caught my eye. She had number 46, painted on her face. Fanny asked why, Jenni responded, "Hey Tony's the star right?" There had to be something goin on between them but neither ever said a word. I grabbed Jimmy and told Billy and the girls we'd be right back.

"Kenny, where are we going?"

"To the locker room stupid. We're gonna wish Tony good luck."

Coach was standing outside the door and sensed why we were there.

"Don't be in there too long"

"No Problem Coach. We'll be out in two minutes"

Coach was the man. "Kenny and Jimmy, Thanks and don't be dumb, you know what I'm thanking you for"

I had to give it back, "No Coach, thank you for everything you did. You had an impact on all three of us. It's something we'll never forget"

Coach opened the door for us, "Hurry up and wish your friend luck"

Tony was in the corner, all by himself. I guess that's where he always got ready. I'd never been in a locker room before a game. The intensity was unreal and unspoken. Tony didn't even know we were there till I said his name. He stood up, I gave him a macho hug and wished him good luck. Jimmy followed my lead, and said, "Hey, me and Kenny will be with you on every play. Kick ass mothafucka"

We got back to the car and the lot was packed! When I die, I'll know I made it to heaven when I smell the smoke from the grills cooking hot dogs and hamburgers on a brisk fall night. My stomach was havin food orgasms. Steph came up and rubbed my tummy, "Everything alright baby?" "Fuckin A Right it is Steph. I got my friends, my girl and a great game tonight. Nothin is better" As Florham Park's team buses started to get closer, some nut stood on top of his car and made the crowd sing the school song. People were goin crazy and Florham knew they were in for the fight of their lives tonight.

The Players were dressed and waiting for Coach to give his speech. The door busted open, "Ya got three minutes to think about the dream we started back in August and everything we did, to get here. When I come back, be ready to play a football game" Time was up. "Let's go" And they filed out like an army getting ready for war.

The team took the field for warm ups and saw the stands were packed. Standing room only. In the last row was some old guy with dark wavy hair and square glasses. All the dads and recruiters kept staring at him.

Tony took his usual spot in the back row. Danny was right next to him." You're playing today, Danny, You better be fuckin ready" Danny didn't say a word. After yesterday, he knew he'd get his chance. He was completely focused. Danny was breathing a rage of fire.

Coach brought the team together for a few last minute inspirations before their Dream chant. He told his Captain to, "Get out there for the Coin Toss." Tony started his slow walk to midfield. Suddenly, he stopped and turned around. "Hey Danny Pintauro, come with me" The freshman joined his idol and in a show of solidarity, they walked step for step to meet the captains of Florham Park. The visitors won the toss and wanted the ball first. They knew all about Tony's mind games at the toss and made no effort to shake hands. Although he was Danny's role model, Danny refused to be his clone. He approached Florham's leaders to offer his hand. They refused the kid. One captain turned his head and spit on the ground behind him, leaving a clear message. Big mistake, he pissed off Danny, "you're gonna pay for that. When I knock your ass to the ground, you'll be lyin in your own spit" The refs told the boys to return to their benches. Everyone in the stands stood up for the kickoff You couldn't hear anything but the noisemakers. Returning to their team, Tony said, "Danny, man that was kick ass!!! But it don't mean nothing if you don't back it up" He assured Tony, "I know, just watch me and you'll learn a little something" The punk kid was cocky?

Three months ago, nobody had any idea.

Steph loved it, "I can barely hear myself think" Jenni put in her two cents, I know, Isn't it awesome??? Florham Park's got no chance" Some older guy in front of us disagreed. "This don't even phase their kids. Believe me, they came here to win" It seemed like the guy forgot more about football than the seven of us could ever learn.

Florham got the ball and Tony got introduced to his ass. Their game plan was clear. Beat Tony and they'll win. He started to get pissed in the huddle and told his teammates they gotta make some fuckin plays. Florham was blocking Tony with two guys and running away from him as well. They were driving down the field like it was practice. On a key third down, he asked the guy who played next to him if he minded if we gave Danny a shot. The guy was all about the team. "Tony, Whatever you think it takes to win, I'm all for" The captain called a time out and went to speak to Bishotti. Coach, I wanna try Danny next to me. Bishotti put his trust in the player. Tony started walking back to the huddle. "Hey Danny Pintauro, get your ass out here" Danny threw on his helmet and the guy he replaced told him to kick ass" Once in the huddle, Tony called the freshman out in front of his teammates. "Danny, you talk alotta shit. Back it up now. You think you're tough cause you took a swing at me? I let you. Those guys over there ain't gonna let you do shit" Danny was getting angrier with each word. Tony focused on the team. "We gave them a few plays, big fuckin deal. It stops now." The play started and Danny blasted his way into the back field. Arms spread like an eagle diving for prey, he dove and took out the quarterback and the ball carrier at the same time. The ball came loose and Verona recovered.

The defense jogged off the field to the cheering crowd. Danny and Tony left together. The freshman kid looked to the captain for approval, but Tony wasn't gonna give it to him. Everyone else did. Tony's message was clear. One play wasn't enough. He had much higher expectations for Danny. Tony believed if he gave him an "atta boy " now, Danny might ease up. By ignoring him, it only pissed off Danny more.. Tony knew the only way to beat Florham was to have Danny step up his intensity. The rest of the team just had to do their job. There was no way Florham was stopping both of them.

The offense took the field and quickly scored on a fluke. The running back broke into the clear and fumbled on a vicious hit. Footballs have a funny way of bouncing and it bounced right into the hands of Verona's fastest kid. The kid ran so fast, you'd think his father was chasing him to give his son a beating. Touchdown Verona!!! .

For the rest of the game, these two teams beat the crap out of each other. Tony was covered in blood, some his and some theirs. He was bloodied but definitely not beaten. Danny did his best to show the same toughness as Tony, but he could only do so much. Florham Park kept coming at Tony with everything they had and they were winning the battle. But every time Verona needed a miracle, Tony reached deep within himself and made the impossible play. It was a different crowd. They, too, were exhausted, watching the war.

Late in the game, with Verona holding onto its 7-0 lead, the offense took the field with 1:56 to go. Coach put Tony in at running back. He hadn't carried the ball since his junior year. Bishotti told the coach, who called the plays, "Give the ball to Tony, get the first down, and the game is over. Tony looked at his coach with a conflicted demeanor. "Why?" he asked. Coach's response was as simple as Tony's question. "Cause you can" He reluctantly put on his helmet and jogged to the team. Everybody knew who was getting the ball. Tony fought for three yards

He was at the bottom of the pile taking punches to his kidneys and every other place on his body that would hurt him enough to let go of the ball. Second down was even worse. He got four yards but wondered if all this pain was worth it. Third down, he carried three Florham kids and more piled on for the last yard. Tony refused to go down till he gained the last yard. First down Verona!!!! Game over. Tony lay there on the ground motionless as everyone erupted in celebration. Danny was the first to see his idol on the ground. He went over and asked Tony if he was okay. The Captain was speechless. Danny gently helped Tony get to his feet and the crowd, both sides, gave him a standing ovation. Tony hurt more with each step. Nothing was broken. He was just completely exhausted.

He finally made it to the bench and drank about a gallon of water and poured the rest over his head. Minutes later, he returned to the field to savor the victory with his teammates. With the state championship at Rutgers, he realized this was the last time he was ever going to play on this field. He cherished the memory of every moment past. Bishotti met him at the fifty-yard line. They both shared the "We fuckin did it" non verbal stare. "Thanks …. Coach" And Tony hugged the man who was a coach, teacher, dad, and friend. Sometimes saying thanks can never begin to say enough.

"Excuse me for interrupting" It was the old guy with the wavy dark hair and square glasses. "I'm Coach Paterno from Penn State and you played a great game young man. Mr. Ferino told me about you a few years ago and I've been watching you grow up. "I'd like you to come to Penn State and get an education. If you want to play football, I'd be happy to have you"

"I'm not interrr.." Bishotti interrupted his captain " Tony, I've never asked anything of you. Coach Paterno is a great man. I think you should at least listen to what he has to say" Tony realized Bishotti was right. Paterno invited him to see the school. "What do you like to study son?" "Uh, to be honest with you sir, I've never been good at studying" "Well, that's okay. When you visit the school, maybe we can find something that'll interest you. Tony, here's my phone number. You can call me anytime about anything. Well Good luck next week Coach Bishotti . Tony. Please call me next week after your game. I want to know how you did." Coach Paterno shook Bishotti's hand. Tony knew the humble demeanor from the man from Penn State was sincere. His instincts kicked in. This guy was alright. Bishotti showed his proud papa look again. "Go enjoy this with your friends. They've been waiting for you."

As Tony turned our way, we gave him a rousing ovation. The girls took their turn hugging him. Jenni was last. Their awkward hug failed to hide the feelings between them. They'd both deny it to each other, anyway. Tony looked at the "46"s painted on Jenni's face . In a shy sarcastic way, Tony said, "nice eyes" Jenni gave it right back, "yeah, thanks," I loved watching Jenni and Tony together. It was like a mystery movie. I couldn't figure out if they wanted to be together or I wanted Tony to have a girlfriend. The guys all gave the star high fives and Billy offered to cover the pizza at Vincenzo's. "So, Tony get in the shower before I get cheap on your ass"

Party of eight. All couples, except the two who were forced to sit next to each other. Tony looked completely exhausted. You could see every muscle in his body hurt. Innocent hanky panky was goin on under the table. Jenni was massaging his leg while fully engaged in the conversation throughout the table. She constantly refilled his glass of water. She was so nonchalant, nobody caught her caring for Tony. He was too tired to appreciate what she was doing. Good thing too. He wouldn't know how to handle it. The excitement made all of us tired. Tonight, it was just pizza, no Italian ices.

We all said our goodbyes in the parking lot. Me and Steph drove Tony home. The girls parade of hugs started with Fanny and ended with Jenni. She gave him a "you're a little more than a friend" hug We've all had it. It's the one where the last squeeze lingers a little longer as her hands slowly let you go.

Tony got in the car and as we pulled away, Steph teased Tony, "I think somebody has a crush on you" He fired back, " What? Ya think she's the first?" Steph knew how to spar. "oh c'mon Tony, you know you love it" "Yeah, yeah, yeah, Steph you think that. Go ahead, believe whatever you want" He was drivin me nuts. Did he like her or not??? I knew Tony better than anybody but, he refused to play his card. He never talked about Jenni. but his eyes did. There was no way I could be misreading the vibe. Tony's house was here and he couldn't leave the car fast enough.

The car door slammed, and my baby couldn't wait to gossip. "So, whaddya think honey? You think he likes her?" "I don't know Steph" "Kenny, don't bullshit me. "Honestly, honey, I don't know. But, if I were to guess, I think he doesn't know what he feels about Jenni. He's never had a girlfriend, ya know. How bout Jenni? You think she likes him" "Oh yeah!!! Do you see the way she looks at him? "Fuck yeah I do Steph. I can't tell if it's a crush or she really thinks she has a shot. I'm worried she could end up hurtin herself. Tony don't date and I don't see him startin now." "You're right baby, it'll be fun to sit back and watch"

I changed the subject. "Can you believe we fooled around today? Doesn't it seem like it was days ago?" "Baby, if you're askin for more, don't ask. It ruins it" "Steph, I'm just sayin it was a really long day" "We arrived in front of her house and she always knew

how to keep things fresh." Kenny, would you walk me to my door?"
Innocent first date love is fuckin hot, and it's even hotter four years
later. We made out and shared a few shy whispers "I had a nice
time". She slowly opened her door, gave one last love look, then
asked me to call her tomorrow.

I slept like a baby. Dad hated when I woke up late on raking
leaves day. I swear the leaf blower always sounded louder when I
needed more sleep. No cheerios this morning. Put on a few layers
of clothes, find your mud-stained work gloves, and go help Dad. I
was the bagger. The size of the pile screamed it was a ten-bag day.

Dad gave me a hard time. "Don't be scared son, fill the bag up
to the top."

We spent a few hours workin on the leaves. Each bag made the
yard look a little better. A fresh leafless lawn is a like a fine piece
of art. But when the wind blows, a few more leaves fall and the
picture-perfect vision becomes flawed.

Jimmy called about four in the afternoon. He invited me and
Tony over to Fanny's house. Her Dad wanted to talk to Tony about
Penn State and Coach Paterno. Tony had a growing number of people in his corner. He better not fuck it up. Thoughts about identity
filled my head again. Tony was the kid who came from a horrible
family. At eighteen years old, he had to choose between living an
angry miserable life or trying to overcome what was so ingrained
within him.. I told Tony I was gonna pick him up in a half hour. I hung
up before he could ask questions.

Tony met me outside and we drove to Fanny's. He asked why
we were goin there and I blamed it on Jimmy."Aww man, Kenny, I
don't have a good feeling about this." "Shut the fuck up Tony, you're
always bitchin about something." " I know, I'm a real bitch." Two
knocks and Mr. Ferino answered the door. He introduced himself
and asked if we wanted something to drink. This was all business.
Mr. Ferino didn't talk about how we met at Harry's.

"Tony, I played for Coach Paterno for four years and it was the
best experience of my life. I wasn't a special player, but Coach made
everyone feel like they were the most important player on the

team. I can still call him anytime day or night if I need his advice. He told me you remind him of Jon. He won the Heisman Trophy which is given to the best player in the country. Jon was strong as an ox but as the country soon learned, his brother was far stronger."

Mr. Ferino handed Tony a copy of Jon's acceptance speech. "I think you should read this and you'll learn everything you need to know about Coach and the type of person he sees in you." Tony took the speech and briefly scanned the beginning. Something caught his attention, and he found a chair in the living room to read everything." Tony didn't know it at the time, but Jon's speech was considered the most inspirational talk ever given by a Heisman award winner.

The last part made Tony's decision easy. He was going to college. Jon finished his speech by saying, "The youngest member of my family, Joseph is very ill. He has leukemia. If I can dedicate this trophy to him tonight, and give him a couple of days of happiness, this is worth everything. "

"Thanks Mr. Ferino. If Coach Paterno will have me , I'd like to go to Penn State. I was shocked, in a good way. "Really Tony? YOU wanna go to college??? I never thought I'd see the day.

"Shut the fuck up Kenny. Ooops Sorry about that Mr. Ferino."

"Don't worry about it. But, Coach doesn't like that language." Mr. Ferino gave Tony a Nittany Lion Cap, which Tony wore proudly. .Jimmy had to bust our friend's balloons. So, when we see you playing on TV, you gonna forget who your friends are? I'm Jimmy and that's Kenny over there. Don't ever forget it. Now, let's get out of here before Fanny's dad sees the real you and changes Paterno's mind".

We made our way to the door. Mr. Ferino wished Tony luck in the state championship and welcomed him in the club. Penn State had some very special guys in their club and now Tony was one of them. We walked home and I remembered our walks when we were kids. I know we're still young, but today made me realize how much we've all grown up. Growin up is pretty cool when ya think about it.

Sunday, I didn't do much. Me and Steph talked a lot about nothing. She had an Algebra test tomorrow which she wasn't ready for. But, who ever is?. Algebra one was the last math class I understood. You had to be a genius to understand Geometry. Jimmy, that bastard, thought it was easy. I didn't study much my senior year. Rutgers was my early decision school. By the time they found out I was cruising, I'd already be accepted. Terry was busy get dressed to the nines. Billy was taking her to some fancy brunch where she was gonna meet his parents. She looked so cute wondering if she looked good enough for his parents. The mirror never lies, but she still didn't trust it. My baby sister worried she only saw what she wanted to see. Why do girls always turn and stare at their butt in the mirror?

Fall was quickly coming to a brisk end. Dad was bored. All the leaves were raked. The cars were ready for winter and the storm windows worked well. He knew it was best to stay out of mom's way while she was cooking Sunday dinner. As he was leaving, he let mom know he was going to Harry's to watch the Giants game. As we all got older, mom didn't get upset when Dad went to Harry's. The years softened Dad as well. He began drinking more coffee than beer. A cigarette, a cup of joe, good friends and Dad was in heaven.

As usual, Fanny went to Jimmy's and convinced Mrs. Fortunato to do some early Christmas shopping at the mall. Jimmy spent the afternoon with his bong and the latest edition of consumer electronics. He refused to give up on the wacky personal computer thing. I still can't believe he thinks every house will have them one day.

Tony woke up to his dad bitchin at him about something. He was throwin all sorts of shit on his bed. Tony couldn't wait to get out of his hell hole. It was the main reason he decided to go to Penn State. He realized if he was gonna spend his life workin on the docks, he was gonna be stuck in hell till his dad died. That would really suck.

Tony cleaned up the mess and got the hell out of the house. He walked nowhere for miles. Thoughts about this weekend and next filled his head. He just gave everything he had for his team and coach. There was nothing left. And, now, he had to give more? He couldn't do it. Tony even thought about quitting. If he played and gave no effort, it wasn't fair to his team. And if he quit, that wasn't fair either. He was fucked.

Again, he ended up in front of Jenni's house. Facing his relationship fear, he stumbled his way to her front door. Standing there feelin stupid for a few minutes, couldn't make him ring the doorbell. Finally, he did and Jenni answered the door wearing his jersey..

"Whaddya wearin that for?" .

"Huh? No hello? Did you forget that already?"

"Hi, now why are you wearing my jersey?"

"Cause I like it. It's comfortable"

"Any other reason?"

"Don't be so full of yourself. It's not you."

"Jenni, can we go for a walk n talk?"

"Wow, it must be serious. You said my name"

"Jenni, please. I'm not fuckin around. I really need to talk to someone."

She stopped kiddin , and playin hard to get was replaced by concern. "Tony are you okay?"

"I don't know. That's why I need to talk"

Jenni got her coat and met him at the door. Showing she cared in a way that neither could explain, she zippered Tony's black leather jacket so he wouldn't feel the chill. He didn't want a girlfriend cause he didn't know how. But Jenni's tender touch sure felt good to him. He was done with the small talk. Tony told her about his desire to quit the team cause he had nothing left. Jenni let him ramble as she was tryin to find the right words. He was a star and a hero to everyone in the school. Jenni wouldn't dare say she thought he was being selfish. She dropped hints like it'd run through the school like wildfire if he did. The game was gonna be on channel nine too. The school would be embarrassed. Tony felt the weight of the world on his heart.

"Tony I'm your friend, not your girlfriend, just your friend and I promise I'll always be there for you; whether I agree with what you're doin or not. I understand how you feel and I really believe your coach and team will too. But, I'm not gonna lie. No matter what you say, they're gonna be disappointed."

Tony remembered disappointment was his greatest fear in life. There was no way he could let all the people that cared about him be disappointed. He stopped to face Jenni. Lookin into her beautiful eyes, he barely uttered the word thanks as he hugged her tight enough to never wanna let go. The stress was gone, and he held her hand for the walk back to her house. Tony smiled and kept true to himself." Just cause I'm holding your hand doesn't mean I like you. It's like you wearin the jersey, it's comfortable"

"Comfort is a good thing" Jenni's eyes made sure he understood.

"I can live with that. No sympathy squeezes though. So don't even try. Ya know Tony, when I first met you, I thought you were a cute asshole. You used all these girls or maybe they used you. It really didn't matter. You didn't give a shit. Being nice to a girl was outa the question. Stephanie told me you didn't even say a word to her till high school. I thought you were a cold angry loser who didn't deserve to be happy"

"Are ya done talking shit about me yet? And no matter what you say, your eyes said you liked me"

"Will ya let me finish? Tony, yeah, I thought you were cute, but I didn't like you. The fantasy seemed a lot better than the reality. Anyway, I'm tryin to tell you I was wrong about you. Tony Matelli, you're probably the nicest guy I ever met. Sure, you hide it, like being nice is a weakness. Whether you see it or not, it took alotta courage to change your mind. Quitting is easy. But, I know you could never let everybody down. It's not in your heart. Besides, Danny Pintauro would kick your ass if you did. "

They shared a laugh about Danny. Tony teased her about some girl in her Spanish class. He asked Jenni to introduce him. Jenni fired right back and told him she'd like to teach Danny a thing or two. They both loved the walk and her house showed up quicker than they wanted. There was that awkward silence again. It was Jenni's turn to hug Tony. He returned the favor by giving her a soft kiss on the cheek. No more jokes, just pure friendship.

Tony walked home feeling really good. The kinda feeling I have about Steph. But, Tony, that idiot, thought it was cause he changed his mind about quitting. He had a lot to learn. He still hasn't said a word to me or Jimmy about Jenni. I think it would make it real to him. I guess it made sense. He hated answering to his dad so if he was alone, he'd have to answer to nobody. He better start learning quick cause he was gonna have to answer to the Italian guy at Penn State. Entering his house, Tony saw his dad already passed out with an empty bottle of vodka by his side. It was only six thirty.

Sunday dinner at our house was good as always. Mom made some fresh minestrone to take the chill off. I snuck a peek in the kitchen and saw the steam floating above the steak pizzaola. It was my favorite dinner. I skipped the salad to save more room for the steak. Dad talked about Friday's game and mom chimed in she had fun too. I know he would never say it, but he wished it was me instead of Tony being the star.. Dad really liked football.

Mom asked Terry about Billy. Terry stayed true to her heart. Mom and Dad finally came around and accepted the fact their daughter was datin a Jewish guy. It's all about happiness and they both saw their daughter was happy. Billy was a good kid, worked hard, stayed out of trouble, and respected my sister. Who cares what God someone believes in? It really doesn't matter and just because two people believe in different ones doesn't mean they're not allowed to care about each other. If we all get along in heaven, shouldn't we be able to do the same here?

We had dessert, warm apple pie with a heaping scoop of vanilla ice cream melting slowly all over the plate. It was okay, but I like blueberry more. Terry helped mom with the dishes. Mom washed, Terry dried, and they shared girl talk. Doing dishes together makes people a lot closer. You can't be mean or ignore the other person. Whoever invented the dishwasher probably fell out of love. You know what necessity is to inventions. Me and Steph will never get a dishwasher no matter how much she complains. Some couples believe you should never go to bed angry. I believe you can't do the dishes together angry.

I excused myself to do my homework. I hate Sunday night homework. Oh yeah, the teachers said if we beat Florham Park, there was no assignments due. Weekends are sooo much fun, but they're really long. I can't believe me and Steph had a "love lunch" two days ago. Missing her, I picked up the phone and dialed her number. Two rings and I heard the sweet music sound of her voice. One day, I'm gonna hear it say "I do"

She said, her, Fanny, and Jenni went to the mall for some Christmas shopping. I was curious. "What'd ya get me? Anything good?" My girl, told me to shut up and wait.. She wouldn't even say what Fanny got Jimmy. Jenni was jealous. She didn't have a boyfriend or a Christmas. Steph said Jenni got all defensive when she asked her why she didn't get Tony something. Me and Steph both thought something was goin on but neither ever said a word. Steph didn't care, she still thought they would make a good couple. "Tony needs someone like Jenni" I backed Tony, "How many times do I have to tell you, Tony doesn't want a girlfriend??? He likes being on his own." Steph was cute, "I know, but.."

I changed the subject. "Hey baby, do you know you're the most beautiful girl I've ever seen?" Steph liked hearing my words but she wondered, "Why are you being so nice to me?. C'mon tell me what you want." "Honey, I don't want anything but you. Sometimes couples get so close they forget why they are. So, I don't want you to ever feel I take you or anything about you for granted." There was a moment of silence and she finally said, "Kenny, that's the nicest thing anyone ever said to me. And don't you go even one day without knowing I love you with all my heart."

I really do hate Sunday night homework. It's stupid. Doesn't the school know how important weekends are to their students. Going to class on Monday is hard enough. Why make it suck more with Sunday homework.?? I did mine half-assed and finished in about an hour.

My mind wandered to Tony and wondered how he felt about the state championship. Did he feel the pressure? This is the game where the Captain has to act like a leader. Till now, Tony believed he was captain only cause he was the toughest kid on the team. Fuck it!!. I know he needed my support so I picked up the phone again and called him.

"Hey, Tony. You awake?"

"No asshole!! I'm talking to you in my sleep. What a stupid fuckin question!!"

"Whoa man. Ease up. I was just callin to tell ya I'm there for ya. I know you. You're hurtin inside about the game Friday night"

"Yeah, outside too!! Florham kicked my fuckin ass. I hurt everywhere"

"Well, I just wanna let you know I'm pretty lucky to have a friend like you. I'm really proud of what you've done. I mean, in four years, you've gone from someone who's never played a second of football to the best player in the state. You're one bad ass mother fucker and you're gonna play that way Friday night".

"Kenny, man, did you get high tonight or something? Did your girl give you a bad shot of the love drug"

"No you asshole. I'm just supporting one of my best friends. When that Penn State guy met you, your life completely changed, and I know you're shittin in your pants now. It's a lot easier to be a fuck-up"

"You're right. I can't lie. This game is on my mind all the time. I just want it to be over. But Thanks Buddy. Don't be surprised if I call you every night this week.

"No problem, Superstar. See ya tomorrow" And I hung up and crashed till the morning.

The alarm clock rang hours before I was ready. I coulda slept till Spring. I hate cold November mornings. They show no mercy. And neither did mom. "You better wake up now or you're gonna be late for school." Easy for mom to say. She doesn't have to go to school, and she doesn't have to go outside when it's 18 degrees. Mom wasn't gonna shut up till I went out that door. Guzzled my hot chocolate, burned the back of my throat and slammed the door on my way out to meet Tony.

The wind was whipping right through my bones. And Billy

came through big time!!! With Terri all warm in the shotgun seat of his car, he gives me and Tony a ride.. Jimmy piled in a block later. He couldn't wait to announce, "It's cold as balls out there" Terri, with a bit of confusion, demanded to know, " What's with the balls???" Hey, that what she gets for ridin in a car with four teenage guys.

Billy dropped us all off at the front door and the shit started as soon as Tony got outa the car. "Kick ass Friday Tony. Good luck. Do it for Verona" and all the high fives made his world come crashin in. He wasn't used to all the attention. It went on all day, all week in the halls between classes. Fuck, even teachers wished him luck. Tony hated it. A few years ago these people didn't give him the time of day. Now everybody was actin like his best friend. It was all fake bullshit. He knocked on Bishotti's door at lunch time.

"Coach, can I talk to you for a few minutes?"

"You know better, my door has always been open to you"

"Why is this game important to everybody but me?"

" I don't know Tony. You tell me"

"Coach I have no idea. Why the fuck do you think I'm askin you"

"Kid, this is the state championship. It's to be the best in the state. Very few people in this world can say they were the best at anything. So, they live through you. Tony, you been given the chance they all want"

"Being the best, what the fuck does that mean??? Who fuckin cares!!! That's not why I play. The only reason I play is to kick ass."

"Really Tony. Is that the only reason??? Do you think I'm stupid??? I knew why you played the first day you were on the field. But, you're different now, and you know it!!! There's only one reason you wanna go back to bein a nobody and that's cause you're scared, scared of something. I don't know what, and I don't think you do either. But, you oughta figure it out quick. ...Not for me, not for your team, but for yourself."

"Coach honestly? You really know why I play??"

"Tony, you think you're the first guy who's ever been pissed at his dad??? C'mon. You've never talked about him and he sure as shit has never been to a game. It's none of my business, but I bet you've never invited him to a game"

"Fuck him, why should I?"

"Like I said, it's none of my business. But Tony, Sometimes ya gotta rise above the tide, cause if you don't, the tide will take you out... if you know what I'm sayin. Now, get outa here, your next class starts in two minutes."

Tony left Bishotti's office and walked right past Jenni. He didn't even acknowledge her. Me and Steph passed him on our way to lunch. He looked lost.

Danny came up and head-butted Tony, "Chin up man. We need ya, Fuck, I need ya. Look man, I never played in a game like this. I'm countin on Captain Bad Ass to piss me off. You and me are gonna kick some fuckin butt. So let's have fun doin it." Fuckin Danny got him out of his funk. "Don't worry 'bout me you punk ass freshman. Worry 'bout yourself. cause if ya don't, I'll do ya sista" Danny fired back, " You gotta better chance doin Raquel Welch". And they walked down the hallway marchin to their bad ass strut. "See ya at practice Captain"

Class was over and the players suited up in their long underwear and pads. Tony chose just the pads. He was sending a message to his teammates. Get tough or Get out. Coach Bishotti put in a few new plays for Tony and Danny at running back. Each was gonna block for the other. Tony was stronger inside and Danny was faster outside. There was no hitting, just execution. Coach wanted his players rested and hungry. The whole week followed Monday's practice.

Thursday, practice ended early. It was rah rah speech day. Coach Bishotti was pretty low key. He thanked the players for the huge commitment they made to the team. Coach talked about quiet confidence and belief in yourself. There was no doubt in his mind the team was ready. He called Tony upfront.

Tony agreed with his Coach. But he preached about the fine line between quiet and overconfidence. Tony wanted it to be very clear. "Pearl River is as good as we are. .Who knows? Maybe a little better. This game has nothing to do with skill. It's all about heart and who wants it more. Now, we can say we do. That's bullshit. Wanting it more means you cross the line. Play harder than you ever believed you could, They're gonna hit the fuck outa us. You can't stay down. You have to pop right up. Keep the pain to yourself. I don't wanna hear it, your teammates don't either, and you definitely don't want Pearl River to see it.. If we win, watch how quick that pain goes away. Let's just kick ass. It's that simple" They joined together for their usual dream chant and hit the showers. Coach and Tony were the last to leave the field. Bishotti felt the need to say something.

"Tony, I've known you for four years and I have to say I've never seen a natural born leader like you. Not only, here, with your teammates. You are with your friends too. I want you to know how proud I am of you. You are the one player I'll remember till the day I die."

Tony, rebutted with a shy smile. "Hey Coach, ya know sometimes you gotta rise above the tide. A pretty smart guy taught me that"

Bishotti cracked up. He messed up Tony's hair and put his arm around his shoulder for the walk back to the locker room.

"Hey Coach, I got one last question."

"Sure Tony, anything. Ask away"

"If we win, are you gonna let me go out with your girlfriend. She's fuckin hot"

Bishotti busted out in laughter. "Sure, Tony... go ahead. all ya gotta do is ask her and I know you ain't gotta rap, so she'll laugh in your face. Now hit the showers. See ya tomorrow, son."

Tony heard the last word. He looked at coach, wanting to say something more than, "Yeah, I'll see you tomorrow too"

Me and Steph have been a couple for years now. She always made sure I kept my promise and didn't take her for granted. While waiting for mom to put dinner on the table, I snuck a quick phone call to my girl. "Steph, baby, wanna go with me to the game tomorrow night?"

She twisted the knife. "Ummm who is this and you're wastin

your time. It's pretty rude askin me out the night before you want to see me. What kinda girl do you think I am? "

I fired right back. "Young lady, My deepest apologies. Last week I was forced to go to Wyoming to help my sick grandmother. She didn't have a phone, or I would have called you sooner. On the way back, my car broke down in Cleveland. I hitched twelve rides, didn't eat or sleep since Monday and all that kept me going was taking Stephanie Demarino to the big game. I just got home, and this is the first thing I did, calling you."

"Well, it sucks to be you. Too late!!! Some asshole named Kenny with a hygiene problem is takin me. How's that feel I'd rather go out with a guy that smells like shit. Next time, maybe you'll call a girl a week before, not the night before"

I love our sparring sessions. It keeps the passion fresh. "Hi baby. You're good!!!. So, what time do you want me to pick you up?' Steph didn't wanna be out in the cold too long. It was gonna be a long night. "Game starts at seven thirty, How bout six?" It worked for me. "that's cool. You call the girls and I'll talk to the boys. Love you, baby" "I love you too Kenny"

Tony finished his shower and made his way to hell house. His mind started to wander, and he found himself knockin on Jenni's door again. Jenni opened the door and before he could ask her to go for a walk., she invited him in from the cold. He'd never been invited in a girl's house before, so he felt completely outa place. "Tony, c'mon I want you to meet my parents." Tony didn't have a choice. He followed Jenni into their family room. "Mom, Dad, this is Tony Matelli" Her Dad immediately stood up to shake Tony's hand. "Nice to meet you, Tony. We've heard a lot about you from our kids." The cocky kid was shy and stumbled through a polite nice to meet you too. I don't know where they came from, but Tony found his manners. "You have a beautiful home Mrs. Ruben and whatever is cookin sure smells good" Jenni's mom lit up and thanked him for noticing."Tony, Please, would you like to stay for dinner?. We'd love to have you." He knew his limit and politely declined. Jenni took his cue and told her parents they were gonna go down to the basement for a quick game of pool. "We are?" "Yes Tony., why are you scared to get beat by a girl.?" Jenni's dad wished Tony good luck for tomorrow night. "We'll be there cheerin you on Tony" Great, that's all he needed, another distraction.

"So what's up Tony? Why are you here?"

"I dunno. I guess I just wanted to be."

Girls never let guys off the hook that easy.

"You don't know? You just wanted to be? What kinda answer is that? Whaddya need? Whaddya want?"

"I want you to stop askin so many fuckin questions again!!!. I'm kiddin ya Jenni. I'm really nervous about tomorrow. Coach told me, sometimes ya gotta rise above the tide and I've been tryin but, sometimes it fucks with my head. I ain't this strong and you know that Jenni"

"Tony, I think you're wrong. You are that strong, You're just scared of accepting it.. You're not gonna like what I say, but I know all about you and your dad. You look at how much he beat you down. I look at how much you endured. A weak person would never be able to survive what you have. I'm really proud of you Tony Matelli.. It's gonna take time but you must learn to be proud of yourself"

"Jenni, are all Jewish girls as smart as you?"

"No, I'm one of the few who's pretty and smart too.. Can a girl give the big football star a good luck hug?"

"Sure, as long as you promise not to suffocate me with your rack"

"You could die so lucky" And Jenni gave him a strong caring hug that ended with a soft gentle kiss on his cheek."

"Jenni, am I gonna see you after the game?"

"Here we go again. Are you askin me out or just askin me?"

"You know me!!! I just askin ya, but I do wanna see you after the game."

"Then you will. Now unless you wanna stay for dinner, you better leave now"

She walked him to the door, and he made sure to say good bye to her parents. Polite Tony...where the fuck did he learn that? He was ready for tomorrow night. Tony got home, went to his room, and listened to music. After about an hour, he heard a loud crashing noise. He went downstairs and saw his dad lying on the floor in convulsions. Tony called 911. The ambulance came and tried in vain to get his father to regain consciousness. He was rushed to the hospital and Tony rode with him in the ambulance. The Doctors took immediate action and controlled chaos surrounded his Dad. Tony overheard one guy say there's a blockage in his heart and the liver is shot. They finally got him stabilized enough to move him to intensive care.

Tony spent the entire night in the waiting room. Too many thoughts were running through his head. He called Coach Bishotti at sunrise and told him what happened. Bishotti called me and Jimmy. He told us about Tony's dad and he was gonna pick us up on the way to the hospital. We met our friend in the waiting room, sat there for hours. Tony never said a word. He stared into space until the Doctor appeared. He took Tony into ICU and told him his father is very sick and Tony should talk to him. "Your Dad can't speak but he definitely knows you're there."

Tony entered the room alone and stood over his Dad. After a few minutes he found the strength to speak to his father. "Dad, please , I'm begging you now. Please stop tryin to kill yourself. I know, no, I believe you know, you made mistakes with me. I forgive you. It's okay Dad. It really is. I'm okay now. I've always tried to make you proud of me. Well, tonight, whether you live or die, I'm gonna make you proud. Ya see, I got this game I gotta go to now so hopefully, after, you'll be proud." He squeezed his hand and walked out of the room.

"Coach can you drive me to the locker room now?"

"Tony, please, you don't have to do this."

"Coach, I ain't gonna say it again. Let's just fuckin go"

Bishotti trusted Tony so he led him to the car. On the drive, he asked if he wanted to talk. and Tony declined. He passed the time lookin out the window and did some world watchin. Getting dressed, sitting at his locker, and staring at the dull grey of the cheap carpet, Tony never said a word. And his teammates followed his lead. He needed space. Danny had the locker next to him and even he didn't get a word outa my best friend.

Outside the fans were gathering. This game was clearly different. It wasn't just family, friends, and students from opposing schools. There were people from all over the state. Our gang, couples, family, and friends sat together in the stands reluctantly nervous. We all made small talk. hoping to distract us from the moment at hand. Everybody wanted Tony to win more than Verona. Everything he'd been through, everything he felt, and didn't feel, made him a special underdog in our hearts. Tonight was the first night I noticed Jenni's open anxiety for her friend. She was talking to my sister, and I swear I overheard her say Tony's name a hundred times. Jenni wore his jersey and numbered face paint really well. I wondered why more people didn't have the "46" jerseys on. Was it something Tony did to make Jenni feel special, without him using the words? Or, Did Coach give her the jersey cause he felt Tony deserved a girlfriend.? I guess we'd never know. Terry schooched through us to go to the bathroom before kickoff.

Back inside, Coach Bishotti lowered his selected locker room music, It was from Man of Lamancha, The Impossible Dream. Players acted like they weren't listening, but how could you not listen to a man who fought when his arms were too weary? Coach reminded his team this season was a dream made by everyone. "It'd be impossible to end the dream now, It lasts until the final whistle when we win this game, Then. it'll continue for the rest of your lives. I've never coached kids like you. You are the best players and more importantly, best people I ever met. Now, let's go out and be the best team tonight." There was no mention of being state champion. Coach wanted the team to be their best, and everything would take care of itself. Before they left the locker room, they had their last "Dream cheer" Tony was the last to leave and Danny walked out with him.

As soon as Verona appeared, the band played, fans cheered,

and fireworks shot up in the midnight blue sky. Their walk to the field had a contagious confidence. Tony was oblivious to everything until his eyes fixed on a pair of shocking pink hi-tops. He looked up and it was my sister. Tony always had a soft spot for her. Before he could say a word, Terry gave him a big warm hug and whispered she loved him and will never forget her favorite lemonade stand customer. Tony finally cracked a smile and hugged back. Danny watched and learned another lesson from the guy who taught him everything about life. When he first met Tony, he idolized him cause of football After seeing Terry hug Tony, it all made sense. Danny began to understand what made his idol so special.

Warmups were charged with an overdose of raging teenage hormones. After their exercises Coach called the team together for last minute instructions. Tony and Danny made their way to the center of the field. I was worried about my friend. He was in his own world. Tony couldn't have been ready to play. Who would? His eyes stayed fixed on the ground and never looked at Pearl River's captains. Danny sensed his silence and called "Heads" for the coin toss., which they won and decided to play defense first. It was time for the ceremonial handshake. Pearl River knew all about Tony's antics about not shaking hands. As they turned to return to their bench, Pearl's Captains heard, "Hey". There was a pause. Tony approached Pearl River, shook their hands, and wished them "Good Luck" Everybody was shocked and confused, but no one would dare ask why he chose now to show good sportsmanship.

As the game finally started, it was crystal clear the teams were gonna kick the shit out of each other. Every play was brutal. The sound of violence created a bond of respect between the fans and the players. Players were completely unaware of the ten thousand people who attended. They coulda played in a backyard just like they did as kids. At halftime the score was tied 3-3. Bishotti led Verona to the locker room where he gave a short one sentence speech. "Keep doin what you're doin and get some rest." Halftime ended too quickly, and it was time to brave the elements. Verona headed back out to the field...

Danny was the last to leave the locker room. He told the coach he wanted to return the second half kickoff. "Danny, you've never practiced returning kicks"

Danny held his ground. "Coach, with all due respect, I'm not askin you. I'm telling you, and I'm gonna score. Ain't no one gonna stop me."

Bishotti was a sucker for passionate confidence in his players and Danny was pourin it on real thick. "You think so, huh Danny? Well, talk is cheap. Show me and then run your mouth."

"I will, Coach. Just Watch me"

Danny kept his word. Tony made his reputation channeling his anger hittin the other team. Danny ran with the same rage, and he was fast. No one could catch him and they sure as shit, didn't wanna get in his way. He scored easily. It even brought a smile to Bishotti's face. Tony had to be Tony, as he messed up Danny's hair," Not bad for a freshman punk kid" Danny fired back by throwing a half filled cup of water on the captain.

Verona stole the momentum and wrestled control of the game from Pearl River. They had an uphill battle, but Verona knew the River wasn't goin away. Pearl River eked out a lousy three points at the end of the third quarter. Fourth quarter was money time. Tony said it's the only quarter that means anything. Win the fourth and you'll win the game..

I'll never forget it. There was about six minutes to go and Verona was shoving Tony right down their throats. He got stronger with each carry. Twenty yards from scoring and putting the game away, Tony took a vicious hit and fumbled the ball. A tale of two stands. Ours were completely stunned in silence. Pearl River's bleachers erupted with its newfound life. Tony came out of the game and threw his helmet at the Gatorade cooler. He took a seat on the bench and buried his face in his hands. Bishotti was furious. "What in the hell do you think you're doing???"

"I fucked up okay? Would ya just leave me the fuck alone???" pleaded Tony

Bishotti wasn't buying it "Are you fuckin kiddin me? Give me a fuckin break!!!"

Parents in the stands were taken back by the coach's bad language. Yet, the strong connection between coach and player made it hard to argue. This wasn't a time to stand on a soapbox and say the teacher was wrong. Meanwhile, Pearl River was slowly marching down the field. Bishotti didn't care. The fight on the sidelines was far more important than the one on the field. Tony was seething. Jenni was hurting in a quiet way.

"I fuckin failed okay???. The one fuckin day I don't wanna fail, and I fuck it all up"

Bishotti kept the heat on. "Poor Tony.. That's all you ever think about, being a failure. And you're right, you are a failure. I spent four fuckin years tryin to convince you that you weren't. And ya couldn't give it up. Yeah, the guy sittin on the bench is a failure. It takes balls to get up and I guess you don't have them"

Bishotti left Tony to drown in his self pity.

This guy just challenged my best friend. It was the most important challenge of his life. Bishotti never asked Tony to go back in the game. Tony went to the ref, called timeout and ran back on the field. Pearl River was fifteen yards and thirty seconds from winning the game. As both teams lined up, Tony told Pearl River's quarterback, "I'm gonna kick your ass" There was testaronic anticipation of the snap of the ball. Tony kept moving around, hoping to guess the best angle to wreak havoc. He timed it perfectly and tackled both the quarterback and runner at the same time. The ball came loose and Verona recovered!!!. Six seconds to go.

The defense stayed on the field and lined up as the offense. Tony was the quarterback. Pearl River put five guys in front of Tony. He snapped the ball and took a knee. Game over. Verona wins!!!!!! Tony's eyes met Jenni's from fifty yards away. Teams exchanged handshakes and Tony waited for Coach Bishotti.

"No balls huh?" Bishotti smiled and reminded Tony balls were the reason they first met. There was the long stare and when Tony hugged his coach, he sobbed uncontrollably between the stuttering countless thank yous and I'm sorrys. This guy completely changed my friend's life. How can you thank somebody for that? The parents who witnessed the bad language, were now envious of the special relationship. Two people, Tony and Coach, were themselves with each other and the love was strong. They put it out there. More kids and parents should do the same. Everybody would be a lot closer. Coach told Tony his father is doing better and he watched the game.

Family and friends gave the two enough space. We were growin restless and Bishotti encouraged Tony enjoy the moment and the memory with us. Me and Jimmy were first to congratulate him. Everybody was givin their atta boys and pats on the back. The girls loved him and stood in line to give him a big hug. Even the moms showed the love. Jenni waited patiently, keeping her eyes fixed on her friend. He'd steal a glimpse; their eyes meeting created a quick spark of electric love. They finally met and held each other long enough to make the witnesses uncomfortable. Tony whispered a nice thank you in her ear and pulled her in tight one more time. These two were just friends?

As my Steph would always say," No fuckin way. They're closer than we are"

I had to answer the bell. "Yeah, but we're havin sex. They're not"

"Steph didn't give up that easy. "Yeah right, look at them. If that ain't the look of desire, nothing is"

"Steph, I'm telling ya. They ain't foolin around."

"Ok Baby, then they sure as shit should be. When they finally do, I wanna watch!!!"

"Steph, you get all embarrassed watchin us do it by the mirror. Ain't no way you can watch other people"

" Awww I know baby , but a girl can dream. Why do you think we read those stupid novels? It's cheatin without the guilt"

I love her so much. She's honest, fun, funny, smart, silly, playful, beautiful and sexy as hell when she wants to be.

Friday night was a day early for Parent date night, but all the adolescent sexuality made the dads horny(well horny as a dad can be) and the moms felt frisky. As kids we loved their code line. A yawn followed by "it's getting late" meant gettin lucky time.. For such an exciting game, there sure was alotta yawnin goin on.

Billy challenged me and Steph. "Kenny, you get us all in Harry's and I'm buyin"

I whispered in Steph's ear, "if you wanna make this happen, you'll probably have to let Fester take ya to the dumpster." "Again? That'll be the fourth time this week." There she goes again. "Billy, you got nothing to worry about. My girl knows people!!!" Tony hit the showers, called Coach Paterno, and met us in the parking lot. Fanny and Jimmy stole a few tokes on the joint. Terry and Jenni were fixin their hair and makeup so they could pass for eighteen. They both looked the part.

Me and Steph led the way in. The crowd was pretty big to-night. A Band was gonna play. Tony and Jenni were the last ones in and the bar erupted with applause. They all went to the game. Verona hadn't had anything to be proud of for a long time. It was an old town fading fast. And this eighteen-year-old kid gave them back their pride. Tony was stunned by the reaction. All of us were happy for him. Fanny insisted he better get used to it. "Tonight it was nine thousand. Next year it's gonna be ninety." Bunny was quick to get us all a beer. Fester bought the round. Bunny reached over the bar to give Tony and Jenni their bottles of Bud. "You and your girlfriend are drinkin on the house all night. "Tony shot back quick, "She's not my girlfriend!!!" Fester's girl could spar with the best. "She's not??? Well, then you better get that cute tight butt of yours over here and let me give you some sugar" Tony didn't back down and wound up with his face buried between her two greatest assets. The bosom strangler struck again!!. I never thought I'd see the day Tony Matelli would get embarrassed. He turned redder than his Bud label, he tried to be cool, but failed miserably as he strutted back to Jenni. Steph and Terry pinched his butt as he went past them.

Fanny came over to talk. She and me never talked much. So, it was nice getting to know her. Steph asked me to dance, I said no. She dragged Jimmy to the dance floor.

"So how's it goin with you and Jimmy?" Fanny tells me, "Good. I really like him and care about him. He treats me right"

I teased her, "Jimmy????"

Her face lit up, "yeah. When I'm cold, he warms me up. When I'm tired, he lets me sleep. And when I'm sad, he makes me happy." She thought a sec and went on, "he always makes sure I have what I need"

This was the most we ever talked.

"Ya know how when Steph talks about you and her, she says "we're one", well if you're one, me and jimmy are "two"

I got what she was sayin, "I understand".

Fanny's face frowned as she got serious, "Can I ask you for a big favor?" Hey, it was Jimmy's girl. Fanny asked me to tell Jimmy to stop doing that sex trick he learned from my book cause it really hurt and made her feel uncomfortable. I didn't know what she was talking about.

"What book? I never gave Jimmy a sex book"

She came back with, "Jimmy told me you'd say that. This is really embarrassing. Please don't make me say the name of it"

"Fanny, I'm not kiddin. I have no idea what you're talking about"

She was upset, "Okay, since I can't say it. I'll show you the famous position. Now, pretend you're the girl and bend over and grab your ankles" I can't believe what I just heard, "WHAT????" "You heard me, Now hurry up, bend over and grab your ankles. Quick, while no one is watching"

I guess curiosity got the best of me cause I wanted to know exactly what Jimmy was doing. Maybe Steph would like it. I turned my back and leaned forward, Before I assumed the position I looked back to ask, "You're not gonna hurt me, right?"

Fed up, Fanny barks back," No!!!! Now stop being a baby.!!!"

Things you do for friends. So, I thought Fuck it and just bent over and grabbed my ankles. At the exact moment, I grabbed hold, the music stopped, and a big white spotlight showed everybody in the bar just how stupid I can be.

Fanny took a few bows. The crowd gave her a standing ovation.

Since I was busted, I figured I'd go with it and mooned everybody. The roar got louder. Steph and Jimmy could barely walk from laughing so hard. Fanny turned to Steph, "told ya I could get him to do it" Steph gave my face a nice one-handed caress with two playful love slaps as she said." I love you baby!! You're so gullible" Acting a little upset, "Yeah this is what I get for love. She's your friend and Jimmy's girl. Lovin you can be sooo fuckin wrong !!!" I pulled her close to me and we had a good laugh. Fanny tapped her on the shoulder, and asked Steph if she was forgettin something. Fanny had her elbow bent and her hand out like a tray as she was tappin her foot. "Oh yeah" Steph reached into to her bra bank, withdrew a twenty and slammed it on Fanny's hand. That's my girl, at least she bet on me. "Fanny, payback is a bitch, so you better watch out. I put my glass down and went to the bathroom. Making my way back, Fanny had her back to me, I snuck up and did the one hand bra release that Fonzie taught me. And the cannons busted out like kids at recess. She turned beet red as she tried to keep the "kids" under wraps. "How's it feel Fanny??? Didn't think I'd getcha back that quick" She did have some personality, though, "I woulda seen you comin Kenny if I still wasn't blinded by the milky white color of your ass"

Tony, with his big stones, talked his way up to center stage and began tappin on the mic. Hey, it was Tony, Verona's celebrity for the night!!!. Everybody turned to the stage and listened. Through his bad days of hangin out all night on the streets, he struck up a friendship with members of the band a few years ago. Tony was gonna sing? No fuckin way!!! As everyone listened, he dedicated his song to someone he took walkin and talkin. "Friends are forever and I'll never forget how this person taught me what a friend is." Tony was thankin me? He didn't have to do that. His next word proved me wrong. "She's been a true friend who always knows the right thing to say. I tried hard, at first, to make her walk away, but she refused to stop believing in me. I hope she's my friend for life cause I'm hers anytime she needs me." Jenni didn't believe he was talking about her, she didn't want to believe it. If she was wrong, she'd be crushed. We all saw the hope in her eyes and heart. From the day she met Tony, she just wanted to be his friend and tonight she got her wish.

Tony carefully grabbed the mic with two hands. His eyes met Jenni's and suddenly they were all alone in a room of a hundred. "This is for you, Thanks for being my angel" And he began a soulful rendition of this song named "Oh Girl."The song was all about how Jenni stood by Tony and how lost he would be without her. The words, the emotion told us Jenni was breakin down his walls. I couldn't believe he sang a song, but dedicating it? That was too much. Steph squeezed my hand as tears fell softly from her eyes. She loved watchin love. The song ended slowly. Jenni marched right up to the stage and her innocence was lost in a "can't live without you" passion. Words were unspoken. She wrapped her arms around Tony and made out with him like it was the last second in time and her kiss stopped the clock. He melted in her arms and when it was finally over. Her eyes electrified his. She turned away and Tony stuttered to ask, "Hey wait, what was that for"

"Ever" Jenni's quick one word answer was perfect.

Jenni returned. Nobody said a word. Terry gave her a big hug. Fanny stood there, with mouth open, enjoyin her visual orgasm. Steph savored the moment. Jenni was like her, one of the passionate people. Steph always told me the "passionate people" are rare and we walk the earth like angels. When we meet another one, it's like knowin the world's a better place and getting better every day. Bunny got Jenni another beer and teased her, "Girl, Damn that was hot!!! I don't know where you learned it, but if he ever says you're just friends. Kiss him again" Jenni cracked up but stood her ground. "Nah, I was just fuckin with him. I don't wanna be his girlfriend." Bunny wasn't buyin, "yeah.girl, sure, you keep telling yourself that"

Embarrassed, but smiling like he just got laid, Tony rejoined us. "No, seriously, Jenni, what was that for?"

Jenni wouldn't give in. I'm guessin it was for two or three minutes, but I'm not sure." I got distracted when you started pressin your barbell against me."

"Yeah, it's a bar alright with two bells you can ring anytime"

"You wish Tony"

We closed Harry's that night. Bunny and Fester let us stay past closing time. Fester bonded with Tony and Jenni stood loyally behind him. I think Fanny and Jimmy found the nice romantic stall in the men's room. If Fanny had the fever, Jimmy was ready, anywhere, anytime. Billy, I kinda felt bad for him. With my little sister on his arm, he always had to be on his best behavior. They'd sneak innocent kisses when they thought I wasn't lookin. Steph told me to lighten up and go easy on them.

It was time to leave. With her innocent eyes, Jenni gently held Tony's hand. " Tony, I know you have to go to the hospital tomorrow, but if you don't wanna be alone tonight. I'm here."

He got scared and stared at the cigarette filled floor. Tony's voice trembled as he forced himself. "Yeah, Jenni, I'd like that"

Jenni asked Billy to call their parents and tell them we were all staying at a friend's house. Billy agreed and told Jenni he'd pick her up in the morning. For all of us, this night would be remembered as the best time we ever had. Hours seemed like years as the game seemed like a lifetime ago. And it was. Four years ago, we were scared insecure kids. Tonight we raised our beers and toasted to the future. Fanny was right, she and Jimmy were "Two" Billy and Terry were tight. My sister felt safe in his arms. That's all I ever wanted out of my teenage make-believe brother in law. Jenni and Tony were who knows what and who cares. Whatever they were together, it seemed to work. And me and my baby, felt like the parents who brought all these great kids together. Yeah, I guess we're pretty proud. We shared a parent kiss.

CHAPTER NINE

Tony and Jenni arrived at his house. The place was a mess and reeked of his dad's addiction to the bottle. Every house has an aura. Think about it, even the word home sounds safe. Tony's house had an empty unhappiness that infected the surroundings. He found it hard to even look at Jenni. She began cleaning up the place. Tony insisted, "You don't have to do that, What the fuck are you doing? Just leave the shit where it is"

"Tony, I'm not doing that. Let me just clean a little. Trust me you'll feel better after I'm done."

"Stop your shit, Jenni. I don't care and he, sure as shit doesn't deserve it"

"Tony, He's your father. I don't care what he did. He should come home to a clean house"

"You don't care what he did? Get the fuck outa here!!! Leave! Have your father abuse the shit outa you and then come and tell me how you feel"

"If you want me to leave I will, but Tony, when are you gonna forgive him? I bleed for you when I think what he did to you. I hate him. But hate is tearin you apart. So, I bleed more when I think I can't be there for the most special person in my life. I guess I should go now"

Tony let her leave. He didn't say a word. As the door shut, the sound of misery echoed through the house. He felt numb and sat there for an hour thinking about everything that nothing could stop. Nothing could stop what happened in the past. Nothing could stop him from thinking about Jenni. And Nothing could stop him from looking for her.

Outside his door was Jenni sitting on the steps. She was crying and freezing. "I had nowhere to go"

"Jenni, I'm soooo sorry. I just can't change. This is all I've ever known. Please, I mean it, please help me.". He extended his hand to help her up and pulled her close to his heart.

"Only if you help me get warm. Tony, you must know I'd do anything for you. You can't be that stupid to not know how I feel about you, Tonight, you did the nicest thing anyone has ever or will ever do for me. Your song melted my core. I'm sorry I kissed you. I mean we're just friends."

Tony gently held her face, looked into her eyes and gave her the softest kiss a man could ever give a woman. It lasted a lifetime of eternities. As it ended, he carefully pulled away, keeping his eyes connected to hers.

Jenni was completely stunned that Tony took control. It left her breathless. She could barely get the words out. " Wow. what'd you do that for"

"Ever, remember?" Tony smiled and led her back in the house.

They cleaned together and the house began to look like a home. Girls make that shit happen. We can't. Women fill a house with love and a tender touch until it becomes a home. Then, as the years go by , they keep feeding the place more love :Little reminders of the happy times grow the home. There's not a safer place in the world than your home.

With the house clean, they went back into the living room. Jenni told Tony to lie down. "Take your shirt off"

Tony fired back, "You take your shirt off!!"

Jenni wouldn't bite. "Oh Shut up Tony!!!! I wanna give you a back rub.. I can tell you're aching from the game"

Tony picked the perfect time to be stupid. "Oh yeah I forgot all about that"

He cooperated and removed his shirt to reveal a body Jenni would kill for. She saw the scars of abuse and it only made her touch more tender. Yeah, Jenni said she bleeds for him and she learned he bleeds for himself too.. Tony was a cutter. She knew it and never said a word. Lost in desire, Jenni thought she was keeping her thoughts to herself. "God you have an amazing body"

"What?" Tony replied in comfortable ecstasy.

He turned over and let Jenni know. "I wanna look at you while you're carin for me."

Jenni continued and resisted making eye contact. You can't ignore pure passion for long. Sometimes passion is a lot stronger than love. Love needs passion a lot more than passion needs love. Heaven was here. Tony pulled her on top of him and they made out with an energy that was powered by their incredible connection. Jenni was completely into it as her body started to shutter. She was becoming a woman far quicker than she was ready for. It was too much. She stopped as fast as she started.

He didn't understand. "What? What'd I do wrong?"

"Nothing Okay????"

"Jenni, C'mon talk to me. You make me talk to you"

"Tony, you really don't wanna know what I'm thinking."

"Yes, I do. I wanna know and need to know"

"Really? You think so?" Jenni got an attitude.

You didn't challenge him." Yeah, I do wanna know. What? you think I can't take it?"

"Tony, What the fuck are we doing??? I mean we're friends and you're making me feel things friends don't feel. You're getting in my heart and that scares the shit outa me. Do you know I think about you all day? Everyday? I wonder what you're doin and I smile when I pretend we're together. At night I go to bed and hold my pillow like I wanna hold you."

"Jenni, I told you. I'm not good at this. And, I really don't know what the fuck we're doing either. I've never kissed a girl and felt what I feel kissing you. I trust you; I depend on you, I think about you. I miss you. Yeah. I feel that way. But, I know, something in my heart is telling me we must be friends first.

I mean how could I have a girlfriend when I have to learn to be friends with a girl first. I can't promise what the future holds cause I don't know. I do know if I ever feel I deserve a girlfriend, I want it to be you."

Jenni felt relieved and gave Tony a long caring hug. "Tony, I just wanna fall asleep in your arms tonight and that's enough for me"

"We can do that Baby. God I wanna have a pet name for you!!! It feels nice to call you baby."

"Tony Matelli , you can call me whatever you want as long as you call me".

He reached his hand for her. As he helped her up he said, "C'mon baby, let's go to bed"

Morning came much quicker than wanted. They woke to playin innocent touch and tender bed games. Jenni reminded him of the reality of the day and offered to go with him to bring his dad home. Tony wanted to go alone, and she should get going so she doesn't get in trouble with her parents.

"Tony, my parents know where I am."

"What? You gotta be fuckin kiddin me"

"No, I'm not!!! They're not stupid. They like you and trust me. Plus, they're pretty cool once you get to know them. You'd know that if you came to dinner sometime."

"Really? Okay I will.... Sometime. "

"I hear ya baby"

He led her to the door and thanked her for the best night he ever had. He won the game and got the girl. But we'd never know. He'd deny it anyway. Tony had to keep his reputation ya know.

Tony met his dad at the hospital. Hoping the trace of love and pride he showed put a "hard to smile" smile on Tony's face. His dad looked tired, beaten, weak and old. They didn't talk much. His father couldn't. Just a muffled," Take me home" The car ride wasn't much different. Tony tried to make small talk telling his dad they won the game.

"I played for you Dad" His father stared blankly out the passenger window and a single tear fell from his eyes. Whaddya do? Tony stared in disbelief hoping his dad would say something to let him know what he was thinking. His father just continued to stare. I guess almost dying leaves you speechless. I don't think two people ever said more saying nothing. My best friend felt helpless to even try and figure out the right thing to do. Hell House arrived just in time.

Tony tried to help his dad but he wouldn't accept it. The walk to the door was his alone. It's amazing what a difference a few hours makes. Tony musta learned a thing or two about caring from Jenni cause he tried to make his dad feel welcome in his own home. Dad found his favorite chair and sat down to continue staring at nothing.

"Dad, Can I get you anything?"

"Yeah kid, get me a cold beer"

Tony was crushed, "Dad, Please..."

"Shut the fuck up and do what I said. Get me a fuckin beer"

Tony obeyed and went to the fridge. He gave his father the beer and his dad told him to sit down. Again, they talked sayin nothing for a half hour. A tear would fall every once in a while.His dad was cryin on the outside and Tony was cryin on the inside. He didn't know why he hurt. Maybe last night was so good and right now was so bad. Who knows? Who cares? When you hurt, you hurt, and the reason don't really matter. We just want the pain to go away, and we don't care how. His Dad was showin that, drinkin liquid death.

The silence was broken.

"I'm dying Anthony."

"Dad, I know"

"That's all you can say son? I know?"

"Whaddya want me to say Dad??? Tell me. All you tell me is you're dying. That's it?

"What do you want son? You want me to say I fucked up everything I ever touched? I wasn't the Dad you wanted? I failed you? I was a horrible husband? So bad that your mother had to go run and hide? I can't live with what I did. Don't you understand???

"Dad, Please, so what. You failed at alotta things. But I have a roof over my head and food on the table. And I'm going to college. Yeah, I played football to take out my anger I had for you. I won't deny that. I've hated you at times. But I'm going to Penn State because of you. Maybe you hated me cause you saw I could be something you weren't. It doesn't matter. I'm gonna be something. And I've never said that before. I'm a part of you and that means you're something too. You gave me life Dad and through all the pain we've both had, I realize you made me strong enough to make it in life."

Tony got up to hug his dad and his father gave a "I'm learnin how to hug" embrace.

"I'm still gonna die Anthony. That's why they sent me home"

"Dad, I've never asked anything of you. So now I have to. Whatever time we have left together, can we just get along? I need that, Dad. I need to know you and me are family.

"Why? We've never been a family, why start now.? Fuck pretending we're something we're not.

"Dad, you called me son. You never did that before. That's why. I ask two things. That's it. Let's go for a slice of pizza sometime. And, Let's take a walk."

"That's it? You think that makes us a family?? That's stupid!"

Tony got pissed, "It's not stupid Dad. It's not what we're doing that's important. It's the fact we're doin something together. C'mon Dad. Give me a memory, Give me a good one. I told you I need that, and I know you wanna give it to me. You're just scared you don't know how."

"OKAY, I'll do it. But you gotta do something for me."

"What Dad? Anything."

"I would like to meet Mr. Paterno"

"Really?"

"Yeah son. He's always been one of my heroes"

"Wow I never knew you even liked football"

"Son, I loved it before I hated myself. And I was pretty good at it too"

Tony was stunned, "Dad, you're kidding right?

"No son, I was the toughest player on my team. I just didn't think I was the toughest on the other team. Tough and scared ain't no way to play"

They spoke for a few more minutes. It was the longest they ever talked and the only thing they fought about was time.

Tony was tired. He didn't get a whole lotta sleep last night. Sleepin with Jenni seemed years ago. The game seemed even longer. But tonight, with his dad, will last forever in his heart. He wished his father a goodnight.

CHAPTER TEN

With the leaves blowin all around and the trees bare, you knew Thanksgiving was any day . Mom raced from store-to-store lookin for those special treats that'll make childhood memories last forever. I told Stef she better learn how to make the rolls just like mom. And the stuffing? no one could make any that compared to mom's. She'd tell us there were all sorts of special ingredients and it was love that made the stuffing so good. Mom promised my girl she'd teach her how to make the feast with all the trimmings. I loved the way mom loved Stef. She was her daughter and old enough to be treated like her friend.

I learned later that his dad died in Tony's arms the day after he got home. It was a week before Thanksgiving. Jenni was the only one he told and she went with him when Father O'Brien put his Dad to rest. Danny Pintauro sat in the last row. I could never imagine someone dying and no one going to the funeral. Jenni went to Tony's house every day and helped him get through the day. Thanksgiving morning came and Jenni was knockin on his door. He took twenty minutes to open it.

"What the fuck do you want?? Can't you fuckin leave me alone for one fuckin day???"

"Tony don't get that attitude with me. We're friends and friends don't treat each other like that. So get some clothes on. You're comin with me whether you like it or not. I really don't care how much you bitch. You have no choice."

With a face that screamed he'd been beaten, he reluctantly turned around and went to get dressed. Jenni stood there, breathless, loving the view of that body she couldn't get enough of, but wouldn't dare admit it to anybody including herself. Sometimes I guess it sucks to be just friends. After a few minutes, she yelled at him to hurry up. He mumbled an obedient "I am". Someday Tony was gonna look back and wonder when he lost control of this friendship. Jenni was takin it from him right from under his nose.

I called Stef and thanked her for everything good she's ever given me. You don't just give thanks for the food ya know. I heard the smile in her voice and it warmed my heart to know she'll never get sick of me lovin her. Stef , her dad and Monica were comin over for dinner. Billy told Terri he'd drop by after he finished. My baby sister... I can't believe she has a boyfriend and he treats her like a princess. Guys, we all try to act tough when we're together but give us a girlfriend? We become soft as teddy bears. Alone though, never in public. The most we do is steal a kiss or hold hands. Ya gotta protect your Rep!!

Fanny invited, no, she insisted Jimmy and his mom spend Thanksgiving with her family. Holidays are never easy for families who lost loved ones. And for families that didn't suffer a loss, we show our love by having holiday dinners together. I realized we did it for Stef and her dad, Jenni did for Tony, And Fanny came through for Jimmy and his mom. I wondered what it'd be like if my family suffered the loss. I looked at Terri and cried inside at the thought of life without her. I know I'm hard on mom and dad, but couldn't imagine not having both of them to depend on. They had no idea what I was thinking and thought I was nuts as I went and hugged each of them and thanked them for being in my life.

Stephanie was curious, "that was really nice. What made you do that?"

"I'll tell ya later"

"Promise? Kenny"

"Yes, I promise."

Mom's dinner was really good and Dad beamed with awkward pride as he was carving the turkey. You'd think in twenty years he'd learn to do it right. But traditions can be funny too. We'd all smirk and wonder if Dad knew the difference between a leg and a wing.

As usual, my eyes were bigger than my stomach and I could barely finish my favorite dessert. Mom would warm a slice of blueberry pie and drop a scoop of melting French Vanilla on top.

Dinner came to an end with the girls clearing the table and doing the dishes. The guys, we just sat there with our hand in our pants trying to make more room for our fat to get fatter. Mr. DeMarino and my dad would find the room to keep their other hand busy. They always had room for more beer. Mom yelled in the dining room asking if anybody wanted coffee. She knew the answer but had to ask. The women sat down at the kitchen table. Stef made me keep my promise .

We took a walk outside and felt the November Jersey cold go through us. Ya get used to it. A Jersey kid could never cry about the cold. My cousin John was from Maryland. We never saw him from November through March cause as he would say, "it's too fuckin cold there" His girlfriend, Shari was even worse. I don't know what high maintenance is but she must be. Steph would always say..." look at her, Honey could you sleep with that? I don't think either one of them know what passion's all about. It sucks to be them. But, they're from Maryland so whadddya expect with their stupid southern accents.!!!!"

Steph looked beautiful with her knitted white earmuffs and matching coat. My eyes fall in love with her look every time I see her. I know I should be a better listener, but I can't help myself. I have to interrupt her thought and tell her she's the most beautiful girl I've ever seen. Her shy smile and innocent eyes tell me she feels lucky to be loved by her guy. She tries to continue our conversation, but I stop her. I have to kiss her.. twice. Once could never be enough. She's come to expect the "two kiss" kiss.

We made our plans for Christmas and New Year's Eve. Christmas would be spent at both houses. We had our Christmas on Christmas Eve. Money was tight so the gifts had to be all about the thought. I had five dollars. Caldor's had to have something. We decided to open our gifts in the parking lot of the elementary school where we shared our first kiss and vowed to never forget where we came to be "one."

Before I gave Steph her gift I had to tell her what her love did to me and for me. I gave her a gentle kiss, handed her the gift, and wished her a Merry Christmas. Girls are so cute taking the time not to rip the paper as they open their gift.. She kept lookin at me with her "little girl on Christmas morning" smile. It was just a small plastic figurine and on the base it said, "I love you so much it hurts" She started crying and between the tears, she uttered, "I'm so lucky I have you in my life." She hugged me like she never has before. Feeling unworthy of her affection, I didn't deserve the most beautiful woman in the world. I didn't need a gift. She was my gift.

It was my turn to open. I ripped the paper like a little boy anytime he gets a present. Steph will tease me forever about my lack of fashion. I knew I didn't look good. She loved me anyway. She introduced a new color of t-shirt to me. They were two black t-shirts. Some fashion brand that I never heard of. But they were much softer than my Hanes. I loved them. She made me put one on right away. Wow. There's nothing sexier than the look of lust in her eyes. I got my "gift" in the back of our broken-down Volkswagen. And she was the gift that kept on giving. Christmas Eves were never gonna be the same.

The world would be a much better place if every day was Christmas. Church bells echoing through the neighborhood, Christmas carols playing all day on the radio, and the smell of Holiday dinners filling each home made the day a memory for everyone. At sunrise, I woke up my sister to give Terry her gift. It was a simple necklace with a "T" pendant. She promised me she'd wear it forever. She gave me the perfect present. I have no idea when or how she got it. But it was a framed picture of me and Steph. We were making out at sunset on the beach as the summer waves were crashing behind us. "Kenny, whether you realize it or not, your relationship with Stephanie is so special to me. I desperately want what you have. Don't misunderstand, I love Billy and he's soo good to me. But you two seem so natural, like you were made for each other."

"Terry, first, thank you so much for this picture. It's got a home on my night table. You do have to understand it took alotta time and even more work to get to where we are. Honestly, I think Billy tries a lot harder than you do. So either you have to try harder or search inside your heart and figure out why you're not trying. As your brother, I'm always here to listen and love you. Merry Christmas little sister"

"Aww, I love you too big brother. Merry Christmas"

We went downstairs to mom and dad and wished them a Merry Christmas. As a family, we were pretty good at doing the Christmas morning thing. Music played and the smell of fresh coffee and evergreen filled the house. Christmas family love was far more important than any gifts we ever got. I cant remember what I got last year, but I'll never forget sittin on Dad's lap and having him read Frosty the Snowman. And every year mom took dad under the mistletoe and made out with him. Why couldn't everyday be Christmas to them?

Fanny invited Jimmy and his mom over. Somehow, Jenni got a key to Tony's house and dragged him outa bed. She noticed Tony was "happy" Christmas morning and the free show made her really happy too. Tony caught her staring at his package of Christmas cheer. "You can dream all you want baby, but you ain't getting that for Christmas."

"And you ain't getting my jewelry box" They shared a laugh. Tony got up and gave Jenni a long warm hug. Friends don't hug like they do. When is he gonna love himself enough to love her? She helped him look nice and they went to her house for Christmas. Jenni's mom and dad were so good to him. Without them, he'd never know what it meant to be a family. And he was learning. He hugged her mom and dad at the end of the night. Jenni drove him home, walked him inside and asked for her present. He felt really stupid. Telling her he didn't get her anything. Jenni reached in her purse, pulled out a cassette player. "Yes you did. I want one dance with you."

"Have yourself a Merry little Christmas" It was the perfect slow song for Jenni to stare into his eyes. Tony had a peaceful smile on his face. As the song was ending, Jenni worked her magic again, and kissed him with perfect passion. The kiss finally ended with Jenni, whispering Merry Christmas in his ear, and slowly breaking away. Tony was stunned as he watched Jenni let herself out. He came back from heaven just in time, running to the door, He yelled a stuttering Merry Christmas to Jenni.

Bunny and Fester invited all of us to the New Year's Eve party at Harry's. Jimmy and Fanny were smoking pot out back. Who knows what else they did back there. They had more sex than all of us put together. I guess they were sex pots. Billy took the floor and toasted to the new decade, the 80s. Jenni teased Tony and reminded him about the song he sang just for her. I don't know how she walked the line between friend and lover but she did it with sensitive perfection. Terry seemed to listen to our talk and she led the make out session with Billy. She pressed him against the wall and attacked him. My little sister wasn't so little anymore.

Steph followed Terry's lead and found us a quiet place. She brushed the hair from my eyes and her tender touch made me wanna live together forever. She looked at me with incredible love that only her eyes could express." Baby this is gonna be our year. We're gonna be closer than we've ever been. After graduation, we're gonna start living our lives together. I've been saving this surprise for tonight. My Dad has been talking to your parents and they all are behind us."

"Behind us? Steph what are you trying to tell me?"

"I'm trying to tell you if you just shut up. My Dad built an apartment for us in my basement. We're gonna have a home. And when you come home from Rutgers, your girl will be waiting for you. All your parents asked was to make sure you spent enough family time with them. Whaddya think Baby?"

"I don't know... I'm speechless. I always knew we'd be together but now it's here. Every night, we can fall asleep in each other's arms. And when I open my eyes in the morning, I'll get to see. Steph. We're gonna have a lot of sex. I mean everyday... a few times a day. "

"Fuckin A right we will !!!! Ain't no way I'm letting you hold back. I've been waiting to show you just how much attention I really need and wanna to give you too. So, Get some rest now. Cause you ain't gonna sleep all summer." I guess Steph liked sex!!

We made out until Bunny pinched my ass. The countdown to midnight was starting and Fester and Bunny wanted to bring in the New Year with us. We shared our news, and I made the toast. "To happiness. If we can be half as happy as you two, we'll be really lucky" Bunny and Fester always reminded us of what true happiness was all about. It's about being in love with your best friend.

Everybody was sexin up in Harry's except Tony and Jenni. She wanted to but Tony just couldn't be a couple, not even for a night. She stood by him though. I didn't understand how it'd feel to need love so much and be able to stand by and not know if it would ever come. Jenni was a lot stronger than all of us. Tony thought he was the only one that knew about Jenni's strength. It was almost as if he was punishing her for being stronger than he was. I wanted to tell him to stop testing her. Didn't he realize he was hurting her? Didn't he care? I mean , I saw them kiss. They got it. Why was he wasting it?

Winter took its time getting out of town. Snow days kept us warm and high. Smokin pot and sleigh riding is like a magic carpet ride. Your head is in the clouds while your body is going a hundred miles an hour. Flyin down the hill is wild until you remember you forgot to stop. Ever panic when you're high? By the time you're panicking you've already met your fate. You wake up and see everybody laughing at you while you believe your marbles are in your ass.

CHAPTER ELEVEN

March came in like a lion in heat or maybe Stephanie did. We started on March 3rd and for twenty eight days, we invented pure passion. She was becoming a complete woman far faster than I was becoming a man. Every night she lost herself in the pleasure of our intimacy. We became so "One" we didn't know where one of us started and the other began. It wasn't sex. It was different. I could tell you everything we never did before, but it's not what I remember. Our "after love" love talks were incredible.

One night she was sated and stared starry eyed at the stars in the sky. We talked for hours about how nice it'd be to live on one of them. We even had an address 717 Diamond Lane. "Baby, what happens there? Do I go to school, Do I work? What do we do?"

"We do one thing Kenny. We have the most beautiful kids you ever laid eyes on. Every day, we make a new one. Days are filled with love and laughter. Our kids make fun of the way we still love each other. But they're happy and they're safe."

"What about them? Do they have girlfriends and boyfriends? Do they go to school?" She loved me going along with her dollhouse fantasy.

"Kenny they're our kids and they're hot. Of course, they date. They hang out two stars over on Roberta Way. They're so cute. They sneak out at night and make out till the sun comes up. Fuck no, they don't go to school. Why would we let some idiots teach our kids. We teach them everything. The most important lesson is love yourself, your family and your friends IN THAT ORDER!!!!

Kenny, baby, I know I've been driving you nuts with sex every night. You must be wondering where I'm getting all the energy. Well, I guess I'm finally learning to love myself. I always felt like a misfit. I don't know if you ever realized it, but have you noticed I never talk to Tony"

"Here I go again being stupid. No, I never did."

"Baby, do you know why? Can you figure it out?"

Awww shit. My mind started to race. My best friend is fuckin the love of her life. I feel so fuckin stupid. My life fell apart. I'll never be able to trust again. Thoughts kept racing. She must like him better than me. He's probably bigger. He turned her into a nympho. That's why we're having all this sex. She fuckin me, wishing it was him. I know he knows more. I felt humiliated. I couldn't satisfy my girl. I wasn't good enough. God this hurts so bad... knowing I gave her the best I got and it wasn't good enough. Steph nudged me. I guess she was gonna spill her guts.

"Kenny, you know I love you and will forever right? "Here it comes. "Would ya get those thoughts outa your head???? I'm not fucking Tony, ok???? How could you even think that? How could you think that little of me? I have to be "One" with you and I always will. You're a part of me and I know I'm a part of you. I need that balance in my life"

"Well then what the fuck are you talking about. So what, you don't talk to Tony. Are you supposed to get brownie points for that? Or are you supposed to get them for not fucking my best friend?"

Steph got real pissed. "Enough with the fuckin attitude. NOW!!! Ya know, every time I try and tell you something important to me, you fuck it up. I was trying to tell you, me and Tony were the only kids from single parent homes. And now, his dad's dead and he doesn't even know where his mother is. I know he feels like I do. All this time we've been together, do you really think I thought I deserved you? Hell no!!! I finally learned to love myself and it changed me. I can't explain how. I just know I can give you more now."

"I'm so sorry baby. You're my life and I got scared. Scared, my life was over at eighteen. But I think you're right. I mean, I think I love you more than I love me. That's no way to live. And if loving myself can make me able to love you more, I'm all for it. I know I woulda never thought those things about you and Tony if I loved myself more. I gave you shit. You didn't deserve it and I tormented myself."

"Exactly, Kenny. This single parent thing has really made me think about Tony though... Well. I mean Tony and Jenni. It's so obvious she loves him. She's completely devoted to him. But it's sad. She's not gonna do it. She ain't gonna get him and she's gonna blame it on herself. But, it's him. Baby, you gotta do something. You gotta get him to love himself even just a little bit. Jenni deserves it and you know it."

"I know but what the fuck am I supposed to do??. This is girl shit. Guys don't talk about this stuff."

Steph smiled, "But my baby does. He's a man, he's, my man!! Honey, I don't care what you do, just do something or you'll never be able to look at him in the eye."

"Thank God Jimmy don't have this shit. He's got Fanny and it works. I don't know how but it does"

"I know, right? "We had a big makeout as she liked to call them. This girl could get me to do anything. I knew I had to take on Tony. I drove home thinking about my baby. How can a girl be so smart, sexy, sensitive, and beautiful? It almost doesn't seem fair. But every day I wake up feelin luckier than the day before. That's what she does to me. I mean she just told me that my best friend and I had to learn to love ourselves. She cares about me in way I never even dreamed about. I pulled in the driveway and as I walked to my front door, I took the time to look up at 717 Diamond Lane.

The morning came and I decided it was time to talk to my little sister. She and Billy were so stable, and I wanted to know why. It was obvious she loved herself. I could tell by the time she spent brushing her hair. After Billy, her hair was her life. "Terry are you happy with Billy? Do you think you love him?"

Terry was stunned by my questions. "What makes you ask that? Why do you wanna know? Did Billy tell you something?"

In my big brother voice, I calmed her anxiety." No he didn't tell me anything. I would tell you if he did. I guess I was wondering what made you two happy."

"Ummm , yes I am happy with him. He is so good at caring about me. I feel safe with him. We're close. As far as loving him, I don't know. But. that's not cause of him. Mom and Dad aren't the best role models for love, so I can tell you honestly. I don't know what love is. How bout you? Do you think you love Steph"

My confidence shined through. "Yeah, I love Steph and every day I fall more in love. She makes me a better kid. And don't worry, you don't have to know what love is. You'll know when you feel it.

Terry was curious. " Kenny where is this coming from?"

I told her about last night." Me and Steph were talking and she told me I couldn't love her unless I learned to love myself. I think she was right."

"Duh. Why are guys so stupid? Of course, I have to love myself first or you guys would walk all over us. Don't you realize the slutty girls have no respect for themselves?"

Yeah, I guess you're right. But me and Stef talked about Tony and Jenni too. She thinks they'll never work out cause Tony hates himself. He never talks about her, and I think that's fuckin weird. I mean I'm his best friend. He should be able to tell me what he's thinking"

"Kenny, you're wrong. You haven't talked to him about Stef in years. He sees the same thing I see, you and her makin out and liking each other. There's no reason to ask you anything about your relationship. But, if there's something you wanna tell me, I'm always here to listen. I love you. You're my big brother.

"Stef told me I gotta talk to him about this shit. I know he'll never be happy acting the way he acts now. I think Jenni is wastin her time."

"I know. I keep telling her she deserves a lot more than what she's givin him. But she doesn't wanna hear it. She doesn't even wanna talk about it. All she says is don't give me shit. We're just friends. I say yeah right, and she tells me to shut up."

"Well, I'm gonna talk to Tony. I don't know what I'm gonna say but it may be time to take a camping trip with him."

"You gonna smoke some of that stuff? I don't know why you like doin that"

"Cause sometimes it's okay to take a vacation in your head. I don't expect you to understand. All your worries fly away like the smoke. Ya also talk about shit you only think about. Hey, the first time I got high, we talked about how fucked up mom and dad are. Terry, don't it bother you about mom and dad? Today, they barely even speak to each other and a long long time ago, they cared about each other like you and Billy do. We both say that'll never happen to us. But, how do we really know? And that's the stuff we talk about while we're getting high. It gets pretty deep. It's cool."

CHAPTER TWELVE

I ran into Tony at school and told him it was time for a campout. I knew it was the perfect weekend cause Fanny and Jimmy were going to upstate New York with Fanny's Family. I could tell Tony hated his time alone in his house. He was up for the campout and told me this was the last time he was getting high. His life sucked and all he looked forward to was goin to Penn State in the fall. He didn't wanna fuck that up. I told him I'd pick him up Saturday night at 6pm.

The rest of the week flew by with Stef attacking me every night. Sex makes time fly ...and me too... to Diamond Lane. Like clockwork, I picked up Tony Saturday at 6pm. Tony hated living in the house where his dad caused him so much pain. Camping out was in the woods a much nicer place. The walls were trees, and the ceilings were stars. It really was a great place to get high and bullshit with your best friend. Tony rolled the biggest fattest joint I ever saw. "Hey this is the last one I'm gonna smoke for a long time. I gotta make it last." Tony boasted.

Last? That fuckin thing will last forever" I said with a little bit of fear and remembered the first time we got high. God, it seemed like yesterday." Remember the first time Tony?"

Tony got all paranoid. "The first time we what?"

"Got high you asshole"

Tony took a second, "Yeah, we've been through alotta shit since then"

"Tony do you ever remember who you were? I mean, fuck, you've changed and overcome so much"

He hated getting credit for anything. "Kenny, All I did was hit people and now I'm going to college cause I can kick ass. Big fuckin deal."

The pot was takin its toll and we got real serious." Tony, shut the fuck up. You just can't be fuckin happy. People would kill to be you. Hell, I wanna be you. You fuckin got it."

Tony was getting pissed. I figured if I got him mad enough, he'd start talking bout Jenni. "Yeah, right . people wanna be me. I live alone in a house that haunts me every night. I'm goin to college where I'm gonna feel outa place. I'm losin my friends, got no bitch. You gotta future. You got Stef. And you're trying to tell me I'm your fuckin hero??? Get the fuck outa here. I ain't shit and I'm cool with that"

I had to keep the pressure on. " Ya know Tony, the only time I ever saw you get called out on your shit is when you fumbled and Bisciotti went off on you. And ya know what? He was fuckin right. I used to feel bad for you. Fuck that. I'm tired of your bullshit. I'm your best friend and I've never seen you happy, really happy. What the fuck is your problem? Life don't owe you shit. You say I have a future ?. Fuck you. You can do whatever you want. Until you learn that you deserve everything good, you're gonna be miserable. You got great friends and a girl that loves you more than you could ever know. And you can't even give her a chance. I think you're scared to be happy cause you couldn't bitch anymore"

Tony was seething, "Enough alright? You say you're my best friend and you give me shit about things you don't even under-stand. Don't you think I know what I've done to myself?? I'm a suc-cess at being a failure and terrified I could fail at being a success. And, I know how Jenni feels, I just can't give her what she wants. I don't know why. It'd be easy to say I don't feel that way about her, but I gotta admit, no girl has ever treated me better."

I took the last hit of the joint and exhaled the smoke while look-ing at 717 "Tony, there's really only two people you gotta give a chance to. You and Jenni. Think about it"

The tension eased. Tony cracked up." I'm turning into a pussy. I shoulda beat the crap outa you for talking to me like that"

I showed some heart. "You ain't man enough!!!"

We decided the deep shit was makin us tired and Tony passed out before I did. I took the time to get lost on Diamond Lane and thinking bout my baby. Even though we were kids, we never let the honeymoon stage end. I guess we both knew if we let it go, we were done. With or without Stef, every night I fell in love with her. I closed my eyes and fell asleep thinking about her eyes, smile, laugh, touch and kiss. I made a promise to myself to make out with her every night of our lives together.

Morning came, Tony busted my balls and blew in my ear till I woke up. I acted pissed, "You asshole!!! You fuckin woke me up in the middle of a sex dream I was havin. I knew it was a dream cause Steph was getting real hot"

Tony piled on, "you fuckin stud!!! The only way you can get your bitch hot is in your dreams. I'd tear that shit up if I were you"

I sank in a funny way, "I know. You doin Steph is my biggest fear. I swear if you do, I'll do Jenni"

"Cool!!!!" Tony was kickin my ass. I tried to change the subject.

"So, Tony, no shit. Are we cool about last night?"

Tony reassured me. "Kenny, don't be fuckin stupid. I heard what you're saying and you're right. But that doesn't mean I'm gonna listen. Look, I don't know how, but if I ever learn, I'm definitely taggin Jenni. You see how hot she is???"

I was fucked, "How the hell am I supposed to answer that? If I say yes, you're gonna think I wanna do her and if I say no, I'm telling you she's ugly"

"But Kenny, why should I milk only one cow when I could have a farm full.?"

My turn to bust balls. "Cause Tony, maybe that one cow gives you fresh milk every day and the rest can make you sick to your stomach"

"Okay Kenny, I hear what you're sayin."

We got in the car and made our way home. I felt good knowing, at least some of it got through. I couldn't tell him he'd be happy with Jenni. He had to take that step. He couldn't expect her to wait forever. Sooner or Later, she was gonna give up and let someone else in. I couldn't imagine loving and leavin Stef. Pretending you're happy with some one else must really suck. I couldn't wait to call my baby. It was only a day , but I missed her.

CHAPTER THIRTEEN

Mom met me at the door and took my laundry, told me I smelled and to go take a shower. The feeling hit me outa nowhere so I had to ask. "ok, mom but I gotta question for ya. Before Dad asked you out, did you know he liked you?" Mom held her ground and promised to answer my question after I took my shower. That's all I needed to hear. I ran upstairs and ran the water till it was the right temperature. I threw my clothes in the empty hamper and hit the shower. Two things I love doin in the shower, singin and thinking, and I do my best of both there. I was dying to know my mom's answer and wondering if Jenni knew Tony really liked her. I think she was so caught up in liking him, she never thought about herself. Mom's answer was callin me. I rinsed the shampoo outa my hair and finished up. Once dry, I wrapped the towel around me, went to my room, and threw on my sweats.

Heading downstairs, I yelled for my mom and teased her about her holding up her part of the deal. Mom fought me a little bit with answers to make me go away. I don't understand girls but I know when they say things like, "in a little bit, let me just make a phone call, not right now, and I gotta get dinner started, means they ain't holdin up their end. I wasn't buyin it and mom knew she was busted. "Kenny honey, you ask really tough questions"

I was confused, "Huh I do? What so tough about askin if you knew Dad liked you?"

Moms need to exhale. "Cause you remind me of a very happy time in my life and it seems so long ago. It seems like we're both so different, it's hard for me to accept that was us. Okay, sit down. I'll answer your question."

I sat across from Mom cause I wanted to see if the happiness was still in her eyes. Mom sat in the middle of the couch and looked so alone. She took a minute to gather her thoughts and exhaled one last time. This one had a reluctant smile. She began slowly, "Kenny, for months I saw your Dad everywhere I went, the beach, dances, my job...everywhere. I was star struck cause he was the cutest guy around. I always thought his girlfriend was the luckiest girl and even pretended I would be his girl one day. But it was weird, he never brought his girlfriend around and he never tried to pick up other girls. I couldn't believe his steady girl trusted him out alone without her. Girls can be worse than boys. I couldn't even smile at him. But my curiosity was killin me. So I started to ask my friends if they knew anything about your dad and his girlfriend. Well, your dad was a pretty good athlete, but he didn't have a girlfriend. My heart raced faster than it ever has but I'd never let my friends know. Then, they'd want him too. I told them I didn't like him cause he seemed so full of himself. And they believed me!!!! I didn't know one thing about your dad but they all agreed.

Well, one night, I'm with my girlfriend and your dad comes from nowhere and asks me to dance. He took my hand and led me to the dance floor before I could even answer him. I liked the way he took control, but it was a different story on the floor. We were full of nervous laughter. Yes, it's hard to believe your dad was shy, painfully shy. But when he looked into my eyes, I knew he was a special guy. The laughter subsided and our eyes connected. I was still nervous, and he shocked me with a sweet kiss. I felt like his princess." Mom took a few moments to savor the memory. "Kenny, I hope you never forget the first time you kissed Stephanie because to make it work, you have to keep it in the forefront of your memories.

And thanks Kenny. I have to take my own advice. I know your dad and I just put up with each other, but I believe if I ever really needed him, he'd be by my side holding my hand. I miss the passionate feeling, but it's okay. After all, I got the guy I always wanted. Now you go down to Harry's and get him home by 5pm. Here's some money. Tonight, take Stephanie out for dinner and dancing."

I knew Mom. "Mom are you gonna have a special night with Dad?"

"Kenny, you said you had a question for me. That means one so I'm not answering your second"

I'd be so lost without her. She ain't exactly that happiest woman but she never forgot the keys to happiness. "Gotcha mom, you're right. I'm goin to Harry's now"

I had to ask Dad the same question. I figured it was a two Bud answer. Harry's never changes and neither do the people. I made my way through the crowd with the usual hellos. Dad was at the end and playin his pleasure machine. All these years and I never saw him win a dime, but I admired his stupidity and persistence. I brought him a fresh beer. His old beer was warm from sittin too long. We had our usual bullshit conversation. You know, How's school? How's work?, and How's Stephanie and her Dad?. I told him about Tony and his problem with Jenni. Dad took Tony's side. "Son, his dad just died a few months ago. Ever think he wants to be alone?"

I admit the thought never occurred to me, but I heard Stef yellin inside my head "That's the last thing he wants or needs. You men are so stupid" I had to listen to her and, besides, I was dying to hear Dad tell his side of the how he met Mom. I got Dad to belly up to the bar and said a few words of bullshit before I hit him with the question. Dad was stunned. "Son you wanna know what? Why? Kid anyone ever tell you that you ask too many questions?"

He laughed at my answer. "Yeah. Dad, Mom did" This had something to do with Tony. I didn't know what, but I knew I'd see it at some point.

"Okay, Kenny. If you laugh at me, I'll kick your butt. Verona was a much smaller town back then. There weren't a whole lot of places to go. But wherever I went, your Mom was there and she definitely wanted nothing to do with me.... Or so I thought.. It pissed me off cause I thought she was really cute. Your Dad wasn't the smoothest operator. My friends would go out on a Friday night and search for "the one night of love" kinda girl. That wasn't me. I couldn't even ask a girl to dance. And there was your mom, making fun of me for just looking at her. I couldn't help it. She was beautiful. I got tired of that snotty look she had on her face whenever I saw her. I learned to sneak in a few peeks every time I ran into her. Kid, I'm not kiddin ya. This went on for months.

I thought it was pretty cool that mom and dad remembered the same things. I kept my mouth shut and told Dad to go on.

"Okay. Well, She was either gonna reject me, laugh at me, or make fun of me. I didn't care. I had to find out her story. One night I asked her to dance. No, I took her hand and told her we're gonna dance. Her hand felt so soft as we went to the floor and turned toward each other. My arms went around her waist and hers could barely reach my neck. Immediately, I saw she was far more beautiful than my sneak peeks led me to believe. All we could do is laugh at each other and I did my best not to stare at her. The faint lights of dance floor reflected in her eyes and her beauty overpowered me. I felt like I was born to kiss her and it was much better than my imagination. After we kissed, the pressure was off and we talked like normal kids. The chemistry was overflowing, and the end of the night came much faster than was fair. I never thought to ask to see her again. I didn't want the night to end and asked her to come home with me. But your mom was great. She wasn't a "one night of love" kinda girl. So, she shot me down. It was okay, we'd see each other from time to time. Each night together made me hunger for more, but it also scared the hell outa me. Your mom put up with alotta shit and she was really patient. It wasn't until we both went through some hard times, that I realized how important she was to me. And the rest is history.

There it was. I got my answer. "Thanks dad. Great story. Can you do me a favor?"

Dad gave me his fed up smile, "Kenny , What? You're really pushin it"

"Dad, I can't promise but I may need you to tell Tony that story. Ya know, I heard what ya said about him being alone, but you don't know him like I do. And Jenni has been amazing. He won't admit it, but he really needs her in his life."

Dad's reluctant feelings shined through, " I got ya. Why do you think it took me so long to be with your mother? I thought I'd be stronger alone, but I was wrong. I found out how much strength she gave me. I got news for ya. Mom and Dad are old and that flame may've burnt out tears ago. But, if I ever need it re-lit, I look into her eyes and see our memories. And those keep me strong. "

We finished our beers, paid our tab, and said goodnight to the regulars. Dad seemed stuck in the memory. I guess guys, as they get older and lose the fire, they take it out on the one who lit their match. Fire can't burn forever. But, why not? I promised myself I'd never let that happen to me with Stef. The Fire is all we got and we gotta lifetime of flame. But were mom and dad any different than us? Dad was still smiling, and I was feeling nothing but fear. No. No fuckin way. I ain't gonna let it happen. I'm bangin Stef as soon as I see her tonight and that fire is gonna burn hotter than ever.

We walked home from Harry's and realized this is the shit that makes memories. I never had a bad walk home with Dad and we both felt close, the way a father should to his son, and the way a son should to his father. Dad was funny. He started telling me dirty jokes. At first, I didn't have the heart to tell him his jokes were old, but I had to after the tenth bad joke. Dad acted pissed, "what? Kid you got any better?"

"Hell yeah Dad" And I started firing jokes at him till he begged me to stop or he was gonna pee himself. Mom was waiting at the front door and didn't know if she should be happy we had a good time or upset cause Anne Heiser spent too much time with us. Mom always teased Dad about his girlfriend Anne and would suggest the two of them separate for a while. Anne's Cousin, Bud Weiser, got along with me and Dad just fine. Mom made me shower away the smoke before I went out with Stef.

With the hot water raining down on me, I thought about my sexual Olympics which was gonna start in about an hour. Stealing Dad's Penthouse Forum was one of the smartest things I ever did. Half the shit couples performed, I never even heard of. How did they get in all those positions. But tonight I was gonna die trying.

Stef better be ready, willing, and flexible!!!. I dried off and dabbed a little cologne on all my dirty places. Stef loved fresh berries.

I figured Jimmy could probably come up with a few kinky ideas. After all, He and Fanny did some pretty sick shit. They've been playin a game of sexual chicken for a year now and neither one wanted to lose. Everybody has a line they won't cross but those two were years away from finding theirs. Yeah, Jimmy was the perfect guy to call. I got him on the phone and told him I need his best sick sex idea. He started laughing and broke my stones. "Fuckin Rookies. Kenny if you can't tap that shit right, I'll hit it for ya."

"Jimmy, shut the fuck up. I seen your shit in the shower after Gym class. I can't believe you think Fanny likes that turtle dick." He had to fire back.

"Kenny, bend over I'll show ya how hard that turtle can snap. And, Asshole don't forget why you're callin me. Alright you pussy. Here's the deal. I go to this hooker every once in a while and she teaches me all kinds of good shit." I had to interrupt him.

"Wait, What? You cheat on Fanny? Does she know?" Jimmy had all the answers.

"Kenny, if you do it with a hooker it ain't cheating. I think of it as adult education. Besides, Fanny is the one who benefits"

"Jimmy, Are you fuckin nuts? You really think that's not cheating?"

"No, I don't. And come on Kenny, don't bullshit me. You trying to tell me you're happy with Stef being the only one to wet your noodle? Ain't no fuckin way I believe you. We're eighteen years old!!!!! We're supposed to wanna fuck anything that moves. And don't judge the hooker shit till you try it yourself." I got a little pissed at Jimmy.

"You fuckin sick Fuck!!! Have you ever heard of AIDS? You get that shit and you're giving a death sentence to your girlfriend. She's been pretty good to you. She don't deserve that. And ya know Jimmy. She'd stay with you if you could never fuck her again. What the fuck are you thinking?"

"Hey Kenny, all I know is I could fuck your girl much better than you. I'd turn her into the bad girl she wants to be but can't be with you!!!"

Great, now I gotta worry about my other friend pleasing my baby better than I can. I played it cool and told him, maybe he could, in his dreams.!! I had to get going so we ended the call. On the ride to Stef's, I admit Jimmy may've been right. What the hell did I know about satisfying my girl.? I did my best and she breathed heavy a few times after we were done. She always gave me the obligatory kiss before heading to the bathroom. Tonight was gonna be different. When we were done, I wanted to see that confused look on her face like I performed pure magic on every inch of her body.

After entering the house, I slammed the door, picked her up by the waist, and pressed her hard up against the wall. I pinned her hands above her head and tore off her shirt . A word wasn't spoken, as the passion in our kiss was stronger than ever. She was gonna be treated like a rag doll tonight and I didn't care whether she liked it or not. Stef learned she had a submissive side, and it made her hotter with each dirty word I whispered in her ear. I looked into her eyes and began telling her what to do. I gave her shit that she wasn't doing it right and she better learn fast or her ass was gonna be really sore. Half the shit I said, I couldn't believe I was saying, but she savored every word. Later that night she told me I had the sexiest voice she ever heard.

We were going at it strong and she wanted to... "release" but couldn't . I wouldn't let her. I decided when that would happen, not her. Begging for an hour, each minute the sex got more intense. Finally giving in to her desperation, she screamed louder than I ever heard a woman yell. It sounded like she was in pain, but no, well yeah, she reached a state a painful pleasure. It felt so good it hurt. After we were done, I lay there knowing my mission was accomplished. Resting comfortably, Stef was confused in bliss. Her insatiable hunger tamed, she kept trying to speak, but couldn't think of any words. Sometimes there are no words. It looked like my baby was thinking "fuck talkin" and she climbed me like a cat to kiss me hard. The kiss made her get off again. She snuggled tight and finally spoke after a half hour. It didn't make sense, but she was talking, and I had no idea what she was tryin to tell me. I didn't care. No more worrying about Tony and Jimmy, I went on pure animal instinct, and it worked!!!!

CHAPTER FOURTEEN

Spring break came and went with the weather breaking. Snow melted and trees started to wake from a long winter's sleep. Flowers bloomed and the fresh morning sun set the tone for the day. As seniors, this was it. A few more weeks and we'd be graduating. Everybody promised they'd be friends forever. I hate to admit it but even the kids I didn't like made me take the time to appreciate and accept them. Talk about the prom made us all feel like this was gonna be the first of many "I'll never forget this night" feelings. I mean it's the prom. It's marriage for a night. In their prom dress, girls become women right in front of your eyes and guys feel like bad asses in their tuxes.

Jimmy wanted to find the best pot his money could buy. He laughed telling us Fanny was gonna wear a huge bud as her corsage. Me, Jimmy and Billy went shopping for our tuxes. Tony had no interest in going to that "bullshit high school" dance. I didn't have the guts to ask him, "Did ya ever think it may be important to Jenni?" I couldn't ask for someone nicer than Billy to be my make-believe brother-in-law. But it was botherin me. After what me and Steph did the other night, I wondered what exactly he had in mind for prom night with my sister. For girls, the prom is all about the dress. Guys? It's all about the sex. It's your fuckin senior prom. The guy's thinking, I can't wait till this dance is over so I can get laid by this hot chick.

Stef set me straight. She teased me saying guys actually think they get us so hot that we can't resist them. I gave her a "well, yeah" nod and she started laughing. "Guys are so stupid!!! . We decide if we're gonna have sex with them before the night even begins." I was completely lost. She went on, "Kenny, when we're deciding what underwear to put on, sex or no sex is already decided. Sexy under wear means sexy sex!! And another thing, if we're not gonna have sex, I'm not takin the time to shave my legs" She was right. Guys really are stupid.

Every prom has the blind date couple where the two can't stand each other. It's sad but funny. There's no way the guy's gonna ask her to dance and she looks at everybody but him. He excuses himself to get her some punch and both are happy to be alone, even if it's just for a minute. Girlfriends stop by and she begs them not to leave. She cries that she'll throw up if she takes one more whiff of his bad hygiene that failed to be hidden by the stench of his Hai Karate cologne. A sorority burst of laughter is quickly silenced by her date's return. Awkward silence is broken by one girl's cough caused by the aroma. He wasn't stupid as he spiked the punch knowing a few hours later, he'd be goin to town and his date's high heels would be poking holes in the convertible top of his dad's car. Jimmy cracked us up with his sick scenarios. He could come up with some pretty crazy shit.

I had to bring up the elephant in the room." So Billy, Jimmy wasn't bullshittin and don't even try and deny you wanna get laid on prom night. Ya know, that's my kid sister and I don't think she's ready for that. You fuck up and I'll cut ya tool bag off and feed it to you" Showing he was behind me,. Jimmy cracked up and threw in a delayed and stoned "yeah"

Billy took a deep breath and fired back. "Look, Kenny, there's something you don't know about your sister." Here I go worrying again. Billy went on, "She really looks up to you and Stef and she refuses to accept anything less from me. Terry always tells me you treat Stef like a princess and your sister dreams of me being her prince. All she wants is to know she's my princess. And Kenny, she is. !! Terry makes me a better guy and want to be even better for her. So, this prom is all about making her feel like the girl she always wanted to be and she wants to be a princess. I ain't gonna fuck that up by doin something she don't wanna do. It's my prom, but it's her night"

Billy wasn't bullshittin me. He spoke with a passion and conviction about my sister. Hell, she's lucky to have him. Terry better not fuck it up. I'll always worry. She's my kid sister and she's always gonna be a kid to me. Terry knows that and she's cool, but. I guess it's part of life, girls fuckin up a good thing. Why does they think it's easier to destroy it rather than accept the good? What is it about getting closer that makes them so scared? Self-esteem sucks and the fear of getting dumped sucks worse. Hopefully, she'll figure out she ain't never gonna do better than Billy.

With our tux trip complete, we headed to Vinnie's for a slice of pizza and more bullshittin. High School just started and was gonna be over in the blink of an eye. We shared some laughs about all our "remember whens" Tony thinking he broke his dick was the funniest moment of the past four years. I know we'll all be old and grey before we forget that one. I won second place for my stupidity in believing Fanny about the sex position. I can't believe I grabbed my ankles in a crowd. We got an Italian ice for the road and headed back home.

Walking in my house, mom let me know Stef called and it was important I call her as soon as possible. Girls get so nervous around prom. I figured she was gonna ask what color dress to wear so we looked like the perfect couple. I called and she asked if I could come over now.

"Now? I just got home from getting my tux and baby, I look really good. Stef, you ain't gonna be able to keep your hands off me."

"Kenny, please. I need ya now baby" Stef sounded desperate. Maybe she was gonna rock my world like I did hers. Man, that would be fuckin hot!!! I grabbed my keys and raced to her house.

She opened her door and gave me a long hug, Something was different. Was she freakin about me going to Rutgers again? I rubbed her back and told her everything was gonna be okay. She broke away and took a few steps back. Staring in my eyes forever, she kept trying to talk. A tear slowly dropped from her beautiful eyes. Those eyes have made me melt for years now. I can't help it. I love this girl.

"I'm pregnant" She never stopped staring and tears fell faster. Seconds seemed like hours. My life just changed at the drop of a tear. A million thoughts went through my mind. What was she thinking? What did I think? I just said I love this girl in my head. Do I? A second ago, we were high school sweethearts. Now, I don't know what we are. Yeah, I do. I'm an asshole. I was being so selfish. You're damn right I loved her. So, whatever she wanted, I was gonna support. It was her body, but our baby . Our silence ended with a hug. Through the years, we became so close, we didn't need words to communicate. She knew I wasn't goin anywhere. She broke away again.

"We gotta talk about this. We can't just love this away. I have to decide whether I'm gonna keep." I got pissed.

"Away? What does that mean?? Look Stef, Yeah, it's your body, but that's part of me inside you and any decision made needs to be okay with both of us. I know I can't stop you from.... You know, but baby, please, I'm begging you not to shut me out." Thank God she began to talk.

"Kenny, baby, you have school and everything in front of you. You don't need this."

I got more upset and spoke in a rage I didn't know was inside me. "Stef, how the fuck do you think you know what I need. You have no right to say that. And don't you ever,ever,call our baby "this". Until we figure it out that's our baby and we both have to realize that"

"Kenny, I am thinking of us. For us to have any future together, we must be smart. I mean, we're not ready to have a baby."

"Stef, do you think anyone ever is??? Who the hell knows when they're ready? Nobody. Life don't work that way. You deal with the cards dealt you. We make our future."

"Kenny , are you saying you want this baby?" This was easy. Stef was my world, and it was a great place to live. I knew not having the baby would haunt us forever. And, loving her, I believe we could overcome anything.

"Well baby, yeah. That's exactly what I'm saying. I mean we love each other, and our baby was conceived in love. So why not? I'll make this work. We'll make this work. Besides, I could never let you do that to your body. We'll be okay. I promise you and I'll never break a promise.

We hugged again, Stef sighed a lot and told me I was incredible. I gently kissed her lips and told her, "Hey we've had alotta practice. We didn't live at 717 Diamond Lane for nothing" Finally, we both smiled. I didn't know if things were gonna be alright, but, for tonight, they were, and that's all that mattered. We talked for hours. She needed time to think it through, but with her Catholic upbringing, she knew she couldn't destroy a life. We decided to keep quiet for a while. Stef asked if we could keep it outa school until after we graduated. "If we keep our baby, let's just live like high school sweethearts for now" I was thrilled, she didn't say keep "this" I called mom and told her I was spending the night. It was like the first night we ever spent together. I watched her breathe for hours and snuck in a few gentle tummy rubs. Life was inside her, our lives.

When the sun began to rise, my eyes began to set. I didn't sleep long and Stef stared into my awakening eyes. We talked some more about fears and futures. She was so scared. No matter what happened, this could ruin us. All three of us. Reality was startin to set in. Were we being fair to our kid? When they figured out we were teenagers, being a mistake could infect their soul. Suddenly, I had a new level of respect for my mom and dad.

All my life I judged them thinking me and Stef would be different. It's easy to judge until you spend time in their shoes. And these shoes I'd wear for all my life, our kid's life. It's a cycle. They were gonna grow up to judge me and Stef. We weren't perfect and our kid was gonna resent any weakness we showed. Mom and Dad were alright. Very few kids remember their mom and dad loving each other. They exist for us. We never see the love. It's not important to us. But the other night, mom and dad told the same story about how they met and they both smiled. Their love for each other was staring right at me and I didn't see it, feel it, until now. Loving is easy, it's life that's hard. My daydream ended as fast as it started and Stef was still staring as she welcomed me back. Stef knew I was thinking bout something. Pullin her close, I whispered in her ear how much I loved her.

"Come on, wake up. Let me make my man breakfast." Her cooking was getting better, but I wanted to IHOP it.

"Baby, you cook like you love, and both are real good, but lemme take ya to the house with the blue roof. Besides, let's walk out your door and face this new world together." A spank on her ass had me jumping up to relieve my morning wood. In the mirror, I watched her change into her IHOP attire. There's something really sexy about watching a girl get dressed. I coulda peed for hours watchin the mirror.

We walked in to see mom and dad at their usual booth in the back. Proper Stef made a point to lead us to them to exchange a few polite hellos. Dad said he'd love for us to join them, but they were finishing up. Teasing us, he said, "ya know we're not like you kids. We can't sleep half the day away." The waitress let us know our table was ready. So we said goodbye and sat down in our booth. Stef got O. J. and I had a big glass of chocolate milk. We ordered fruit for Stef and French toast for me. Looking up, dad was at the register payin his check while mom patiently stood three steps behind him. After they left, the waitress stopped by to let us know Dad picked up our check.

"Awww. That's so nice." My baby was a sucker for good will. We shared countless meals together but this one was different. Our world wasn't changing, yet, but it sure felt like it was. Living in the moment, Stef began talking bout the prom. She wanted to dance every song, slowly. "Promise me that night will never end Kenny and make love to me slowly at sunrise." Stef, sex and sunrise are my three favorites things I like to see everyday. This was an easy promise to keep. Breakfast was over and the day was just beginning.

I drove her home and we shared a goodnight kiss at noon. After dropping her off, my drive wasn't easy. I wasn't good at keeping secrets from my family or Tony and Jimmy. This was different. I had no right to go against Stef's wishes. I knew the longer we kept this quiet, the better we'd be at telling people. Perfect timing, I got home, and dad was watchin the Yankees. Talkin baseball with the ol' man saved me. There's nothing like the Yankees to clear your mind. Reggie was barely battin his weight and Dad was yelling about the overpaid bum. It's all about playin in New York. One day you own the city and the next day you're a bum. Reggie hit one out and Dad clapped yellin the "Reggie Chant".

CHAPTER FIFTEEN

Prom week arrived and the senior class was all fired up. Me and Stef were doing okay and still hadn't told anybody what happened. Oh yeah, we decided to keep our baby.. On Tuesday, we met for lunch. Nobody caught it , but her pregnancy glow looked more beautiful every day. Stef was so excited about the prom, she asked , " Baby, are we gonna have sex on Prom night?" I hesitated for a little bit and Stef wouldn't shut up. "Come on Kenny, I know it hasn't been that long , but you haven't touched me, since I told you I was pregnant."

She was right but, I had to ask. "Stef, are you sure it's okay? I mean I don't wanna hurt the baby."

Stef shook her head and laughed at me, " You're soooo stupid. Why do guys even think that's possible. Baby, go read a book and learn all about me down there cause you really don't have a clue. I mean, what did you expect me to say, "Kenny, you stud, you're way too big and I'm worried about what you'd do to the baby.. Ya know, you're not exactly a yardstick down there"

I had stupidity and defeat written all over me. She was my baby!!! "Awww Kenny, you know how I love the magic you perform with that wonderful wand of yours."

I hate when she lies to me!!!! My appetite was gone, and I headed to class. She wouldn't let me get away. "Baby, you forgetting something?" I went to kiss her. "No you idiot, you never answered. Are we gonna have sex or you gonna make me look for it with someone else?" I gave her a dejected cooperative answer, "Okay if I have to" She smiled and I melted but refused to let her see.

I gave jimmy a ride home after school. What a nut. He wasn't kidding about the bud corsage. Jimmy's corsage was huge, and the bud was tucked in at the bottom. No one would ever know and it wasn't leavin the prom hall anyway. We started to bullshit about Saturday night. He began, "you believe that shit about Tony not going? Ya ask me, he's a fuckin pussy or an asshole. Either way, it don't matter. "

"Yeah, it's bullshit. He'd have a kick ass time and all he's gonna do is sit home and play tug-a-war with his own junk."

Jimmy never failed to disappoint. "We should sneak out of the prom and peek in Tony's living room. I'd throw a rock through the window a second before he was gonna "win". I bet he'd shit in his pants.

He amazed me. "Jimmy where do you come up with this stuff.?"

"Smoke da weed mon and your brain will come alive"

Once home, I talked to Terry about Jenni and the prom. Jenni told her she was happier bein with Tony at his house than she would be goin to the prom alone. I asked her if Jenni was disappointed. She said Jenni denied it but thought it was written all over her heart. I'll never understand Jenni and Tony, but whatever they have, it seems to be enough for both of them.

Finally, Prom night was here, and it started with, Prom Evening. I took an extra-long shower to make sure all the dirty parts were clean. This was a high school kid's most memorable night, but my memory was filled with thoughts about Stef's pregnancy. I felt a little cheated that my kid days were being cut short. It was selfish. i felt a little ashamed, but it made me realize there's nothing perfect in this world except the love me and Stef share. She was my soul and we'll be "One" forever. Our pregnancy wasn't gonna ruin this night, it was gonna be the reason we celebrate it. I was determined to make it like the night my Stef dreamed about as a little girl.

Standing in front of the mirror, wearing Stef's favorite boxers, Dad came in and sat on the bed. He made some shallow excuse about being bored and mom was helping Terry get ready. His thoughts seemed to race and the look on his face screamed, it isn't fair. His kids weren't kids anymore. He looked like he was stumbling to say something fatherly to me. And a great conversation began.

"Dad, you don't have to"

"Don't have to what son?"

"I see my life passing through your mind and yeah, I'm grown up. You don't have to tell me to wear a condom or anything stupid like that. I mean, Dad, you did your job. I didn't understand everything you did but I'm proud to call you Dad. I learned everything by just watching you. Do you know I'll never forget that song "Thunder Road" cause of you?"

"Huh? Kenny, ya lost me. What are you talking about?"

"Dad, as a kid, I remember you and mom were fighting a lot. You came home from work and drank your beer while sittin in the dark. I didn't know if the hell you lived was at work or here, but you looked beaten. As the song played, you listened to every word. It definitely took you somewhere, and when you finally said the song's name, it was clear you were trying to tell me something. I began to understand when life sucked, you take it out on the one you love the most. I didn't like the way you treated mom and while listening to the song it seemed you realized you didn't like the way you were treating her either" The song reminded you how much you loved mom. I hope if me and Stef ever fight, I'll never forget the vision she is."

"Kid, I'm sorry you thought that, and I can't deny it was true. But that's what relationships are all about. If every day were easy, nobody would ever break up or get divorced. You and Stef just have to hold on during the rough times. And you'll find that's really hard. It's a lot easier to give up. If you think you're unhappy and lonely in your relationship, try giving up on it and being alone. Only then you'll realize what true unhappiness and loneliness are all about. Son, there's one thing I want you to never forget. When you have everything, you want, you better want everything you have. And if you and Stef are together as long as me and your mother, if she's half the vision I think your mother is, you'll have everything.

Dad hugged me and went downstairs to get a beer and I

finished getting dressed. Mom was leaving Terry's room as the gifts of a mother/daughter love were overwhelming. Once I heard her downstairs, I knocked on Terry's door. She let me come in and looked absolutely beautiful. This was my kid sister and she left me speechless. Her precious smile was sensitive and shy. Doing my best to act like a gentleman, I extended my arm and escorted her downstairs. Mom and Dad beamed with pride. Mom started to cry and Dad held her tight as he leaked a tear or two as well. Me and Terry played parents and comforted mom and dad. It only made the moment better.

Billy saved us and knocked on the door. Stunned by the beauty of his Princess, he gave her a dozen roses. Terry melted and lovingly gave Billy a kiss on the cheek. We took plenty of pictures and I finally made my way to Steph's house. Looking at her, I realized, I've never seen her look more beautiful than she was right now. Her dark hair fell softly on her dress which was made for royalty. I didn't need the prom. Her eyes gave me a million slow dances and kisses. Life with my baby was gonna be incredible. And Dad was wrong, Steph was and always will be twice the vision. She was perfect and will be forever. It looked like Mr. D. stopped trying to be strong an hour ago. I know Steph. I'm sure she told him, "you're Italian!!! You're supposed to cry when you see your daughter all grown up." We did a family hug and left for our "honeyprom"

Holding hands for the car ride, we talked about what Fanny and Jimmy were doing right now. Yeah, we knew they were having sex, but how many times and were they gonna do it there too. Tony and Jenni were the next topic, and I wasn't gonna let my anger for him ruin one second of tonight. We arrived at the hall and walking in, I knew I had the best-looking girl in the school on my arm. Steph whispered in my ear that everyone was staring at us with envious eyes. Then, as only she could say, "Don't do anything stupid like trip and fall" Whoa!!! I never knew my baby loved to be the center of attention. We did alotta loving, laughing and dancing. Jimmy and Fanny were blissfully stoned, and Billy kept true to his word. The prom was a fairytale to Terry, and she loved it.

As the band was getting ready to start their next song, the doors to the hall opened and the music began, Tom Petty's "Here comes My Girl" Tony and Jenni appeared holding hands and walked straight to the center of the dance floor. Everyone was stunned in silence. Stef, Terry and Fanny's eyes filled with tears that couldn't fall. My best friend did the right thing, and I knew this was a never forget moment. No one would dare join them on the dance floor. It was theirs. Facing each other, their eyes were locked in perfect passion. They couldn't hear the song. What they felt for each other was screaming love.

Tony stared at her soft blonde hair and loving eyes, as he pulled her close, he remembered the first day they met. With a kid's smile, he said, "Hi my name is Tony"

She squeezed his hand, blinked her eyes, and answered him. Hi Tony. I'm Jenni and I'd love it if you kissed me right now" They shared a huge make out and when they finally broke away from each other, the entire prom gave them a standing ovation. I never saw Jenni look this happy. Tony was a different person. Happiness was new to him, and he loved it. He had some more words for Jenni.

"From this moment on, I'd like you to be my girlfriend and to-night, let's have the night both of us have wanted for so long" Jenni softly kissed his lips and told him, "I'd like that"

How fast things change!!!! Once their dance was done, Jenni led Tony to all of us. In the shyest unsure voice, Jenni greeted us. "Hi everybody. I'd like to introduce you to my boyfriend" The girls had their say. "he's very cute." And Stef had to be Stef, "yeah and he's got a great ass too!!!" They were so tight. Jenni could tell Tony was getting embarrassed and kissed his hand which she never let go. They wore each other well.

Terry had to speak up. "You bitch!!! You're my best friend. How did you ever keep this a secret from me."

"I didn't. Tony came to my house yesterday and asked my dad permission to take me to the prom"

"Wait. What? Are you trying to tell me Tony asked your dad? No fuckin way!!!! And Tony, you're an asshole. You let me give you shit, and you never said a word."

Tony was cool. "It's not like I didn't hear ya. But look at her. I ain't stupid. She's fuckin hot. There was no way I was gonna let her get away. Watch! "Hey Jenni. C'mere. She was mesmerized by his charismatic magical voice. Two kisses and his arm fell below her soft exposed shoulder. Jenni just moved and her new address was in Tony's arms. Home is where the heart is. The rest of the night was spent dancing and loving. I think Jimmy and Fanny broke their sex record. I would sneak in a few rubs of my baby's baby belly. The party moved to Harry's and the guys bonded with beers and shots. Once lit, we belted out a drunken version of "I gotta be me" All the customers joined us in the chorus. Bunny and the girls loved it!!!

After the standing ovation, we made it to our girlfriend's arms and Jenni was hypnotized by the private passion seeping from Tony's eyes. She returned the stare. Tonight was their special night and the end of it couldn't happen fast enough. Slowly taking her hand, he pressed his body to hers in a way that melted their souls together. You could tell by the way the made out. Their breathing was silent and breathless. They didn't need to breathe. They breathed each other. I looked at Steph starin at them like she was watchin passion porn.

Bunny yelled last call, and everybody hugged each other and reminded us this was a night we'd never forget. Billy promised me he'd be good to Terry. He didn't have to tell me something I already knew. Jenni and Terry hugged like sisters. Jimmy and Fanny shared a cigarette as their sex prom gave them a feeling of exhaustion and complete satisfaction. Too tired to stop, they waved goodnight. Tony hugged me, shook my hand forever while he said just one word, "Thanks"

I just nodded. That's what friends do.

Fester sat in his seat at the end of the bar and Bunny let us stay after closing. It was cool. Me and Steph didn't want this night to end. As Bunny was clearing glasses from the bar, she asked, "So you two, how long Stef been pregnant?" We were shocked, fumbling for words. Did we deny it? Bunny kept the pressure on, "Come on Stef. You've been coming here for a year and every time you get two beers and never finish the second. Tonight, your prom, everyone is partying, and you order water, barely take two sips and you're in the bathroom peeing every ten minutes. You think I'm stupid?"

Me and Stef looked at each other and knew we were busted. I guess if anyone were gonna figure it out, we should be happy it was Fester and Bunny. They don't judge. It made me escape for a minute. Who the fuck judges and what gives them the right? I know I was wrong to judge my mom and dad. I'll never judge again. Anyway, I fessed up and we talked till sunrise about everything. Fester was so cool. He told us to, " Be cool to each other and fuck everybody that gives you shit. They ain't your friends. And whatever you need from me and Bunny, you got it. I mean that, anything!! But, I gotta tell ya, the longer you keep this from your parents, the more pissed they'll be. You're gonna need them. And don't worry, they'll come around. Remember, parents never stop lovin you. And if they give you a problem, I'll talk to your dads" Stef went over and hugged Fester. I followed by going to Bunny. Remembering the first time I met her, everybody teased me about starin at her rack, I still get all red in the face. It cracked her up. . .

They were right. We were gonna have to tell our parents before we planned.

Their Night

Tony unlocked his door, picked up Jenni and carried her right to his bedroom. They had all night, and he was gonna savor every minute. So was she. Letting her fall softly on the bed, he climbed beside her and gently stroked her face for an hour. Tracing her lips slowly while loving her eyes, she looked scared and full of anticipation. It was too much for Jenni as a few tears filled her eyes. Tony pulled her close and cleaned the tears. They didn't last long. Jenni cried because of her incredible love for Tony. She didn't waste her time telling him she loved him. She showed him every day knowing she may never feel the love returned. And tonight, she was gonna feel every ounce of love within him.

He took his shirt off to reveal the body she never forgot. Feeling his smooth skin and muscles everywhere, Jenni was filled with infatuation. She loved his shoulders the most and carefully stroked them. They were incredibly strong and Jenni felt safe surrounded by his strength. I guess feeling safe can be pretty hot. Jenni was losing hold of her heart. Tony was in control and slowly unbuttoned her shirt. Once removed, he gained a new appreciation for art. She was as sexy as she was beautiful. They took turns removing the rest of their clothes and it almost seemed unfair how natural they were together. The strength of his hands moved all over her body like a wave comes to shore. Gentle, yet forceful, he knew exactly where he was going.

Jenni returned the favor moving her hands in a way that sent shivers down his spine. Tony couldn't take it and kissed her hard. Their passion was out of control and he pushed his way through her heart and soul. She wasn't ready for the power of his penetration and dug her nails deep into his back and screamed in passion. Each movement made her keep "the feeling. " They rolled all over the bed and even fell off which joined them closer. Both were too turned on to even think about what was happening. When neither of them could take it anymore, they came as one. Their "four play" never stopped as they made out until the feeling hit them again. ..and again.. and again.

They knew this was the beginning of something real. The whole night changed them forever. Sexual satisfaction rocked her to sleep on Tony's chest. Feeling this good to Tony was new and weird,.he promised himself to learn to accept it. In the fall, he was gonna go through a lot more changes than tonight and he needed Jenni in his life. Having her, drove him to wanna kick ass at Penn State so Jenni would be proud of him. His Dad died a few months ago and it still hurt that his dad never made him believe he was proud of his son.

Day one of the Jenni and Tony family began with him bringing her gourmet coffee in bed. Girls love their coffee. It's like foreplay to start the day. Tony sat on the side of the bed and watched her savor the morning flavor. He kissed her cheek and told her come to the kitchen when she's ready. She found his t-shirt and made her way downstairs. The table settings were covered fresh flowers and fruit. Jenni was stunned he did this. Well, she returned the favor and attacked him right there on the kitchen table. For these two, sex was for breakfast. Lunch wasn't bad either. And Dinner only made them hungry for breakfast again. Tony and Jenni found time for a midnight snack. Prom weekend worked magic. Before Jenni would call home, Tony turned up the TV so it sounded like they were just hangin out. Her parents were cool. They knew what prom weekend was all about and respected Tony. He was the only senior who asked his date's parents permission to take their daughter to the prom. Her dad knew he never would've done that if he didn't have deep feelings for his daughter.

Sunday afternoon came and it was time for Jenni to leave. As they sat on his couch, she got quiet and started to cry. Jenni's tears were kryptonite to Tony, and he pulled her close. "Jenni, please don't cry. Look, this is our beginning. This weekend, I realized three things, I needed you in my life, I need you in my life, and I'll always need you in my life. "

"Tony, baby, ever want something so bad when you finally get it, you think it can't be real? I know we're real and I wanna be everything you need. Being your girlfriend is something I've dreamed about. And I'll tell you right now. I'm really territorial so if some girl tries to hit on you at Penn State, you think you're tough? You ain't seen nothing till you see how tough I can be. I will kick her ass in a heartbeat."

Tony smiled, "Baby, you're really sexy when you're mad!!!" Her protective nature lit his passion, and they went at it one more time before she really had to go. They quickly showered together and hoped to erase their sex smell. He drove her home and walked her to the door. Billy, Terry and her parents were hangin out in the living room. Jenni's mom insisted Tony stay for dinner.

It seemed a little awkward, but they played the role of innocent couple perfectly.

CHAPTER SIXTEEN

After the prom, Graduation came, and we bonded one last time at Verona High. There'd be other times, but you only graduate high school once and we made sure the day would never be forgotten. Our parents let us have our day, our moments. They beamed with pride. I don't know if it was cause of the diploma or the friendship family of which we were all a part. There's a memory I'll never forget. Stef was in the middle and joined by Jimmy and Tony. They walked arm in arm to Jimmy's mom, then Stef's dad, and finally to Coach Bischotti. The moment was a remembrance of the lost ones and the parents who raised the three of them. I knew Tony thought of his coach like a dad. From Bischotti, he learned about life and the way it was supposed to be. Danny Pintauro showed up late to thank Tony for making him love the violence of the game. He promised Tony he'd never let the game be tougher than he was.

Me and Stef were hanging out with our parents when I asked mom, "When are you gonna make one of your famous holiday dinners? You know like the last one, when we talked about sex, drugs, and rock n roll. ? Mom told us anytime that was good for the Demarinos , was good for her. Stef chimed in, "Okay we'll be there next Friday. Won't we Dad?" Her dad agreed. Stef knew we had alotta thinking to do. I had a bad feeling about this. Steph gave me a "two kiss" kiss and told me I worry too much. Easy for her to say. Did she forget we were 18, not married, and pregnant? Oh yeah. And I was going to Rutgers in the fall. It's all about timing and this wasn't a good time.

Terry's a great sister and made sure she had a date with Billy for Friday night. I thought "yeah Billy's my age, but if he got Terry pregnant, I'd kill him myself." So what's different about me doing the same thing? I couldn't answer. I mean I love Steph and our baby with all my heart. But how am I gonna convince our parents we're different? Dinner was gonna be a disaster.

Mom set the table with her favorite linen table cloth. The rich Italian red contrasted nicely with bright white plates and green candles. Mom loved the colors! Our finest silverware and crystal champagne glasses finished the picture-perfect table. I guess we'll be celebratin something, but after I drop the bomb, we'll see how fast the bubbly flows.

We sat down as soon as mom started serving the salad. Dad and Mr. Demarino had fresh Budweisers. And Monica poured a glass of wine for mom and herself. Me and Steph weren't exactly thirsty. Dad started the table conversation talking about everybody's plans for the summer. He wanted to see alotta Yankee Games. Mr. Demarino rented a house and a boat for a few weeks on Lake George. He encouraged all of us to come up for a few days. Me and Steph mentioned our boring summer plans workin another season at Seaside Heights.

Mom cleared the salad plates and yelled for Dad to help her in the kitchen. He hated getting his lazy ass outa the chair during sit-downs. Mom rocked!! She made her homemade stuffed shells and gravy. Dad brought out a bottle of Korbel. He loved showing off as he bet Mr. D he could pop the cork and hit the front door. He came up short by a foot. Showing he had manners; he filled the ladies' glasses first. I peeked at Stef. She was gonna fake a sip. With our glasses full, Dad sat down and raised his to make a toast.

"Stephanie and Kenny, the four of us are so proud of you. High School's four years bring more changes than anytimes in your life. You started out as kids and graduated as men and women. With all of the changes and your experiences, you stayed together, and we can see you grow closer every day. How many of your friends can say they stayed with the same person through high school? So we raise our glasses to the people you are and the couple you've become. Salute!!"

This went far enough. I had to tell them, and Steph nodded in agreement. The sooner we knew their reaction, the better off we were all gonna be. Here goes nothing.

"Dad, thank you so much for you toast and Mom, Mr. Demarino, and Monica, we appreciate the acceptance and support. I hope we can always count on you for the guidance we need. Stephanie and I have something to share with you. Please know we've spent countless hours talking about what I'm about to say."

I took a deep breath and began, "Stephanie is pregnant, and our baby is due in late January."

Dad stopped me as fast as I started. His face became blood red, as he became more enraged. He rose from his chair and stared me down as he threw his champagne glass crashing on the wall, followed by mom's and then mine. Glass flew everywhere. He went off!!!,

"You let me say those words and make me look like an ass! Kid, I fuckin trusted you and you spit in my face. Your mother and I gave you all the freedom you wanted cause we believed you loved Stephanie. Be a man, son. Look Mr. Demarino in the eye and tell me what you see. And don't even try and tell me you love Stephanie, cause if you did, you never would've let this happen. You didn't protect the one you love."

I heard enough. It was my turn to go off. I stood up and got right in his face. Nobody was ever gonna question my love for Steph. "You talk about love?? Are you kiddin me?? You don't even know how to spell the word. Ok, so yeah, I got Stephanie pregnant. You did the same fuckin thing to mom. And I'll tell ya this. We'll never raise our kid the way you did. As a little kid, do you have any idea how many nights I didn't sleep, because I heard you yellin at mom and her crying? Terry was so scared; she'd come into my room whimpering. You didn't have to hold her tight till she fell asleep. I DID!! Yeah, you wanna tell me what love is all about. Do you know I had to tell Stephanie you and mom didn't love each other when I was thirteen? You made me feel so ashamed. So, I'll tell you and everybody else here, I will love her and be in love with her forever.

Don't fuckin doubt me. I'll never put our kid through the hell you put me,"

The table was silent. We were all digesting the news and the ugly fight. But Dad didn't have to question my love or devotion to the only woman I will ever love. I hated to admit it, but no parent would've trusted us like the three of them. They had to understand everything was gonna be okay. Dad had his back to all of us and just blankly stared out the window. He was my dad, and we both said some fucked up shit. But I hit him twice, first with the news and then with the blame. Ya don't talk to your dad like that. I was wrong. I walked up to him and put my hand on his shoulder.

"Dad, I'm so sorry for talking to you like I did. I love you Dad, and the truth is I'm proud of you and mom. Neither of you ever claimed you had the best marriage, but I do know your love for each other is real. I never told you, but I feel lucky to be your son. You may not be proud of me now, but I promise, you will be. Dad, do you remember when you won the pool at Harry's? I'll never forget it cause, without saying it, you let me know you trusted me to always do the right thing Dad, please turn around, I can't take you not looking at me"

He slowly turned to show a few tears falling. Dad never cried. He hugged me hard and apologized too. I may've felt ashamed as a kid, but he felt ashamed of being a dad. I begged him to realize how good he was to his family. Tension eased as Dad told me to go to Mr. D and convince him everything was gonna be okay. Four steps seemed like four miles. Before I said a word, he stopped me to say, "Look Kenny, I didn't like seeing what I just saw between you and your dad. But you did show me the passion of your love for my daughter. You've made her very happy, and I owe you for everything you've done for her. So now, I guess, as parents, we want you to know we'll all be here for you two."

Mom called Dad back to the table and also had a few words to say. "Well, no one can ever say, the Mancuso's dinners are ever boring. Stephanie, honey, as my future daughter-in-law, I am your worst nightmare. Soon, you will have a mother-in-law!!!!. As I prepare for that role, you will have no say in my next few words. Monica, I could sure use your help in planning a fast wedding." Monica had a big smile, "of course, how bout we make the date two weeks from tomorrow.?"

Mom chimed right back, "Sounds good to me. Stephanie and Kenny make sure you take off that Saturday. Tell your bosses you have to go to a wedding"

Steph finally spoke, all the fighting and lovin made it hard for her to speak without losing it. I mean, all this worry was about her. "Thank you,.Thank you all so very much." She reached over to give me a long hug. .Our parents witnessed the pure love we had for each other. Dinner ended just before midnight and there was alotta huggin at the door. In time, everything was gonna be okay. .

Two weeks flew by like two days and all the couples came over after the rehearsal. While Father O'Brien kept his feelings to himself about the reason we were getting married, he agreed to perform the wedding and he told us me and Stef had the love in our hearts to last a lifetime of lifetimes. After dinner, friends and family shared a few stories about us. Jimmy's was the best as he tactfully told the story about when I called him for "love advice." When the toasts were over, I asked Stef to go on a walk outside to see 717 Diamond Lane.

We were both a little nervous and looked to our home in the stars for comfort. It worked. There's nothing more serene than the night sky full of twinkling diamonds. After a few breaths, I told Stef I wanted to give her something that I learned from her dad. It was a letter.

My Beautiful Baby, Stephanie,

I don't even know how to express what we share, Passion with you is soo easy. I could try to explain for hours what's going on in my heart and never begin to come even close. I just know you feel exactly the same way. With you in my life, I'm able to see what it means to truly love. Without you, I'd be walking around like a blind man. I never know what tomorrow brings, but I know it brings me you. I may love today but can't wait for tomorrow.

You've made my life. I'll be in love with you forever,

Kenny

Stephanie held her hand to her heart and was shaken by my words. Filled with emotion, she tried to speak and failed. She fell into my arms, and I held her tight until she got herself together for a long romantic kiss. Our next big makeout would be as husband and wife. Stef looked in my eyes and told me she picked out our wedding song. She said it was perfect and I'd find out the name when we danced for the first time as husband and wife.

On June 18th, I married her, and Stef looked beautiful. Tony was my best man and Terry was her maid of honor. Tony loved having my kid sister on his arm. As her dad and Stef walked toward me, Mr. Demarino wore his emotions about their Daddy Daughter talk. I'm sure it was the moment he's been waiting for all his life. Stef would later share the highlight of his day. He told Stef she was as beautiful as her mother on their wedding day and right now she's crying pride in heaven.

Father O'Brien gave us a traditional service. His sermon told the story of two kids who grew up and fell in love. He stressed the importance of treasuring this honeymoon love and committing to never letting it fade. The ring ceremony activated my anxiety and the only thing that saved me was looking into her eyes. While I sounded like an awkward idiot reciting my vows, Stef was a natural woman. Father pronounced us man and wife and our first married kiss was just like the first one outside the elementary school.. We'd never forget either one.

We held the reception in our backyard. Mom and Monica did an amazing job. It was just friends and family. Bunny and Fester were there cause they were both. Our first dance, wow, Stef had a sappy side, but I have to say she picked the perfect song. It was sung by Tony Bennett and Stevie Wonder, "For once in my life" Verona was a town where we were bound by the struggles, we all endured. And to overcome anything, you had to have someone to love and need.

We invited all the couples out to join us. Mom and Dad were beautiful together. God knows they've been through a lot. Tony and Jenni were great. She still had that tender starry-eyed stare and Tony had his shy reluctant smile. And for once in their lives, Jimmy and Fanny shared a moment of love not lust. Terry and Billy will always have a special kind of puppy love. Bunny and Fester loved watching and "emotioned up" as she reached for his hand to hold tight.

It was a great day. Tony gave the toast. Other than football, this was the first time he ever spoke to a crowd. "Stephanie and Kenny, you're commitment to each other has had an effect on everyone here. I don't know whether to admire or be jealous of what you have. Look what you've done for your closest friends. Jimmy is with Fanny and I'm with Jenni because of you. We strive to have what you have. Everyone here does. So, may you share the incredible love between you forever. Salut!"

As the night slowly came to an end, Fester had to give me shit about our wedding night. He told me to try all new stuff since she couldn't say no!! There's a shocker!! I asked him, "if the girl can't say no on the wedding night, why haven't you married Bunny?"

Immediately, he puts me in my place. "Cause Bunny ain't said no yet. Why ruin it by getting married? Ya think I'm stupid???" I was smiling as he made me shake my head. Leave it to Fester to fuck with me now. I mean all I ever saw or heard was married sex wasn't all it's cracked up to be. Fuck that!! Me and Stef will never allow that to happen.

Once everybody cleared out, we spent a few minutes talking to our parents. How do you thank anybody for unconditional love? We tried but all they could say was, "you can thank us by unconditionally loving each other forever. " Stef held my hand and told them we'll do that. As we exchanged hugs, I hugged Monica first. She was pretty cool and smart too!!. When we first met, Mr. Demarino didn't care for her that much and she accepted the reality. But, without him realizing, he became more dependent on her. You always depend on the one you love. Who knows what their future holds, but I think they're gonna be happily stuck with each other for a long time.

I looked in mom's eyes and hugged her tight. Telling her how much I loved her, made her cry. She taught me well. When a woman cries, you hold her till she stops. She finally did and I made my way to Dad. Believing marriage made me a man, I gave him a strong handshake. He wasn't big on man hugs, but he couldn't help himself. He pulled me in and gave me a few pats on the back. With a funny smile, he said, "Good Luck tonight son"

We spent our honeymoon night at the shore. Walking along the beach, we talked about yesterday, today and tomorrow. Marriage can be pretty scary. We laughed about how easy it was to love each other, but in marriage, you *have* to love each other!!! It seemed to take some of the fun out of it. Stef promised me she'd never let the "M" word get in the way of the "L" word. "L" came before "M.!!" I reminded her of the were three "L"s . If we liked, loved and lusted, marriage was gonna be easy This wasn't gonna be one of those "easier said than done" things.

I'd like to say our wedding night was a dream come true, it wasn't. But, God, it was nice. We snuggled on the beach, made out for hours and only took breaks to stare at the stars and listen to the waves crash. Seaside Heights was heaven on earth. The sky was getting lighter, and desire was getting stronger. We finished making love in time to welcome the rising sun. Sex with Mrs. Mancuso was amazing and it always will be.

CHAPTER SEVENTEEN

Summer was racing by and the high school friends forever bullshit was already starting to show. Stef was growing bigger every day. Tony was working out hard to get ready for football. Jimmy started searching for an apartment in Newark. Terry was worried about losing Billy to NYU. Jenni dedicated her life to being there for Tony. The girls had it much harder than the guys. None of us had to change their lives for them. They had no say in what we were doing. Our dreams became theirs and all they could do is make the best of the situation. Yeah, Dad worked, but I had no idea how hard mom had it, having to keep her mouth shut.

Registering for classes encompassed me and I would come home telling Stef about all my courses. College already was making me stupid. I never even asked Stef how she was feeling or if there was anything I could do for her. Responsibility sucks. It can make you selfish.

Tony left for football camp in late July. Jenni seemed lost without him. Hours on the phone turned to minutes as he became more focused on football. She worried she was becoming a football widow before the season began. Girls worry way too much. Tony called and invited her to spend the weekend with him. It was gonna be one of those walk n talk weekends. He gave her the tour, introduced him to his friends and they had dinner at Coach Paterno's house. Mrs. Paterno had done thousands of these dinners and treated Jenni like a daughter. Jenni's mind and heart were racing. It'd been a few weeks, but Tony grew up so much and that perfect body, became even more perfect. She couldn't wait to be wrapped up in his arms. Dinner ended around ten and Tony asked if it was okay to show Jenni the stadium. Coach Paterno loved the idea and welcomed Jenni into the Penn State family. Jenni showed her sincere appreciation to the Paterno's for making her feel accepted.

The stadium was only a few blocks away and Tony introduced Jenni to his new world. She was in awe of the vastness of the stadium. Back home a thousand people may come to a game. and she could look into Tony's eyes as he came off the field.

"Tony, how many people come to a game here?"

"I don't know. Maybe a hundred thousand"

"Oh my God Tony!! That's ten times the size of Verona"

"So what. That doesn't mean anything"

"You're trying to tell me that doesn't make you nervous?"

"Fuck yeah, I'm nervous. I'm not starting so that makes it easier. I don't know maybe it makes it harder."

"Honey, I know you. Something's wrong. Talk to me."

"Jenni, I've missed you so much and didn't realize it till just now. I don't know if I'm happy out here. I feel lost. Playing football was a way for me to get out my anger. But Dad's gone and I don't have any anger left. I feel like I'm faking it out there and I don't wanna let Coach down. He's been so good to me in such a short time. I know I'm a lot tougher than my teammates, but they want it more than me"

"Tony, I love you. Please don't do this to yourself. You're not gonna fail cause I won't let you. You think it was your anger that made you good. It wasn't. Yes, you were angry, but it was the passion of your anger that drove you. And Tony, when you make love to me, the passion of your love is far stronger than the passion of your hate. Trust me, I know. So, this game you play is all about passion and you have to find it within your heart to play like you can. I don't care if you do this for me, your friends, Coach Pacelli, or yourself, just do it and be great at it.

"Jenni, you don't know what you're talkin bout. There are fifty guys here with stories worse than mine. Every one of them is stronger, faster, and meaner than me. Big fuckin deal, I was the toughest guy in Verona. You said it yourself. Only ten thousand people live there"

"Tony, it's okay to be scared and feel like you can't do this., I know in my heart you can. If I honestly didn't believe that I'd tell you it's okay and we'll get through it together. But Tony, baby, you told me your biggest fear in life was disappointment. If you quit now, no one will be more disappointed than you and it will eat at you. You just have to, what'd your coach say?; oh yeah, Rise above the tide!!"

Tony realized she was right and remembered how lucky he was to have Jenni by his side. He wore the shy seductive smile that drove her crazy. "Something's rising right now baby"

"That's one thing that will never disappoint me. So, come on, give me the best you got. I want it, I need it. I gotta have it! "And they went at it right there. It was the first of many scores he'd have in his stadium, but none would be as memorable or as important as tonight. Tony was learning to love the after sex talks he had with Jenni. He couldn't wait any longer to let her in on his surprise.

"Baby, I almost forgot. In two weeks, we're playing back home in Giants Stadium. We're playing in this new game called the kickoff classic. Some big ass farm boys from Nebraska wanna kick our ass. I won't play much, but that's okay. If I get a chance, I'm gonna knock the cow shit outa somebody""

Jenni couldn't believe his first college game was gonna be a few miles from Verona. Everybody would come to cheer him on. She couldn't help herself though. She had to ask, "Tony if this is the first one, how can it be a classic???"

"Baby, you'll never stop askin me questions. And think about it, the first time we fooled around was definitely a classic. I see you smiling, you're thinkin bout it right now, aren't ya Jenni?" She gave him a reluctant smile and they shared a kiss. ·

Two weeks passed, As we were getting closer to Stef's delivery date, time was racin. Tony's game was a distraction from the fear of being newborn's parents. Everybody was there. We sat in the upper deck. Ya think being his best friend, he'd hook us up, but nooooo. He gave his two 50 yd line seats to Jenni's parents. Tony played a little bit in the fourth quarter and got a rude introduction to big time college football. Nebraska had the big farm boys, but they also had guys faster than lightning. Nebraska's best players, Turner Gill and Mike Rozier, made Tony look real bad, but the whole team looked bad too. It was Coach Paterno's worst loss in eighteen years of coaching.

After the game, we went to Harry's. Bunny had a tent put up behind the bar and we had about 20 people there. Tony appreciated the support. Danny Pintauro showed up and he and Tony shared a big man hug. "Tony, we're gonna play together again. When I graduate Verona, I wanna go to State." Danny owed everything to Tony. He was the high school star now and was nailin all sorts of women. Being the best has its benefits. Jenni was incredible. She really knew how to love Tony and he knew it.

He was different though. Maybe, the month away made him grow up a little bit. Living in a small town in Pennsylvania changed him. I could tell he was happy to be home, we seemed to grow apart a little. I was always his closest friend, but in the month, he was away, we didn't call each other. He called Jenni. If he was closer to her than he was to me, I was happy for him. Me and Jimmy didn't know what changes college would bring. We hadn't gone yet. In another week, I'd be starting college and my life would suck. Between making a pregnant wife happy and my teachers happy, I was miserable, but I'd never let Stef know. And that was my problem, hiding how I felt, was lying to her. The reason I'd lie would make her feel bad but lying about it could make her pissed too.

Jimmy had it pretty good with Fanny. Maybe they were better at this love thing than us. All they did was get high and have sex. Sure, they did other stuff, but they kept it simple and taught me it's simple to be happy. Why make everything so complicated. Just do a few things together really good so it connects you. I was really worried all our bullshit would make us lose our connection. We needed to go out on a date. Something we'd never forget. New York City was callin me and Stef.

I told Stef we were going to the city Friday night before school started. She was cute. "ummm just because I'm your wife doesn't mean you can tell me where you're takin me. Baby, you must ask me out, and you'll ALWAYS have to!!

God, I love her. She is amazing how she keeps me wanting her more every day. Fuck the bullshit. We'll deal. But Friday night, I'm takin my baby out and we're gonna make out till sunrise..

We hit the south side of the city and had dinner outside at this small Italian restaurant. The sunshine was setting, and she looked beautiful. Her eyes will forever paralyze my heart. The city noise couldn't distract me from the song of her voice. She didn't like me staring, but I couldn't help it. A woman will never be comfortable in her beauty. Telling her how good she looked just made her shyer. She is the perfect date.

We shared a sensual piece of cheesecake. Slowly feeding each other was just foreplay to makin out. We didn't have to talk to each other. I'd cup her hand as she fed me. The last bite, she smeared all over my face and then slowly licked my lips clean before kissin me like only my woman can. I finally broke away, paid the check, and took her for a walk in Central Park. We found a spot by this beautiful fountain. Stef loved people watchin and NYC has lots of people.

All this lovin made Stef realize she was gonna miss me in a few days. She cried a little. "Kenny, I can't do this. You've been with me every day since first grade. Maybe we weren't together, but you were always there. And in a few days, my world is gonna be rocked. I've known that if I ever needed you, you'd be right there in a few minutes. It made me feel safe. Suddenly, I don't feel safe anymore and I'm scared."

"Baby, I'm gonna be an hour away and I'll be home every week. I'm doing this for us"

"Honey, you don't understand. I'm alone again. I hate that"

I got pissed, "Look Stef. I'm just leavin here I'm not leavin you. Do you fuckin hear me? I'm not leavin you. I'll be in your heart, your soul, your mind. We're "One" and that will never change!!! Ever. You're the most important thing in my life. I told you.. you are my life!! You need me for anything, I'm dropping everything. That's just who we are"

I took her hand, and she wondered where I was takin her. Stef thought I was crazy. We were goin in the fountain! As the water rained down on us, we made out for a long time, a real long time. We didn't know it but a crowd of couples watched our love. There were old couples, new ones and everything in between. After a standing ovation, a few joined us in the fountain. I guess love really can be contagious.

Tony was already back at school. Me, and Jimmy left on Saturday. Billy stayed home to learn his dad's business. Jimmy was convinced there was money in computers. I thought he was nuts and only big companies could afford them. Jimmy told me I was wrong and by the time we graduated, there would be computers for use in the home. He heard some guy on the west coast was tryin all sorts of weird shit, but he was makin something cause IBM paid him to keep working. The only thing I was going to college for was four years. I'd have a family to support in a few months and I had no idea what I wanted to do. I had to get my shit together real quick.

Vietnam ended less than ten years ago, but the guys going away to school and the girls staying home seemed similar. They were on their own and they all looked out for each other. Between workin at the mall, and checkin on Jimmy's mom and Stef, Fanny stayed pretty busy. Jenni and Terry hung out at school and the boys knew they were off limits. Every week the four of them would hang out together. Freshman year, I picked my classes based on schedule. I wanted early classes on Tuesday and Thursday. Late classes worked best Monday and Wednesday. I went home Tuesday afternoons and spent the night. Weekends were a little longer with late classes on Monday. I thought Stef would appreciate my schedule, but she had her own routine and told me I was in the way. I knew she was kidding when she'd tell me to go back to school, but there was a little truth there too.

Jimmy would come home once a month and he and Fanny would have a weekend sexathon. Weren't they ever gonna get tired of constant sex? They reminded me of Bunny and Fester. Both couples had been goin at it for years. I always thought Fanny was pretty simple and maybe she was, she decided a long time ago she was gonna be great at pleasing her man. She never had to decide anything or want anything either. All she wanted was to be with Jimmy. How many people can say they have everything they want. Billy, Terry, and Jenni would drive to Tony's football games every weekend. A year ago, we were all together and now we were worlds apart.

Jenni was getting bigger every day. Thanksgiving was tough on her. There's way too much traveling during the holidays. She'd be tired, uncomfortable and moody. I knew she was tryin to love me, but there were days it was too hard. I understood, but I missed her. Yeah, we'd steal a nice kiss occasionally, but sex stopped a month ago. Even lying in bed together wasn't what it was. She was just too tired. I didn't care. I'd caress her face and get lost in the silkiness of her hair. I even would watch her breathe like I did years ago. I felt selfish. I wanted my Stef back, but I knew it was impossible, for now.

December was packed with school papers to finish. I found a part time job on campus.

Mom and Dad were buggin me about Christmas. Stef had her baby shower, it was awesome. We got everything we needed but couldn't afford. She was the happiest I've seen her in months. I took the time to savor the beauty of her pregnancy glow. So what, we weren't high school sweethearts anymore. She grew up a lot in nine months and now it was my turn. In another month, I was gonna be a dad.

Winter break was here, and we all met at Harry's It was great to see my friends again. Bunny almost cried seeing Stef. She walked a fine line between mother and big sister to my Baby. Stef didn't care, she needed both. Fester won't change. He had his seat at the end of the bar with a beer and a cigarette. We went to him, and he had a subtle smile like he was too cool to show he was happy seein us. Ten minutes hadn't gone by and Jimmy and Fanny already disappeared to find their "place" Tony, Billy Terry and Jenni hung out together in the corner. Billy was still respectful with Terry around me. And

Jenni had a new confidence. She'd climb Tony like a cat. Tony was all about kitty contact. He always had a hand on her ass. We had so many great memories at Harry's. I still can't believe Fanny made me grab my ankles here. Tony and Jenni's first kiss, My dad winnin the sex bet at my expense. Fester teachin me about dumpster sex. Stef was done talking to Bunny. She came back and kissed me like the early days at the shore. With a beautiful smile and Christmas lights twinkling in her eyes, she told me, "Baby, Merry Christmas" She's the best gift I ever got.

We spent New Year's Eve at home. Stef was too tired, and we were asleep long before midnight. Danny Pintauro. had a big party and everybody went. Jimmy and Fanny did it again!! They fooled around right on Danny's bed while the kid was tryin to find some early love in the night. Danny was the star now. It didn't take him long. Jenni never left Tony's side and they also fooled around in Danny's house. Tony went big and snuck Jenni into Danny's parents bedroom. High School and college kids didn't hang out together, but we didn't give a shit. What? Were we supposed to be better cause we were in college? It don't work that way in Verona.

January was cold and snow fell every day. Splittin time between school and home wasn't easy. Sometimes the hour ride would be three. It gave me time to think about my two babies Time wasn't stopping and by the end of the month, We'd be parents. I remember it was January 26th and I was getting ready to back to school. Stef was sittin up in bed watchin me pack. " Kenny, please don't go. I'm scared." Her eyes pierced with fear and desperation. There was no decision to be made. I sat next to Stef and held her hand. "It's gonna be okay baby. I promise."

We hugged each other till she exhaled in relief. This was my moment to shine, and I was gonna do everything for her. The rest of the day I met her every need.

About midnight, Stef told me she felt something weird. It was like a tightening from her back to her front. It didn't hurt. It was different. That's all. Who was I kiddin thinking I wouldn't panic? She called her doctor and found out it may be a contraction. If it happened again, we had to write down the time. Contraction? Isn't that the start of...? Oh God I was panicking, but only on the inside, or so I thought. Stef started laughing at my emotional disarray. Was it that obvious? Well, at least I had time to get my shit together. She was more worried bout me than herself. Tony may think he's tough, but my baby is a lot tougher. Every mother is.

Stef tried to sleep. She was gonna need her strength. I couldn't even close my eyes. I watched her every breath. After every contraction, I softly patted her body down with a warm wet cloth. It felt good to her and to me. I was doing something right. These contraptions things looked like they hurt. Morning came and our baby wasn't ready to join the family. Maybe they were stealin the last few moments of alone time. While the world inside Stephanie was much smaller, it was a lot safer too. I called mom and dad to fill them in and mom told me not to wait to hear from the doctor, just get to the hospital. She'd know, she's been through it a few times before. I called my dad-in-law for Stef. He and Monica would meet her there. God, I wondered what was goin through his head. The birth of your kids are the happiest days of your life. But, for him, there was happiness followed by incredible pain. When I saw him, my eyes had to convince him everything was gonna be okay.

I let Stef rest while I got the car ready. The ride was gonna scare the shit outa me. I can't deliver a baby in a car, much less a Volkswagen where, for all I know was where they were conceived. No I'll drive careful but real fast. Car packed, I almost left without her. Stef was shakin her head as she was watchin me from the window. I had to laugh at myself walkin back to the house. It was the second thing I did right. At the door, she was waiting to waddle to the car. I took her hand and the most confident voice one could muster said, "C'mon Let's Go!!"

Openin her car door, like a first date, she fell awkwardly to the seat. "Kenny, it just started snowin so you drive careful!!!" Great, now I got a nagging wife and mother, all in one.

We made it to the hospital without crashing And Stef kept her yelling under control. The Emergency Room people took over and admitted us to a room on the floor where everything would happen. The tension was getting to us. I figured the T.V would a good distraction. Big Mistake!!! She yelled, "Shut that fuckin thing off!! And hold my hand" Her dad and my parents showed up at the perfect time...when I was fuckin up. I didn't know what I was doing. I never went through anything like this before. The soon-to-be grandparents eased our anxieties. Her Dad was amazing with his baby girl. His strong soothing voice relaxed Stef. Mom was great too. She was the only one here who went through this and reassured her about everything going on in her body.

Soon after she was calmed down, the Doctor came in and the parents excused themselves. Dr. Muise explained the examination he was going to do. He said he was gonna check and see how much Stef was dilated. This would give him an idea of when our baby was coming. Dilated? Your eyes dilate when you go outside on a sunny day. That thing dilated? I had no idea what he was talking about and I wasn't gonna ask. My job was to hold her hand. I'm used to that.

After Dr. Muise left, the contractions became faster and more intense. I felt so helpless. Seeing her in this much pain tortured me but it wasn't a time to think about myself.

Stef asked me to get the nurse cause her water broke. I ran as fast as I could to the nurse's station. They were cool. It's hard to believe they do this every day. I brought mom back in the room just to reassure Stef. Mom did her job and left me and Stef together for our private time. We were the only two people there when we made our baby. So, we should be the only two to welcome them into our world. Stef was dripping in sweat, and I had plenty of cool wash cloths to gently caress her face. She said it was the only thing that helped as she could focus on the cooling of her head. Anything to distract her from the pain.

Dr. Muise returned to check how much she had dilated. It was about ten hours since we arrived. It felt like ten days. Stef was a perfect ten. The doctor told us she was dilated ten centimeters and it was time to get to the operating room. The staff was ready and wheeled her in while I was scrubbing and putting on my scrubs.

I realized the past nine months flew by and I never even thought about our baby being a boy or a girl. What did I want? Was I gonna be disappointed if I was wrong? It hit me. I didn't care what we had. This was gonna be the luckiest baby in the world cause me and Stef would love them in only a way we could. We'll love our baby the way we love each other.

Entering the operating room overwhelmed me a little but I didn't have time to freak. Stef reached for my hand and the doctors were great. After every push, they'd tell her , she's closer. "Push Stephanie!!! We can see the head. Push!!! One more!! Stephanie and Kenny you have a beautiful baby boy!!!!!" The doctors did a quick check to make sure he was okay. His cry was a music we'll never forget. The nurse brought him to Stef and she was a natural mother. Holding our baby and me, holding his incredibly soft and small fingers made us both cry. I gently brushed the hair away from her face. She looked more beautiful and happier than I've ever seen her.

Staring into my eyes, she asked me, "Kenny, honey, if it's okay can I name our son?"

"Of course, baby, you did all of the work. Well, most of it. I was there when it counted"

She smiled, "Honey, I'd like to name our son Anthony James. We can call him T.J."

"Really Stef, baby? You wanna name him after my best friends?"

"I do. I think that'd be nice,and I've always loved a kid who goes by his initials. They seem to be the happiest kids."

"Baby?"

"Yes, Kenny?"

"Can I hold T.J." She was right. It did sound nice. Stef asked to be wheeled to the room where our parents could meet their grandchild.

Stef held our son for the ride to the room and I couldn't believe how peaceful his world was. I gave the news to our parents "Anthony James Mancuso was born on this day, January 27th, 1981" Everybody cheered, and Mr. Demarino was relieved for his daughter. We all walked in the room together I put my arm around her dad and brought him to his daughter. "Hi Daddy. Look at your beautiful grandson."

Mr. Demarino stared at the two miracles in his life. T.J. rested in his arms while Stef savored his happiness. Mom and Dad worked their way in taking turns breathing in from our cute little fountain of youth. Mom loved Grandmotherhood and the two dads weren't wild about realizing they were Grandpas. It sounded so old. With everyone settled, I let Stef know I had some calls to make. Tony and Jimmy were speechless about the name. Terry, Jenni, and Fanny were sitting by the phone waiting to hear the news and they went nuts!!! "Tell T.J. his three aunts are stopping by tomorrow and we're gonna spoil him rotten!!" Girls love babies!

We left the hospital a few days later. Jimmy had to bust my balls. "Kenny, since he's your son, you sure they had enough room to do the circumcision." I told him he did, cause I felt his pain. I had to get back to school a day after we got home. We were pretty lucky with help staying with Stef for a few months. Mom was amazing and Monica and Stef grew closer. Mom and Monica grew closer as well. I gave her a lot of credit, Monica knew she wasn't family, but she treated Stef and Mr. Demarino like gold. Mr. D was softening, and his dependence continued to grow stronger every day. Me and Stef noticed they were getting more affectionate with each other.

Everybody grew closer except me and my wife. With me at school, and Stef taking care of T.J., Romance was gone. On the days I was home, we were too tired to be nice to each other. T.J. was the only thing we talked about. Parenting held us prisoners of our distance. And sex? If we ever had it, it was obligatory. Same thing every time. No Passion, No eye contact, No kissing. She was listening to hear if T.J. was crying and I was listening to hear if I was. I was no longer the love of her life. A distant second was the best I could hope for. If we talked about it, she said I was being selfish, and she was right. Was I wrong to fight for our marriage? If we weren't close, it wasn't fair to T.J. School was my haven and I would walk around looking at other girls, wondering if the love and passion between me and Stef wasn't enough to go the distance. Was I missing out on college life?

Freshman year came to an end and our first summer with T.J. didn't start off well. The baby was five months old, and he was going through major changes. He was adorable as he was becoming a cute little man. Maybe me and Stef could get back on track. It was a Friday night. Earlier in the week, I asked mom to baby sit. Me and Stef were gonna go out for a few drinks and dinner. As Stef was getting ready, T.J. started to cry. I was watchin T.V. in the other room. when she came in with the baby..

"Kenny, T.J. has a little fever, and I don't feel right about leaving him"

"Aww Stef, it'll be okay. My mom is gonna be here and I'm sure she'll call us if it's anything to worry about."

"But I've never left him before, and I don't feel right about leaving him for the first time when he's sick"

"Baby, come on don't worry. Trust me he'll be fine. We really need this"

"As usual, Kenny, you're not listening!! I said I don't feel right about this and I'm his mother. I need to take care of him!!"

"Stef, who's gonna take care of us? WHO THE HELL IS GONNA TAKE CARE OF YOU AND ME?? Do you even care that we're growin apart so fast??" Stef was speechless. "No!!! I guess you don't!!!"

I stormed out of the room to call mom "Don't worry bout comin over. T.J was a little sick." Stef stood there with a tear in her eye. I didn't give a shit as I told her "I'm goin out" and slammed the door behind me. Driving around for an hour didn't give me any answers. It only made me more pissed off. Fuck it. Time to go to Harry's. Walking in the door, Bunny was behind the bar and I ordered a beer and a strong shot of something. Fester was in his usual seat at the end of the bar with cigarette in hand.

Bunny questioned my order, "Whoa a shot? You wanna a shot?"

I was in no mood to deal with another woman." Bunny, just shut up and get me my drinks" Fester got pissed, "HEY, you don't talk to her like that!!!" I didn't need to hear his shit either.

" You too, Shut the fuck up and mind ya own business"

Fester left his chair and came at me. Never fuck with age. He had me jacked up against the wall and was gonna kick the shit outa me. Giving me one last chance, he screamed, "What the fuck is your problem??

My answer stunned both of us. "MY MARRIAGE, OKAY??? It's fallin apart and there's nothing I can do to stop it."

He pulled back and just stared at me breathing out the fear of God. Fester put his arm around me, and we walked back to his stool." Bunny, my babies, get Kenny his beer and shot on me." She brought my drinks, and I gave her a big hug and apology. Bunny and Fester were my relationship idols and I just treated them like shit. I treated Stef like shit too. What the fuck was wrong with me? I have the most beautiful girl in the world as my wife and our kid is just a baby who needs us now more than ever. I spent a few hours with Bunny and Fester. Watching the two of them made it so clear to me. They were best friends and Stef was my best friend. Through all the bullshit of the overwhelming changes of the last year, I forgot that. We were One and it's time to get back that feeling.

I returned home about midnight and Stef was up cradling T.J. Sitting on the side of the bed, I told her how selfish and stupid I've been. This was all my fault. It was my responsibility to make it right. "Baby, you've had a rough night with T.J. Let me take care of him tonight and you get some rest"

"Kenny, no. you've been at Harry's, and you reek of smoke. How much have you had to drink"

"Baby, honestly, I had one beer and a shot four hours ago. If you want, call Bunny and ask her. As far as the smoke, I know it's not good for our baby, so I'm gonna take a hot shower to get nice and clean. When I come out, if you don't smell smoke, can I take care of him for us?"

"Stef smiled and agreed. She seemed relieved to have her husband back. After the shower, I carefully took our son and gave Stef a sweet kiss on her forehead. Sure, we didn't make out, but a trace of love returned between us. And a trace felt really nice. With the baby in one hand, and the rocking chair in the other, Stef turned on her side and was asleep in a matter of minutes. I parked the chair by the window in the other room. He struggled at first, but the chair was rockin like waves to the shore. Staring out at the window, I told him all about the moon and stars; I tried singing songs to put some weight on his eye lids. Regular lullabies weren't his style. Exhausting the baby juke box in my head, I finally found his song. "Father and Son' by Cat Stevens did the job. I couldn't sing but he liked the soothing sound of my off-key lyrics. I did too. We both fell asleep in the chair around three am.

Looking as beautiful as the day I met her; Stef woke us up around nine. She had French toast on the table waiting for me and T.J., a nice fresh bottle of milk, the breakfast of champions. Sleepless nights turned Stef into a coffee addict, and she savored her cup this morning. This seemed kinda easy. All the three of us had to do is care for each other a little bit more and we'd be okay.

Two years later, T.J was mobile, and his world was growing every day. I had school down to a science as I was about to enter my senior year. It was gonna be tough finishing my double major, journalism and communications. Stef signed up for a baby class at the YMCA. T.J. was startin to make friends and play dates were a time for me and Stef to start enjoyin sex again. It was like ridin a bicycle but, two years older, we were much better. There's something really hot about not knowin the next time you're gonna get laid. Just our luck, T.J was the well-behaved popular baby and he had a full schedule of play dates Lightning struck again and Stef got pregnant on a hot summer night in July.

This time we talked a lot about all the changes to come. T.J came to us at the start of my college years and our next child would arrive close to the end. Jimmy, Tony, and Billy had some major changes too. Billy understood his father's business and they were opening a second location in Montclair and Billy was going to run it. Terry was working at a local crafts shop. After graduating from N.J.I.T., Jimmy and Fanny were gonna move to Seattle to work for this company named Microsoft. Years ago, when we were smoking all that pot, we thought Jimmy was nuts talking about computers. Today, this company had about fifty million dollars in sales. Tony was gaining national attention as the starting fullback for Penn State. Fanny's Dad told me he was going to play in the NFL. Poor tough guy was gonna be rich. As he was becoming famous, Jenni was the only one he trusted. People would approach Tony, Jenni, a psych major could read them in a heartbeat. Tony would look into her eyes, and they told him whether to listen or tell them he's not interested.

Emily Megan Mancuso was born on April 5th, 1984. And She was all Stef!!!. Like her mom, she looked beautiful wrapped in a soft white blanket. Who knew she would become a star softball player at U. Va.? Now, she was as precious as the sunshine. I lost myself in the operating room dreaming about the mother daughter fights when Emily would run to me with sulking eyes. This kid was gonna play me bad. How could I ever say no to daddy's little girl? With T.J., we had a kid, Emily Megan made us a family. While your second kid doesn't get all the hospital fanfare, the adjustment was easier. I said easier, not easy. Here I was, a soon to be college graduate who never knew one plus one does not always equal two. Sometimes, it equals two hundred. My graduation was uneventful as I focused on my family and upcoming job at Conde Nast in New York City. Life was good. We had balance and even found a little time for sex. Quantity was replaced by incredible quality.

FINAL CHAPTER

Twenty-eight years had passed and Tony's retirement as the head football coach for Verona High brought us all together. Jimmy made millions working for Microsoft. He and Fanny had one child; a girl named Christina. She graduated from the University of Oregon. Jimmy and Fanny never changed. They still fooled around everywhere they went. He loved having sex with Fanny in as many countries as they could. The pot smoking fuck up actually had a private jet to take them wherever and whenever they wanted. To us, he was still Jimmy. We didn't give a shit what he had. He bought his mom a mansion in Florida. Billy and Terry lived in Montclair with their two boys, Danny and Kyle. Mr. DeMarino never married Monica. They were dating for 30 years and counting. It worked for them. Mom and Dad never left Verona, stayed young by hanging out with Mr. D and Monica. Jenni became a adolescent psychologist and she and Tony had two kids, a boy named Matt and a girl named Maddy.

Coach Biscotti surprised Tony with his arrival. He said a few words about his prized player and introduced Coach Matelli to the crowd. On stage, they shared a long hug. Biscotti saved my best friend from a life of hell and Jenni lead him to heaven on earth. Biscotti left stage to let Tony have his moment. Staring out at the audience, he saw Danny and immediately called him up to the stage where they shared a glory days moment. Tony wasn't big on speeches in public. He thanked everyone he ever encountered and passionately spoke to the students about following their impossible dreams. Be relentless in your pursuit and never let anyone stop you. Kids listened to Tony. They didn't know his history growin up in Verona. Yet, they sensed he lived the words he spoke. And that was enough. Tony received a standing ovation, left the stage to meet Jenni and his kids at the bottom of the stairs. They shared a family hug for a minute. Then Jenni made out with him like they did the night he sang for her. Once again, Stef and Fanny had a visual orgasm watching their electric passion.

T.J, being the oldest, got all the kids together and planned a wild night in Asbury Park. We asked them to be home in time for brunch tomorrow. The "old people" were going to Harry's !!!! Bunny cried when she first saw us. She was stunned with how much we grew up. The girls all had pictures in hand showing her their kids. An earthquake could happen, and Fester wouldn't get up from his favorite stool at the end of the bar. Me and Stef slowly made our way to him, and his weathered smile couldn't hide the fact he missed us. Of course, he had to check out Stef's ass with a playful touch. "Nothin better than a nice big ass to keep a marriage hot" Stef was hysterical rubbin it all against him. She hadn't laughed so hard in years. For me and Stef, and Bunny and Fester, the twenty-eight years never existed. The four of us laughed so hard, at one point, I almost wet my pants. Seeing me hold my tool bag, Fester went for the kill and made me laugh even more. I busted my way to the bathroom and hit the stall from ten feet away. Supposedly you can't go back, but we did. The years ago defined us.

Growing up in Verona, I didn't see then, what I see now. We thought we were bad kids growin up in a loser town. We smoked pot, we drank, we had sex, and me and Stef had a baby. Nobody would ever give us a shot at makin it in life. But we did, and we all loved our wives like the days when we were twenty-one. Our kids were no different than us, but we didn't judge them. Seven good kids knew how to party and not fuck up their lives. So, we must've done something right.

The clock struck midnight and we had to leave Harry's. Everybody pretended they were in high school again. Naturally, me and Stef were the last to leave. Bunny and Fester invited us back for Labor Day Weekend. They rented a house in Wildwood. Stef had never been there so Bunny and my baby finalized the plans. "See ya soon" was followed by a few long goodbyes. I thanked Fester for everything, including not kickin my ass years ago. I loved the sound of the door slammin at Harry's. Stef and me held hands walkin to the car.

It was a beautiful night and I convinced her to make a road trip to Seaside Heights. With the window down, her hair still fluttered in the wind. We arrived at the shore, walked along the beach and savored the feeling of fallin in love all over again. We stopped to face each other, and the moon reflected in her deep dark eyes. We looked in the sky for our make-believe home in the stars. But it couldn't have been better than the home we created here. There was a little bed of sand, and I carried Stef to lay her down gently. Once again, we became so close I couldn't tell where my body ended and hers began. We were "One" in a way I never knew possible. Stef slowly drifted off to sleep and I watched her breathe for hours.

God, I love her.